WHAT HAPPENED THAT SUMMER

LAURA PEARSON

Boldwood

First published in Great Britain in 2025 by Boldwood Books Ltd.

Copyright © Laura Pearson, 2025

Cover Design by Lizzie Gardiner

Cover Images: Shutterstock and Adobe Stock

A CIP catalogue record for this book is available from the British Library.

Paperback ISBN 978-1-83603-485-8

Large Print ISBN 978-1-83603-486-5

Hardback ISBN 978-1-83603-484-1

Trade Paperback ISBN 978-1-80656-168-1

Ebook ISBN 978-1-83603-487-2

Kindle ISBN 978-1-83603-488-9

Audio CD ISBN 978-1-83603-479-7

MP3 CD ISBN 978-1-83603-480-3

Digital audio download ISBN 978-1-83603-481-0

This book is printed on certified sustainable paper. Boldwood Books is dedicated to putting sustainability at the heart of our business. For more information please visit https://www.boldwoodbooks.com/about-us/sustainability/

Boldwood Books Ltd, 23 Bowerdean Street, London, SW6 3TN

www.boldwoodbooks.com

For Elodie, my favourite reading buddy.

1

EPISODE 1 – A TALE OF TWO FAMILIES

Danny: Hello, I'm Danny Drake: journalist, podcast host and 1990s obsessive. And this is *What Happened That Summer?* A seven-part investigative podcast looking at the sudden and shocking death of American teen pop megastar AJ Silver. He was killed in a rollercoaster accident at Wildworld theme park in West Wilding, near Birmingham, here in the UK, on 20 June 1996. Some of you may be aware that the Hunter family who ran Wildworld were later fined £500,000 for negligence and the business went into administration. John Hunter has always maintained the family's innocence.

I've spent hundreds of hours individually interviewing the Hunters and the Campbells (that's AJ's family), AJ's team and the residents of West Wilding, to bring you a more comprehensive record of the events of 1996 than has ever been available before. Along the way, I've uncovered brand new information that casts the incident in a whole new light, and will be revealing secrets that are guaranteed to shock you.

Over the next seven weeks, I'll be talking to everyone who was around in the run up to AJ Silver's tragic demise. For the first time, we're going to reveal exactly what happened in microscopic detail and from all angles. Were the Hunter family really to blame? What was it like to be AJ Silver, and did his own actions play a part in his untimely death? And how do you cope with living in the shadow of the death of one of the world's most famous teenagers?

Today, in episode one, we're giving you the lowdown on the two families at the heart of this tragedy. The Hunters, who owned and ran Wildworld theme park, and the Campbells – AJ Silver's parents and his brother. If you want to join in the discussion, you can find us on all the usual social media channels at @WhatHappenedThatSummer.

Pea: It's funny, because you know that you'll end up with some big before and after moments in your life, and maybe you can guess at some of them, like before or after you got married, or made this big international move, or became a parent. But others just come at you out of nowhere. And this was one of those. Before, I was just doing whatever teenage girls do. I was taking my GCSEs, hanging out with my friend Alex, pining after boys who didn't give me a second look. And after... Well, I guess we'll get on to after.

Danny: That's Pea Hunter, daughter of Cathy and John Hunter, who owned Wildworld.

Cathy: We were an ordinary family. Me, John, and our two children. Sebastian and Penelope, who we all called Pea. We just happened to have a theme park.

Danny: That's Cathy.

John: There's no such thing as normal, is there? Sometimes I think, so Cathy and I ran a business together? What's so unusual about that? But Wildworld wasn't just any business.

Danny: That's John.

Sebastian: I know now that it's a weird thing, to basically live in a theme park. But it was all we'd ever known. It was just normal to us.

Danny: And finally, that's Sebastian, Cathy and John's son, and Pea's older brother. Now that you know who everyone is, let's hear about the park, and how it came to be theirs.

John: My grandfather opened Wildworld in 1932, and it was mostly gardens with a couple of carousels, a helter-skelter and some playground equipment. He had the house built just beside the entrance, so he could always be onsite at a moment's notice. He didn't really believe in time off, my grand-dad. And a business like that, it's twenty-four seven. He worked hard to get it off the ground. My dad took over when Granddad retired, and he made some pretty big changes, adding a lot of rides and making it more 'theme park' than 'park'. I'm an only child, and I grew up in that house, with the park on my doorstep. It was all I knew. I worked alongside Dad after finishing school, and when I married Cathy and we found out we were having Sebastian, he said we should be the ones to live in the house onsite, and him and Mum found a little bungalow nearby. I pretty much took over at that point but he kept working there for another few years.

Pea: All my earliest memories are of the park. Dad was always working, so Mum and Sebastian and I would spend most of our spare time there, because it was the only way we got to see him. We'd just find him, usually operating one ride or another, and we'd hang out nearby. Mum didn't have a job when we were little. A couple of years after we'd both gone to school, the woman who worked in the office left, and Mum stepped into that role. It was just part of us, properly ingrained in our beings. We *were* Wildworld, effectively.

Sebastian: Has anyone explained the layout of the place to you? Would that be helpful? So it was supposed to be a world, right, and there were five cities within it. I know, it doesn't make much sense, but you'd have to take that up with my granddad. There was Water City, where all the water rides were, Adventure City, which was all the biggest rides and always the most crowded one, Fun City, which had lots of rides and play areas for really young kids, Fantasy City, where all the rides were based on fairytales, and then Animal City, which had a farm and also a few exotic animals. They were arranged in a rough circle, and in the middle there was a huge building that housed a few food places, a handful of little rides and the gift shop. The noise level in there was always insane, and if it was raining, everyone in the park crowded in and it was horrendous. But other than that, I think it worked pretty well. Something for everyone, you know?

Cathy: I actually haven't been to many other theme parks. Busman's holiday and all that. We were smaller than Alton Towers and Thorpe Park, but people still seemed to come from all over. I think we had a nice mix of things for younger children and rides for thrill-seekers. And it was all very manageable, very walkable. John's dad had done a good job with it, really. John was proud of it. I mean, I was too. It was a great little theme park.

Danny: So there you have it. A great little theme park. Did you ever visit Wildworld in the 80s or 90s? We'd love to hear from you if you did. Find us at @WhatHappenedThatSummer on all the social media channels.

Next up, we got onto the subject of the theme park's future, something Pea in particular was quite het up about.

Pea: Wildworld had come down the family on the male side, right? Dad's grandfather, then Dad's dad, whose two sisters didn't get a look-in, then Dad, who was an only child. Sebastian knew Dad wanted him to take it on, but he didn't want to. It just wasn't his thing, and him and dad were always arguing about it. And then there was me, practically waving my arms around trying to get their attention, because I really wanted it. I wanted to run that theme park more than I'd ever wanted anything in my life. I knew every ride, every operator, every bit of space that might have potential for a new ride in the future. I spent every hour I wasn't at school roaming around. When we got old enough that Mum didn't have to supervise us all the time, Sebastian spent most of his time inside the house, watching TV or sketching these incredible battle scenes. He used to use reams of computer paper, you know the stuff with the holes down each side? He liked being on his own. And I spent pretty much every waking moment in the park.

Cathy: Oh yes, it was an issue. It was clear to me that Sebastian didn't want it and Pea did, so pretty obvious, right? But John was so adamant that he wanted it to be Sebastian. I don't know whether it was an age thing or a gender thing or what. When we talked about doing our wills, I said we should leave it to both of them, like you would with a property, but John thought if we did that, they'd sell it and split the money. He wanted it to stay in the family.

Pea: I would never have let that place go. I would have fought tooth and nail to keep it in the family.

Sebastian: I guess I might have sold it, if the right offer had come along. I don't know. It's all a bit immaterial now, isn't it? What I do know is that Dad was obsessed with me taking it over, and it didn't matter how many times I told him I didn't want to.

Cathy: John felt like he owed it to his father and his grandfather to keep things running. And I don't think Sebastian had that same compulsion. He's never seemed to care as much about family as the rest of us. He's just... wired differently, I suppose.

I always had this feeling, while this was going on, that it wouldn't matter, that it wouldn't survive beyond our working lives. But I couldn't say that to John; he would have been crushed. So we kept putting it off and putting it off. And in the end, I was right.

Pea: Mum often says after the fact that she knew stuff was going to happen. I'm not saying that to be unkind. I think she genuinely believes that she knew.

John: Did I want Sebastian to take over Wildworld? Yes, I did.

Pea: He said outright – even now – that he wanted Sebastian to have it? Jesus Christ. I don't even know why I'm surprised.

Sebastian: I don't know why we're dragging it all up, to be honest. None of it mattered in the end.

Pea: Of course it matters. It shows what our family was like, the cracks running through it.

Danny: Sounds like trouble brewing, doesn't it? Don't worry, we've got plenty more where that came from. Now, shall we backtrack a bit? I bet you want to hear the story of how Cathy and John met, don't you?

Cathy: I was nineteen when I met John. He was ten years older. My parents weren't happy about it, and I didn't understand it, because I was an adult in the eyes of the law and ten years didn't seem like a big deal to me then.

John: We met in a pub in town. She told me she was twenty-one, I think. But when I found out that she was nineteen, it didn't really bother me. She was mature for her age. I never really noticed the age gap.

Cathy: He came over to where I was sitting with a few of my friends and he looked straight at me and said he would like to buy me a drink. I didn't have a lot of confidence, and I always thought I was one of the least pretty in the group, so the fact that he'd picked me and not any of my friends really meant a lot.

John: It all happened fast, really. We went out a few times and within six months we were engaged.

Cathy: He told me about the park very early on. Everyone knew Wildworld. Everyone had been. I thought it was pretty cool, I think. I mean, I was young and it was the early seventies and I was just glad he didn't have a typical corporate job. What could be more exciting than a theme park?

The wedding was small and it felt rushed. Do I wish I'd waited? Perhaps. But you can't do that, can you? You can't imagine yourself a whole different life. If I hadn't married him, I wouldn't have the children I have, and my life might have been better, of course, but it might have been worse, too.

John: It's easy to look back on a marriage that's ended and say, with hindsight, that it wasn't the right thing to do. But you don't know that when you're young, do you? I thought Cathy was the most beautiful woman in the world and I wanted more than anything to make her my wife.

Cathy: Yes, I loved him. Of course I did. I wouldn't have married him otherwise. But I was naïve, and I didn't know much about the world, or about what I could expect from a husband.

John: It's hard to pinpoint when it started to go wrong. There's never just one thing, is there? We just stopped being nice to each other, stopped being patient and making time. Started to let our irritations show. Now and again, and then always. Until it really wasn't clear what we were doing together.

Cathy: By the time the whole AJ Silver visit happened, things were pretty bad. With the park, with our finances, and with our marriage. I think neither of us wanted to admit it. We're both stubborn, and we don't like to admit defeat. And there were the kids to think about. I used to think that if we could just get through another handful of years together, they'd be grown up and it wouldn't hurt them so much if we split. But that's no way to think about your life, is it? Gritting your teeth and getting through it.

John: Look, Cathy was a hippy, right? I knew that from the start. And I was no free spirit. I didn't see that causing problems in the early days, but it did. We were fundamentally different. She liked to go with the flow and I worried endlessly. When we started to get in trouble, financially, Cathy would say that everything would work itself out and there I was, lying awake at night, trying to see a way out of it. It drove me crazy.

Cathy: John's drinking was a big factor.

John: Look, I had a drinking problem later on. But not then. Cathy's parents didn't touch booze and it was always an occasional thing for her. Back then, I'd say I just liked a few beers of an evening, a glass or two of wine with dinner.

Cathy: He never opened a bottle of wine without finishing it, and then he'd always open another.

John: When all the stuff with AJ Silver started, we were on the rocks. We were hanging in there, just about, but I think we both knew where it was headed.

Cathy: I can tell you exactly when I knew it was over. It was a few weeks before the call from AJ Silver's people, and we were eating dinner. The kids were both off out somewhere and it had been a while since it had been just the two of us, and I realised that I didn't have a single thing to ask him or tell him. I didn't have anything to say to my husband. That's never good, is it?

Danny: From first meeting to the end of a marriage in five minutes, there. Now, there's someone else I'd like to introduce you to, and that's Alex. He's not a Hunter, but he was Pea's best friend and he was around so much that he was practically part of the family. Now, Alex Robb is obviously a household name these days, rarely off our TV screens and one of the most successful presenters of our time, but back then he was just Pea's friend Alex. Here he is, telling us about that friendship.

Alex: We'd been friends for, let's see, at least ten years. We just started playing together at school, pretty early on, and then we were a pair. When we were eight or nine, people mostly split down gender lines where friendships were concerned. The boys would chase the girls and vice versa, and there was a lot of competition. Girls are stupid, boys smell, that kind of thing. And I wondered whether it would happen to Pea and me, but it just never did.

Pea: Everyone noted pretty early on that my family was a bit... odd. My mum was kind of a hippy, and Dad used to turn up at school looking wild. Covered in grease from fixing rides. I didn't have the right clothes, either. I mean, I had school uniform but it was always a bit wrong. Like all the girls would have pale blue and white gingham dresses in summer and mine would be navy and white because Mum had found it in a charity shop. Or I'd turn up in knee-high socks when everyone else had switched to ankle socks with those little frills on them, as if by secret committee.

You'd think having your own theme park might be the sort of thing that could make a child really popular, I guess. With me, it was kind of used against me. People said Wildworld was rubbish, that they'd rather go to Alton Towers.

Alex: Oh man, Wildworld was absolutely a perk of our friendship. Pea and I used to spend every weekend there, just hanging out. I remember the first time she invited me. We were only about seven so my mum took me, and Pea met us at the gate and waved us in. There was a queue of people waiting to pay and they all had their mouths hanging open when I was ushered through. I felt like I was famous or something. Ha. Pea's mum was with her, and she was wearing these rainbow dungarees and I honestly thought that maybe she was performing as a clown or something. I didn't know, then, that that was just how she dressed. We went all over that day. Every ride. Pea just made her way past the queue, pulling me along behind her, and the ride operators would all smile at her and nod for us to get on. It was the best day of my life up to that point.

Sebastian: Alex and Pea were always together. I mean, always. At school, after school. Weekends, too. I didn't have a friend like that, one that I was with all the time, so I often felt like I was on the outside. Mum and Dad were a unit, and Pea and Alex were another unit, and then there was me. I didn't really mind. That's just how it was.

Alex: I was in and out of that house a lot, but I never saw much of Sebastian. He was one of those people who marched to the beat of his own drum, you know? He kept himself to himself, shut himself up in his room, drawing for hours on end.

Cathy: I always thought if we had two children, they'd play together. But Alex was there so often it felt like we'd got three, and three is never an easy number for friendship, is it?

John: Why are we talking about Alex? He wasn't part of the family.

Danny: Alex may not have been part of the Hunter family but he plays a big role in everything that followed, so it's worth introducing him early on. Now, when I talked to the Hunters, something that came up over and over was their financial situation. Let's hear what they've got to say about it.

John: We'd never had a lot of money, and the kids were used to that. Clothes were often hand-me-downs. And we never went on days out, because I was always working, and besides, they had access to an actual theme park all day every day.

Cathy: I often felt guilty about the things we weren't able to give to the children. Lots of people were starting to go abroad on package holidays, but we just didn't have the money for it. We had this old Volvo and the exhaust was always just about falling off. There was never enough money to get a new one, so we just kept fixing the things that went wrong and hoping for the best.

John: I loved that Volvo. Good, reliable car, that.

Sebastian: I wouldn't say we were poor, exactly. I think a lot of kids these days are kind of spoiled.

Pea: Money was tight. I was very aware of that. Sometimes I'd ask Dad if Wildworld was doing all right and he'd always run a hand through his greying hair and then fix on a smile and tell me things were fine.

Kids at school were brutal if you didn't have the right stuff. We had these occasional non-uniform days and I'd stress for weeks about what to wear. About what I had that was right, or at least right enough to let me go unnoticed. The last thing you wanted to do was stand out.

Sebastian: I don't remember anyone at school talking about money, or what we were wearing, or any of that. It wasn't a fashion show, was it? We were there to get an education.

Pea: I had these trainers once, and I thought they were just like the ones everyone else had, the ones people were talking about. For once, I couldn't wait for the next non-uniform day to come around. When it did, I paired my flash trainers with some jeans and a Naf Naf jumper and a denim jacket. I knew double denim was where it was at. I walked into school thinking I was it, and two minutes later Nicole Waddington pointed at my trainers and burst out laughing. Said they were fakes and my mum had probably got them from the market. The thing is, she *had* got them from the market. I didn't know there was anything wrong with that.

Danny: Nicole Waddington. Remember that name. She's going to make a comeback.

Cathy: Things were steady for most of the eighties, but from about 1991 onwards, there was a slide. I don't know what it was. People always said we must be raking it in. There were hundreds of people there day in, day out. But none of them considered all the outgoings. The staff, the upkeep of the rides, the electricity, the cost of bringing in new rides so there was always something to shout about. The outgoings really stacked up, and gate numbers dwindled. 1992 was worse than 1991, and then 1993 was worse again. John was drinking a lot. I was trying to hide how worried we were from the kids.

Sebastian: This whole narrative about Dad's drinking is a bit of a mystery to me. Yes, it became a problem in later years, but back then I don't think it was. I think they're looking back on it with the knowledge they have now of what came later, if you see what I mean.

Pea: Sebastian lived in his own little world. He didn't pick up on some of the stuff I did.

John: 1994 was a good year. I really thought things were picking back up, that we'd have an upward trajectory from there. But then 1995 was bad again. I had to take out a couple of loans, make a few people redundant, and it was tough. Some of them had been with us for years and years.

Cathy: John used to get up and pace around at night. It was like when the kids were small and we'd walk up and down the landing trying to get them off to sleep after a night feed. John used to say, back then, that I'd wear out the carpet. And I lay in bed listening to him going up and down, wondering what he'd say if I said the same thing to him then. We didn't joke or laugh much by then. We didn't have much to laugh about.

John: It broke my heart to do it but I looked into how much we might get for the place, if we sold up. The irony was, the longer we kept going and the numbers kept dwindling, the lower the selling price would be. So I thought it might be in our interests to sell up as quickly as we could. I went to see Dad. Mum was gone by then and he was in a nursing home. Dementia. When I brought it up, he set his jaw and said Wildworld stayed in the family, no matter what.

Cathy: I went to my parents to ask for help. I don't think I ever told John. I wanted to present it to him as a fait accompli because I knew he'd feel emasculated by it. My parents lived half an hour away, and on the drive I repeated the speech I'd come up with over and over.

Mum opened the door to me and said, 'Well, this is a surprise,' as if I never went to see them, when in reality I made sure we got over there at least once a fortnight. I drank half a cup of weak tea and then rolled out the speech. My dad's eyebrows started rising early on and just kept going, disappearing under his hair. It would have been funny if I wasn't so stressed.

I was almost finished when Dad put one hand up to get me to stop. I waited. And then he said they would have a look at their finances and see if they could move some things around. I was grateful; it sounded promising. I stayed for lunch, and on the drive home I felt lighter than I had for weeks.

Dad phoned three days later, and I stretched the cord to pull the phone into the downstairs loo, shut the door. He said that they could lend us two thousand pounds. It was a drop in the ocean, not enough to make any real difference. But I couldn't say that, could I? I thanked him and tried to keep the tears out of my voice. When it arrived in our joint account, I'm not sure John even noticed.

John: We came *this* close to closing, we really did. And then, out of nowhere, the call came.

Cathy: That call. We thought it would save our lives.

Danny: Right, let's get to it. It's time to hear about the call from AJ Silver's management that came out of the blue and changed the Hunters' lives forever.

John: It was a Tuesday afternoon.

Cathy: I think it was a Wednesday.

Pea: I didn't hear about it until afterwards. I would have been at school when it happened.

Cathy: We had this little office that I was based in during opening hours. It was a glorified shed, really, but it was where people would come if they had any problems, from losing a rucksack to losing a child. Usually, when the phone rang, it was people asking for our opening hours or admission prices. But not that day.

I was surprised to hear an American accent. We did get some international visitors, but not many. It was a woman, and she said she was calling from Los Angeles, and that her name was Maggie McGee and she was the manager of AJ Silver. Had she got through to Wildworld theme park?

Now, if I'd had a bit of time to think about it, I probably would have known who AJ Silver was. I mean, his face was everywhere. But off the top of my head, the name didn't mean anything.

Maggie: I'm pretty sure that, when I made that first phone call, Cathy had no idea who AJ was, but she hid it pretty well.

Danny: The woman you've just heard for the first time is Maggie McGee, manager to the stars. She'd been looking after AJ Silver for a little over a year at this point, and had gone from managing a roster of celebs to just looking after him as his career snowballed.

Cathy: She said that she was in an unusual position. That was when Sebastian stuck his head around the door. I put a hand up to tell him to wait, asked Maggie McGee very politely if I could put her on hold for one moment. 'AJ Silver?' I asked. 'Who is he?' And Sebastian said, 'Mum, he's, like, the most famous pop star in the world.' He turned on his heel and left then, no doubt to go back to the house and start making his way through a loaf of bread. He didn't want to know why I'd asked. I took a couple of deep breaths and went back to the call. Apologised. Maggie sounded like she was smoking a cigarette. She told me that AJ Silver had an extensive UK tour booked for the following year, 1996, and he had requested exclusive use of a theme park for the duration of his trip.

Maggie: Was AJ Silver a pain in the ass? Of course he was. He was a kid. But what you have to understand is that, back then, that kid was a licence to print money. He was idolised, all over the world, and anything we put his face or his name on sold in the millions. So when he came to me and said he wanted to stay in a theme park when we did the UK tour, I had to work really hard not to roll my eyes. Because he could have got rid of me just like that. And I knew that I would never find another him.

I knew right off the bat that we'd need exclusive use, that we couldn't have him just roaming around a theme park while it was open to the public, so I had a look at what we could offer to pay and I started making calls. The big parks weren't interested in the offer – said people would lose trust if they closed to the public for that long. And then I stumbled upon Wildworld.

Cathy: I was stunned. I had to stop myself from asking why she'd chosen us. But all I could think about was how something like this could get us out of a hole, financially. So I asked practical questions. How long would they need to use the park? Six weeks. What were the dates in question? They were in May and June, mostly term-time, so it wouldn't even interfere with the summer holiday, which was our most lucrative time of year. What sort of budget did they have in mind?

Maggie: I could tell she was blindsided when I made the offer. It made me wish I'd gone in a bit lower.

Cathy: I had to ask her to repeat it.

Maggie: She did ask me to repeat it, yes. I was tempted to lower it. But she seemed like a nice enough woman, and I knew we'd make the money back with some merchandise, no problem. So I said it again. Two million.

Cathy: Two million pounds. I said, 'Where do we sign?' Maggie laughed and said that it wasn't quite a done deal just yet. She and AJ's brother would be flying over to assess the place. Could we accommodate that? I said we could, and she said she'd be back in touch. I put the phone down, feeling like I'd just woken from a dream. When Pea came in, I must have been staring into space, because she gave me a funny look.

Pea: I remember her saying, 'You won't believe it, Pea!' Then she sent me to get Sebastian and find Dad. Told me to get everyone in the office as quickly as I could, because she had something to tell us all.

Cathy: It took a while to convince them.

John: Had I heard of AJ Silver? I think I knew that song about ice cream that was on every time you walked into a shop. I couldn't have picked him out of a line-up, though. And it was this kid, this famous, American kid, who was going to save us?

Pea: I thought she must be joking, but then I couldn't work out why she would be. It was just too bizarre a story to have come up with. AJ Silver. Here. At Wildworld.

Cathy: John made me tell them everything I could remember from the call, over and over. And then he made this noise, this sort of cheer. It was the first time I'd seen him look happy like that for weeks. Months, maybe.

Sebastian: I asked whether we were going to say yes. It seemed to me like it would be a massive upheaval, and I didn't know whether we needed it.

John: I made it very clear that this wasn't something we were going to say no to.

Cathy: I stressed that it wasn't a done deal. I explained about Maggie flying over from LA – John did a little clap when I said LA – with AJ's brother.

Pea: I asked why his brother. I thought that was weird. If only I'd known.

Cathy: I guessed his brother was coming because he knew what AJ liked but wasn't as busy as him, and that it would be easier for him to travel without getting mobbed. I'd seen the Beatles at a tiny hall in the sixties as a kid. I knew what teenage girls were like.

Pea: I called Alex straight after we dispersed. It was the strangest thing that had ever happened to me, to us, and I needed to hear his reaction to know how I felt about it. He went quiet after I told him. He said his name a couple of times. 'AJ Silver? *The* AJ Silver?' And then he was screaming and laughing and telling me this was the best thing he'd ever heard and he couldn't wait until those bitches at school found out. Later, when I was lying in bed, I repeated that to myself. Those bitches at school. He meant Nicole Waddington and her friends. Kelly and Fay. They'd had it in for me for years, and I guess Alex thought this was like getting one up on them.

John: I was on a high for days. I wanted to get some champagne, but Cathy said we should wait until it was more certain. I think she still thought it might come to nothing. At the time, I would have felt absolutely devastated if it had. But now? Now I wish we'd never heard from Maggie McGee again.

Pea: The next morning, Mum and Dad said we should keep it to ourselves until it was all signed, and I looked down at my cornflakes and hoped they wouldn't know I'd already told Alex. Within a week it was all over school. I was in PE one day when Nicole threw a netball at my chest and said, 'I heard you think AJ Silver is coming to your sad little theme park.' Her friends laughed in this mean, high-pitched way. 'As if,' one of them said.

Sebastian: I didn't tell a soul. Why would I?

John: It's hard to keep a secret when it's something huge like that, isn't it? You tell one person and then they tell someone else. It was a small town. It was impossible to keep a lid on it. I had to call a meeting in the end, because nothing was getting done. I told the staff I could confirm the rumour was true. Nothing was definite, but the wheels were in motion. The atmosphere was electric. I reminded them that we had a park to run. They all filed out, and it was business as usual for a while.

Pea: The rumour wouldn't go away at school. You have to wait for something bigger to come along, but there wasn't going to be anything bigger than this, was there?

Danny: I tracked down Pea's old headteacher, June Pears, to ask whether she heard the rumours.

June Pears: I'd been a headteacher for twenty years, and I knew a thing or two about teen heartthrobs. When you're around teenagers that much, you get to know who the big stars of the day are. And I'll tell you what. I hadn't ever seen so much excitement about anyone as I saw about AJ Silver in those mid-nineties years. Even I could see that he had something. Underneath the baggy jeans and the floppy hair, he had these eyes that made you feel like he was looking just at you. I remembered what it was like to be a teenage girl. All those hormones. I understood. So when I first heard the rumour about him coming here, coming to Wildworld, I just laughed. He was from LA. He might as well have been from the moon. But it didn't die down the way unsubstantiated rumours usually did. After a couple of weeks, I called Pea Hunter into my office and asked what she knew about it. She squirmed a bit, and then she told me it was true. Or that it was half true, and his management were coming over to have a look at the place. I think my mouth was hanging open. She'd never been in trouble, and she wasn't the sort to make up lies in the head-teacher's office. I let her go, and I just sat there behind my desk for five minutes or more, thinking about the absolute carnage this would cause, if it ever came to pass. Little did I know.

Cathy: I bought one of his albums. Pea laughed her head off, but I just wanted to know what all the fuss was about. Once, I picked Sebastian up and I'd forgotten to turn it off, and he looked at me with absolute disdain. 'Mum, this music is for pre-teen girls.' I told him I was just curious. I listened to that album from start to finish three times, and I didn't connect with it at all. It was manufactured pop, with meaningless lyrics and synthesised sound.

Pea: I couldn't wait for this visit to happen, to be honest. Because then we would know one way or the other, and things could go back to normal if he wasn't coming. And if he was... well, I didn't know what would happen then. But at least it would be a definite fact and not just something people thought I'd made up to make myself sound interesting.

In one way, I wanted it to happen. Because Dad had looked so happy since the call, whistling and bustling about the place like a younger man. Mum, too. Plus, I was fifteen and I was desperate for anything to happen, like all teenagers are. But another part of me just wanted it to be over.

Sebastian: It was all anyone talked about for weeks, and it was just boring, to be honest. When Mum told us Maggie had called again, and that the visit was set for the following week, I was just glad it might soon be over.

John: We all went into a kind of meltdown when we heard the visit was booked. Ever since that first call, I'd been tarting the place up as best I could. Giving some of the rides fresh paint, getting the staff to pick up every last piece of litter, but when we had the dates, it was so real, and it felt like what I'd done wasn't enough. I started working late into the night, giving all the rides a really thorough going over, making sure they were all serviced and running smoothly. We had this one chance, and it could change everything, and we needed to make sure we didn't blow it.

Cathy: John worked himself into the ground in the run up to the visit. I did what I could, too, of course. Smartened up the office and made sure the house was looking its best. Pea was excited, I think, but she didn't really show it. One night, the week before they came, I said to her that it was okay to be enthusiastic about something, even if it wasn't quite your thing. She just shrugged.

Pea: I didn't tell anyone at school when we had the dates for the visit. Didn't even tell Alex.

Alex: I knew when they were coming, yes. I'm pretty sure Pea told me.

* * *

Danny: Now, let's leave the Hunters there for now and go across the Atlantic to talk to the Campbells.

Grace: We knew AJ was special from the time he was about two years old.

Danny: That's Grace, AJ's mum.

Grace: He was always a performer, always lining up his soft toys and dancing or singing to them. It was just in his nature. With Zak, our first son, I had no idea what he'd do as an adult, but with AJ it just seemed really clear from very early on.

Ken: Those early years with Grace and the boys in Atlanta were the happiest of my life.

Danny: And Ken, his dad.

Ken: We'd been together a couple of years when we found out she was pregnant with Zak. It wasn't planned, but we were both in our twenties and I had steady work as a builder and we were in love, so I couldn't have been happier.

Grace: It was hard, adjusting to that first pregnancy. I'd been a dancer as a child and teenager, and I'd never quite made it to the top. By the time I met Ken, I'd stopped training, but I don't think I'd fully let go of that dream. But with that pregnancy, I was forced to. If I was going to be a mom, I was never going to be a professional dancer. It was a beginning and an ending, for me.

And then Zak was born and he was a hard baby. Or maybe he wasn't, and it was just that he was my first. But I remember really struggling with the lack of sleep and the fact that he wouldn't eat sometimes and he had these allergies. There was always something, you know?

Ken: I wanted to have a whole bunch of kids, yeah. Four or five. When Zak turned one, I said I thought we should start trying again and Grace looked at me like I was nuts.

Grace: He had no idea. He was at work all day and I was at home dealing with tantrums and dirty diapers. And it had taken a toll on my body. I'd lost the weight but I was a different shape, somehow. I told him I wasn't sure about having another.

Ken: I was floored at that. We'd never discussed it but I'd just assumed we'd have at least two or three. I didn't want Zak to grow up lonely. It was clear that Grace was serious, so I started petitioning for just one more. She said I should give it another six months and then she'd think about it. I marked it on the family calendar.

Grace: I think I told him I wanted to wait another year. But he didn't.

Ken: Looking back, I think that was maybe the beginning of the end for us. We wanted such different things. So I just kept on working, and at the weekends I'd play with Zak for hours. Take him swimming and chase him around the garden. Sing songs and push buttons and fit puzzle pieces together. He was a joy to be around. And Grace was there but she wasn't, somehow. She was always in the kitchen fixing lunch or doing a load of washing. It was like she didn't want to just be with us. It was hard.

Grace: By the time the weekend rolled around, I'd sung the 'Hokey Pokey' a hundred times and I needed a break. He had this plastic ball with holes in it and different shapes that you could slot inside through the holes, and I sometimes felt that if I had to pick up those pieces, all wet with slobber, and put them away one more time, I would just start screaming and never stop.

Ken: When six months had passed, I asked her again. I laid it on thick, said I thought Zak needed a little buddy to play with, which was true. And yes, I seduced her. Made dinner, arranged for Zak to be with my parents for the night so we could have some guaranteed privacy.

Grace: You hear about people spending years trying to get pregnant, don't you? Not us.

Zak: I was two when AJ came along. I don't remember him being born, obviously. It was like he'd always been in my life.

Danny: That's AJ's older brother, Zak.

Grace: AJ was such a different baby. He slept well, he grew at exactly the rate he was supposed to according to all the charts, and he ate everything I put in front of him. Plus Zak adored him. I thought it would be harder with two, and it was in some ways. Getting out of the house was a nightmare, getting anywhere on time was impossible. But the long hours I'd spent with Zak, not knowing how to fill them, that didn't happen so much the second time. We'd go to playgroups and toddler classes I'd been doing with Zak and AJ would just slot in. And when we were at home, Zak kept AJ entertained because all AJ wanted to do was follow him around the room with his eyes. He started walking before he was one, AJ, because he just wanted to be able to do things with his big brother. And his first word was Zak.

Ken: Grace loosened up a lot that second time. It was a lot of fun, being a family of four. We did trips to the zoo and took them camping. All of that. As Zak got a bit older, I started teaching him practical things, like how to fish and how to swim. Everything my dad had taught me.

Zak: I loved doing stuff with my dad. I think it was just about having his attention, looking back. I think I always had this sense that Mom loved AJ more, and the way I dealt with that was by getting closer to Dad, I guess.

Ken: All the stuff I did with Zak, I thought I'd do with AJ too, when the time came. But he just wasn't interested in any of it. He was always off in some imaginary game or other, making up songs, putting on shows. He learned how to do magic tricks, loved playing pranks, that sort of thing. Always a performer.

Grace: AJ was born to be a star. He went to this club for kids who were into theatre after school and on Saturdays. They would put on these shows every few months, and AJ was just head and shoulders above everyone else. He had talent to burn.

Zak: I remember going to see AJ's early shows, yeah. Mom was always super nervous and pretending not to be, and Dad was tapping his legs with his fingers like he was playing an imaginary piano because he hated being still. I loved to see AJ on stage. He was my little brother, and he was awesome.

Ken: I don't remember when Grace started talking about getting him signed to a talent agency. He was young, I know that much. Maybe first grade? Or second? I wasn't sure at first, but she was the one who'd taken him to all the classes and spoken to the people who ran them and she said it was essential if he wanted to have a career in show business.

Grace: Yes, I signed him up to an agency young. They wouldn't have taken him if they couldn't see the potential, would they?

Zak: Mom was obsessed with AJ's 'career'. That's what she called it, even when he was auditioning for the odd commercial or to model kids' clothes in catalogues. It was all about him. I wouldn't say I was jealous, because I never wanted to do that kind of stuff, to be in the spotlight. But I did want my mom to notice me. Doesn't every kid?

Ken: It felt like it happened kind of gradually. He was doing some acting, some modelling. Sometimes, at weekends, Grace and AJ would be off doing auditions or whatever, and Zak and I would go camping or fishing. I asked Zak what he thought about it all once. We were sitting by a campfire, and I remember the way the flames were reflected in his eyes when I looked at him. He was maybe ten or twelve. I asked whether he minded that we were so rarely all together, and he shrugged, and I thought I wasn't going to get anything out of him, which wouldn't have surprised me. He was a fairly quiet kid. Always lots going on in his head but he didn't often give you access to any of it. But then he said something. He said it didn't feel like we were a family any more. That it felt like the AJ show. I knew I had to talk to Grace about it, then.

Grace: Ken engineered this big family talk about where AJ's career was going. He took us to our favourite Chinese restaurant and waited until we'd ordered. I guess so no one could storm off if the conversation didn't go their way. He said he wanted to hear from everyone, starting with AJ.

Zak: Oh yeah, that dinner. AJ said he didn't care much one way or the other about all the performing, and Mom looked horrified. It was like he'd gone off-script and she didn't know what to do with him. It was kind of funny. The wait staff were bringing out sweet and sour noodles and chow mein and every time we thought they'd finished, they'd bring out another dish of rice or some prawn crackers. So AJ was saying he could give it all up tomorrow but he quite liked the money, and Mom was staring at him like he was an imposter, some kid she didn't even know.

Grace: AJ had had a bad audition that weekend. He'd just heard he hadn't got the part. It was for this candy bar commercial, and it was massive. I'd thought it was going to be his big break. But they went for this goofy kid with teeth like a beaver. I have no idea why. AJ had great teeth. But who hasn't felt like giving up now and again? It doesn't mean you give up, does it?

Ken: I looked at Grace for a long time after AJ finished speaking but she would not meet my eye. Later, in bed, I said to her, as gently as I could, that I thought some of what she was doing with AJ was more about her than him. That she was trying to make sure he had the fame she missed out on with her dancing. She was lying very still, next to me, not speaking. For a second, I thought maybe she was asleep. But then she sat up, very suddenly, and said that I might not care about helping our son to be the best he could be, but she did. And she wouldn't be talked or bullied out of it, or made to feel like she was doing the wrong thing. She picked up her pillow and left the room. She slept in the spare room. Started sleeping there a lot.

Zak: Do I think Mom and Dad would have stayed together then if it hadn't been for the situation with AJ? I don't know, man. I doubt it. It's never just one thing that leads to divorce, is it? I feel like most of my childhood they were heading that way. Not screaming at each other, no violence. Just quietly living different lives. So I think it would have happened regardless, but I also think that AJ's fame probably sped it up a bit.

Ken: I still thought it was worth rescuing, then. Our marriage. I asked my mom to watch the boys for a week and I booked us a holiday in Miami. Did it all as a surprise. I even talked to her boss and got her the week off work without her knowing. And then the day before we were due to leave, I told her to pack some swimsuits and she asked me what I was talking about. I showed her the brochure, which I'd stuffed in a drawer. It was like she didn't understand at first. But then she did. She started asking why I'd done it and saying she couldn't go tomorrow because AJ had an audition and he couldn't miss it. I said I thought he could, just this once. I had honestly never considered a scenario where she refused to come with me.

My mom arrived and there was this heavy silence in the house, and I opened the door and said something like, 'Shit, I forgot to cancel you,' and then she was furious because that's no kind of welcome when you've driven three hours to your son's place to take care of your grandsons for a week. I was making Mom a coffee when Grace came into the kitchen and said she wasn't going and that was final. She looked at Mom and said, 'We don't need you here, it's all been a misunderstanding.' They'd never got on, Mom and Grace. Mom thought Grace believed she was better than her, and to be fair, Grace probably did think that. And Grace thought Mom was a busybody. She was, a bit, but she was still my mom, you know?

So there I was, with these two tickets to Miami and a half-packed suitcase. I went upstairs and started taking things out of it. Shorts and T-shirts and a book and my toothbrush. All of it. Zak came into the room then and asked what I was doing. And when I told him, he asked whether we could go. Me and him. I stopped unpacking.

Zak: I know a week in Miami with me isn't what Dad had been planning, but I thought it was probably better than wasting the money altogether. And we had a good time. Days on the beach, nights in the hotel restaurant, me with a Coke, Dad with a beer. It was pretty sweet.

Ken: That was the beginning of the end, if there even is such a thing. I realised on that holiday that there was probably no going back. I remember lying next to Zak in the hotel bed, watching his chest rise and fall in the darkness. I remember crying, and trying to do it silently so he wouldn't wake up. I didn't know what I was going home to, but I didn't think it was a family.

Zak: AJ came to me not long after that Miami trip and said he didn't want to do any of it any more. That he wanted to have a normal life. I think he was twelve. He liked playing video games. It was pretty much the only thing we did together. We played a lot of *Pac-Man*. Sometimes he called me Zak-man. I said we had to speak to Mom and Dad, but he was pretty reluctant. I said I'd do it with him, that no one would get mad. So I went with him, and we told them, but it was like Mom didn't hear it. He mentioned something about liking the singing the most and she just took that and ran with it, saying she'd tell the agents to focus on the singing from then on.

Grace: It was AJ's choice to narrow our focus to just the singing. We started travelling a lot, doing whatever shows we could. He had a great voice, and so much charisma. I realised he was right. He was good at the acting, but it wasn't his thing. He came alive when he sang.

Zak: When AJ was at home, I used to ask him if he was okay, if he wanted to carry on with it all, and he said he did. And to be honest, every time I saw him performing, he was magic. Just...

it's hard to find the words. He was really special. I knew he was going to make it big, because how could people not recognise that in him? How could they not see?

Ken: Grace started going all over with him. Some weeks I didn't even know what state they were in. She hired a tutor because he was missing so much school, and we could barely afford it. I was getting ready to tell her it had to stop, that it was enough, when he got offered *The Friday Show*.

Grace: He was thirteen when he landed *The Friday Show*. It was huge. Everyone watched it. Kids singing and dancing and cute comedy sketches, and it aired on Friday afternoons when school was out and kids had that feeling of freedom. There was no way we were ever going to turn it down.

Zak: I had watched that show when I was younger. Everyone did. I couldn't believe it. I remember giving AJ a hug and telling him I was proud of him. We went out for this fancy dinner, and even Dad seemed pleased. And then, when we were waiting for our dessert, Dad asked Mom how they'd manage the travel, how often they'd have to go back and forth, and I thought, *Oh yeah, of course that show is filmed in LA*. And Mom said, cool as anything, that we'd have to move there. Dad just sat there with his mouth hanging open, and when he finally spoke, his voice was like ice and I knew from experience that that was much more dangerous than when he shouted. He said she couldn't just uproot the whole family like that, on a whim, without even discussing it with him. And she said it wasn't a whim, it was the fucking *Friday Show*. Everyone turned to look at us. We weren't used to that back then. AJ got up and walked out, and the rest of us followed, Dad throwing down some money and shouting for our dessert order to be cancelled.

That night, I lay in bed listening to them arguing. I wondered whether AJ was listening too. I'm sure he was. For my part, I didn't want to move. I was fifteen and I had a good group of friends and I liked my high school, and there was a girl I'd had my eye on for months and I was planning to make my move any day. But I knew that none of that mattered to Mom.

Grace: Ken just wouldn't even entertain the idea of moving. He was a builder, and he could have worked anywhere, but he said he couldn't move further away from his mom, who was getting older. It was bullshit. It was just an excuse. He'd always been cautious, afraid to try things. One night, when we were in the kitchen making tacos, I told him me and the boys were going, whether or not he came with us, and he turned around from where he was standing at the fridge, left the door wide open and walked right over to me. Didn't stop until our faces were inches apart. I don't think I was breathing. I thought he was going to hit me for a second. But he wasn't that type of guy. He said, very calmly, that I couldn't take his boys away from him. And I said, 'Watch me.' I'm not proud of that, but I wasn't going to ruin my son's career before it had even properly got started because Ken was too chickenshit to make a change.

Zak: Mom presented it to me as a fait accompli. We were going, he was staying. I said I would stay with Dad, but then AJ came to my room and said he didn't want to live in a different state to me, and he looked like he was going to cry, and I asked him whether this was what he wanted, and he just told me how much they were offering to pay him, which was kind of a

mind-blowing amount. I felt like he needed me, like it would be too hard on him if it was just him and Mom, day in and day out. But I felt like maybe Dad needed me too, though he never asked me to stay.

Ken: I wanted to ask Zak to stay, but I couldn't bring myself to do it. One person leaving a family is one thing but having it torn down the middle, separating brothers, that's something else. I talked to a solicitor, asked about my chances of winning custody if I took her to court, and I was told they'd more than likely give the kids to the mother. That that's the way it pretty much always went. And I thought it was what AJ wanted, so I knew that I'd be fighting against him as well as Grace. And I just... didn't. I let it go. Let them go. Worst mistake of my life.

Zak: It all happened pretty fast. Mom found somewhere for the three of us to live and we packed up and went. AJ started filming a few days after we got there. Meanwhile, I didn't have a school to go to for a month or so. That certainly reinforced Mom's priorities for me. I used to go with AJ and hang out on set, and I saw this totally different life. There were people there to do the kids' makeup and hair and style them and there was a fridge full of free soda and fruit and candy to help yourself to. It's funny the things you remember, the things that impress you when you're young. That soda fridge really stuck with me.

And it felt like AJ became famous overnight. He used to get recognised when we were out for dinner or at the grocery store. It's such a crazy place, LA, and everyone's either writing a screenplay or starring in one, or waiting tables while they wait for their break. AJ had this money – Mom made him put most of it into savings, but he had more cash available than either of us had had before – and life was sweet. I missed Dad.

Of course I did. But I was fifteen and my head was easily turned. In LA, it felt like the sun was always shining and everything came easy.

Grace: I don't regret that move for one second. AJ was going places and who was I to hold him back? He fitted right in with the cast, and he was making good money and I was making sure he put a lot of it away for the future. At first, Ken and I pretended the marriage wasn't over, that this was a trial and we'd see how it went. But I think we both knew we were heading for divorce. He used to visit every couple of months to see the boys, and on one of those trips, about a year after the move, he brought it up. Said he thought it was time to face facts.

Ken: Yes, I was the one who said we should get divorced. There's only so long you can sit on your own eating microwave dinners with your wife and two sons in another state before you make it official. There was no one else. It was just a sad inevitability. After that I stopped visiting so often and I'd arrange for the boys to fly to me, but Grace didn't like it. There was always some excuse about AJ needing to rehearse or film. Sometimes Zak came alone, and we'd hang out and fish and it would be like the old days, and when he left, the house would feel so unbearably empty.

Zak: I know Dad missed us. I used to go to see him as often as I could, but it wasn't long before it just felt like our life was in LA, and all those years in Georgia had just been some kind of warm-up. I didn't fit there any more. I made some good friends, once I finally got to go to school. For a long time, I kept quiet about my brother being on *The Friday Show*, but it didn't last. Once word was out, girls would come up and ask me about him, try to score an invitation to the house.

There was this one girl, Melissa, who sat in front of me in history and who I obsessed over for months. I used to stare at the back of her head, at her long, blonde hair, and will her to turn around. And then one day she did, and I couldn't believe it, so I didn't hear what she said at first, and I zoned back in just as she was talking about hanging out, coming over, and I was so fucking happy. But when she came, all she wanted to talk about was AJ. He wasn't home, and I was hoping I could get her to forget about him. But then I heard the door open and she jumped up and then he was in the room and she was blushing and twirling her hair around her finger. And it was hard, man. He was my kid brother. He was, what, thirteen? And we didn't look so different. It was just that shine that fame gives you, I guess. I had to get used to it.

Grace: I don't think AJ's fame was hard on Zak in particular, no. He was proud of his brother, happy for him. And he got to enjoy some of the perks, too. We were invited to premieres and parties – there was always someone's pool to swim in or some- one's new role to celebrate. They were good days. We didn't know then that he'd get so famous it would be hard to go anywhere. Back then he had the money and the start of the fame, but it hadn't gotten out of hand.

After about a year on the show, one of the producers took me to one side when I was picking AJ up and asked if I'd like to go for dinner with him. I wasn't expecting it – there hadn't been anyone since Ken. But he was a good-looking guy and I was ready to have a bit of a life of my own, so I said yes. Over dinner, he told me that a record company had been sniffing around, that they were looking for a new teenage singer to turn into a pop sensation. I remember he used that exact phrase. He said he thought AJ was the perfect choice, but that they were looking at a kid called Luke too. He made it clear that he had a certain amount of influence over the decision. When we were driving home, he took me to this clearing where you could see the Hollywood sign, and he kissed me, his hands sliding under my dress, coffee on his breath. Let's just say that one thing led to another.

And a week or so later, we met with the record company boss. He said he thought AJ was exactly what he'd been looking for.

Ken: I remember the phone call when I heard about AJ's record deal. It just wasn't the kind of thing that happens to people like us. Grace told me and she was all excited and the money they were offering was just crazy. I asked to speak to AJ, and she put him on. I said, 'So you want to be a pop star?' And he said he guessed he did. I could imagine him standing there, shrugging. I used to watch him on *The Friday Show* when I was lonely. He'd shot up and he was such a good-looking kid and I could see why they wanted him, I really could. I told him that it would be a lot of hard work and not all parties and fun. He said he knew that, but I'm not sure he did, really. I asked how he felt about people recognising him on the street, and he said that already happened. I didn't know that, hadn't thought about it. It was a reminder of how much I didn't know. When I talked to Zak, he sounded kind of sad but he said it wasn't about the record deal. After I got off the phone with them, I just sat on the couch drinking a beer without the TV or any music on, and I thought about AJ being a real star. And I knew, I just knew, that it wouldn't lead to anything good. But I knew, too, that Grace wouldn't listen to me if I said that.

Zak: It felt like it all happened really fast. One day AJ was on a TV show and got recognised a bit, and then the next, he was a star. This one day, it was summer and he and I went to the beach after school. His first single, 'Ice Cream', had come out a week or so before and gone straight into the charts at number four. It was massive, but I hadn't realised the impact it would have. We were mobbed by teenage girls, asking for his autograph, just wanting to touch him, really. We ended up going home after half an hour because it was just too much, you know? I think it was a bit of a shock for both of us, that this was how it was going to be now.

Grace: They made an album and got a single out really fast. The first time I heard 'Ice Cream', I didn't think it was going to be a hit. Shows what I know.

Ken: I started to hear AJ's songs on the radio when I was at work. It was the strangest thing. And I loved it, because it helped me feel connected to him, but I was scared of it, too. Of how fast it all happened.

Grace: Next thing we knew there was a US tour being organised and I had to pull him out of school altogether. The record company organised for a tutor to travel with him, but I usually went too. Zak was old enough to stay on his own. Sometimes he came, but he had schoolwork to do, so often he didn't.

Zak: That sucked, to be honest. I spent a lot of time alone. I was old enough to look after myself, yes, but I was still too young to be fending for myself. Once I had this party, and it got a bit out of hand, and I was preparing myself for Mom to be mad when she got back, but she didn't even notice. It was like she couldn't see me.

Ken: I used to call the house and it was usually Zak who answered, and sometimes he'd tell me he was home alone and I'd say 'huh' and I'd think about the two of us, both on our own but thousands of miles apart, and it seemed like we'd got something wrong somewhere along the way.

Zak: By the time he was fifteen, AJ was the biggest pop star in the world. Even saying that now, I can't believe it. Even having lived through it. He just had the perfect combination of looks and talent and that thing you can't describe or really put your finger on. He was just a star. Once he was, it was hard to see how he'd ever not been. How we hadn't known forever. I think most of the time he loved it, but sometimes he'd come into my room and he'd look like he was on the edge of crying, and I'd ask what was up and he'd say nothing. He used to ask if we could just lie on my bed and listen to some music and pretend we had different lives to the ones we had. I remember him saying that, and thinking about how many people would have killed to have what he had, to be where he was. But I'd do it, all the same. I'd put on *Nevermind* by Nirvana and we'd lie back and close our eyes, our shoulders touching on my narrow bed. He used to talk about Kurt Cobain, how he died at twenty-seven. Just like Jimi Hendrix, Janis Joplin, and Jim Morrison. He said he sometimes thought he wouldn't even make it that far.

Grace: Fame has its downsides. Of course it does. But the upsides outweighed them, no question. AJ was living every teenage boy's dream. Girls and money and fame. He could buy

anything he wanted. He bought us a house, bought three fancy cars – one for me, one for Zak, and one for him to drive when he was old enough. That cracked me up. He was living the high life. Lapping it up. Loving every single minute of it.

Ken: I felt like they were moving further away from me as time passed. They were already so far, geographically, but as AJ's career really blew up, there were more and more people around them who I didn't know. People who were spending a lot of time with my family. Managers and security and God only knows what else.

Grace: The staff was something I hadn't thought about, but when you're making the kind of money he was making then, you need a team behind you. We had a bit of trouble with managers. We couldn't keep them, for some reason. I'm not an idiot. I know AJ could be a bit of a pain, but these people seemed to quit so easily. Then we found Maggie.

Zak: Maggie was great. She knew how to handle AJ and she always seemed to have time for Mom and me, too. She used to come over for dinner every Wednesday night and we'd talk about what was going on with AJ's stuff, but she'd also ask about school and how basketball was going and treat me like my stuff was important too. Her and Mom got on great, and AJ had this quiet respect for her.

Ken: One day I got this call out of the blue and it was from AJ's new manager, Maggie. She said she knew our paths probably wouldn't cross but she was going to be a part of AJ's life and she wanted to introduce herself to me. I really appreciated that. It made me feel like I was a part of it all, for a while.

Maggie: I'd been in the talent management game for a while by the time I started working with AJ. He was a good kid at heart. Moody, demanding, impossible to please. All of that. But underneath it all there was a scared little kid, I think. Getting to know Zak helped me understand AJ, and talking to Ken did, too. I liked Grace, but I could see how she'd pushed him, how she was still pushing him. And I had this sense that it might all end badly. AJ liked being famous, liked having teenage girls trailing behind him everywhere he went, of course he did. But sometimes he came to my office and closed the door and said he just needed an hour away from it all. And I understood that. He was so goddamn young.

The first time we went to Europe, I tried to prepare him for the fact that he was just as big over there as he was in the US. But I don't think he believed me. He hadn't left the States before. And then we got off a plane in France and we were jetlagged, our body clocks all messed up, and there was this crowd of girls outside the hotel. I remember he said that these girls lived on the other side of the world from him, that he didn't even speak the same language they did, but they knew his name and his songs and wanted a piece of him. It was hard to take in.

The travelling was pretty punishing. People talk about these young stars getting all these opportunities, flying all over the world at such a young age, but that's all bullshit. That kid was on planes, in hotel rooms, rehearsal spaces and auditoriums. There was no sightseeing. No culture. We were on our way to a radio interview once and in the car he asked me which country we were in.

Zak: I was there when he came up with the theme park idea. We were hanging out at home. He couldn't really go anywhere by then without his whole entourage. I'd made us packet mac and cheese because it was his favourite – had been ever since he was small – and he was telling me about the tour that had just been confirmed for the following year. It was going to be the biggest one yet, all huge stadiums in huge cities. He asked if I would come. I said I would. And then he went off on this rant about how he never got to actually see any of these places or do anything fun and how he was sick of fancy hotel rooms with windows that didn't even open.

He went quiet for a bit, and we put MTV on, watched some girlband jumping around, hair flying. I knew AJ had kissed one of them. Maybe two. Then he turned to me, eyes wide, and said what if we stayed somewhere cool instead. I asked him where. He said maybe a theme park. I laughed. I thought it was a joke. But the next day he went to Maggie with it, and before I knew it, the wheels were in motion. I mean, it was a crazy idea, really. That's what happens when you give a teenager a lot of money and a lot of power. No one could say no to him. Maggie was pretty good at calling out his bullshit but even she knew he was paying her wages and he could stop at any time. I thought of the whole thing as this out-of-control car, which is ironic really, given how it all ended.

Danny: And that's where we're going to leave it for this week, but be sure to tune in next week for a sweet love story. Can you guess who it might involve? If you've ever been a teenager, you'll relate. Thanks for listening to *What Happened That Summer*? Don't forget to leave us a review if you've enjoyed listening.

SamJBakeford
Well, John seems like a dick #WhatHappenedThatSummer

LucyLou

My God, I used to go to Wildworld as a kid. I couldn't believe it when I heard AJ Silver had died there. It was like hearing Madonna had died at the Spar. Hearing Sebastian describe the place brought so many memories back. Adventure City was my favourite! #WhatHappenedThatSummer

DeanoJones

Wow, AJ's mum is not coming out of this well, huh? #WhatHappenedThatSummer

The_Paul_Wilson

I always thought people who ran theme parks were absolutely raking it in. Things are never what they seem, huh? #WhatHappenedThatSummer

Smithy562

I never knew there was a connection between AJ Silver and Alex Robb! Small world #WhatHappenedThatSummer

KatwithaK

Wildworld was always Alton Towers's shitty little sibling #WhatHappenedThatSummer

MimiShepherd

Great episode! Can't wait for next week! Who's the love story going to be about? Surely not Pea and AJ?! #WhatHappenedThatSummer

JohnnyG63

Let's get straight to the juicy stuff! I want to hear about this new info that's come to light! #WhatHappenedThatSummer

2

EPISODE 2 – A LOVE STORY

Danny: Welcome to episode two of *What Happened That Summer?*, the podcast looking into and around the mysterious death of pop superstar AJ Silver. I'm your host, Danny Drake. Since our first episode aired, AJ Silver's music has had a resurgence, with his *Greatest Hits* album riding high in the download chart and a new remix of 'Ice Cream' bringing him to the attention of a new generation.

Last time, we heard from the Hunters and Pea Hunter's friend Alex about their life before they got entangled with pop royalty and everything came crashing down around them, as well as the call that changed their lives. We also chatted to AJ's family, the Campbells, about AJ's origin story and how his fame impacted them.

I mentioned at the top of the first episode that new information had come to light recently and we've had tons of emails asking what that is. We'll get to it all in good time, but I will say this. There are some people who believe that AJ Silver's death wasn't an unfortunate accident caused by lack of care, but a deliberate malfunction caused by someone in or close to the family. But we'll get to that.

First, a love story. Everyone loves a love story, right? Over to the Hunters.

Pea: Mum let me have the day off school when they were due to arrive. I'm pretty sure Sebastian would have gone into college but it was a teacher training day or something like that. They were landing mid-morning, and Mum had offered to pick them up from the airport.

Cathy: Oh yes, I did offer to pick them up. Maggie laughed at that, said she'd already booked a car. When it pulled up, John was standing next to me looking out of the window. 'A bloody stretch limo,' he said. We couldn't believe it. They were from a different world, and I think that was the first time I fully realised that. Sebastian and Pea were in their rooms, and we called them downstairs. Pea had more makeup on than usual, and I was pretty sure she was wearing a different outfit than she had been when I'd seen her eating breakfast, but I knew better than to say anything.

Pea: Mum and Dad called us downstairs and we were all just standing there, like we were waiting for the queen.

Sebastian: I felt like an idiot. I was a seventeen-year-old guy, waiting for a pop star. And not even the pop star, but his manager and his brother. I would have preferred to be at college, quite honestly.

Maggie: First impressions? I thought the place looked like a dump. I'd been expecting something more flashy. I was starting to understand the way Cathy had reacted when I'd mentioned the budget. But we were there and I hadn't found us any other options. I thought we should make the best of it. Zak had his headphones on, Discman in his lap, and his eyes were closed. I reached up and pulled the headphones off, then said his name right in his ear. He jolted awake. The family were at the door, Cathy and John standing side by side on the front step with their kids in front of them, looking awkward. I got out and Zak tumbled out after me.

Pea: Now, I don't know why, given that I was a teenage girl and 80 per cent of my brain space was taken up with teenage boys, but I hadn't given much thought to the brother. I didn't know his name, even. I think the whole AJ Silver thing was so overwhelming it didn't leave space for anything else. But when he got out of the car, I stopped breathing for a second. He was tall, he had to sort of unfold himself, and he had a similar look to his famous brother. Baggy jeans, long-sleeved top with a T-shirt over it. Hair in curtains that fell over his eyes. And his eyes. I don't remember whether I noticed them at first, but they were like staring into space. It wasn't the colour. They were brown, like mine. It was the flecks that looked like little stars. But I'm getting ahead of myself. I couldn't have noticed all that when he'd just got out of the car. What I will say, though, is it was like he was magnetic. That's the only way I can describe it.

Danny: Ah, first love. And did Zak feel the same way? Let's just say not immediately.

Zak: I didn't want to be there, man. I was eighteen and I was pissed. My baby brother was one of the most famous people on the planet, and what did I have? No job, no girlfriend, no plans of my own. I'd been sort of incorporated into the whole AJ Silver machine. I knew they'd always find things for me to do and ways to give me money for it. But it wasn't what I wanted. This trip was costing a ton, I knew. And all because AJ had decided he wanted to run around a theme park for a few weeks. But if AJ said it, AJ got it. So I wasn't exactly delighted to be on this trip, checking out some dumb park in the middle of nowhere to see if it was fit for the mighty AJ. I barely looked at them, the Hunters. I just wanted to get into the park so we could check it out and be on our way. Maggie had booked us two nights at a hotel nearby but I was hoping we'd split after one.

Cathy: I think I asked whether they'd like to come in for a cup of tea or go straight into the park. Maggie looked at Zak and said she'd kill for a coffee. So we all trailed into the house and I put the kettle on. John showed them into the lounge. I don't think we even knew Zak's name at that point, but I could already see that Pea was smitten. I must have asked them both three times how they took their coffee. I was so nervous. A lot was riding on this.

Maggie: They were very pleasant, very welcoming. The coffee was terrible.

John: I was eager to get out and show them what they'd come to see. I wasn't great at small talk, but when it came to talking about that park, that's where I would shine. I knew every inch of that place inside out and back to front. There wasn't a question they could have asked me that I wouldn't have been able to answer. Having said that, she did throw me with the very first thing she asked when we stepped outside.

Maggie: I asked whether they'd have room for three or four tour buses to park on site, and for mobile toilet and showering facilities. He looked surprised but he recovered well. Said he thought everyone would be staying in a hotel, like we were for this trip.

Zak: I laughed at that. I said it was one thing for me and Maggie to stay in a hotel in the middle of town and drive over to the park each day, but AJ couldn't do that, or wouldn't want to, at least. They'd obviously never come into contact with fame. Most people haven't, of course, but it was ingrained in me at that point. Anywhere AJ went, they found him. The fans. If he checked into a hotel, even if he used a different name, they were there before he'd ridden the elevator to his suite. I hadn't seen much of this place on the ride over but I was pretty sure it was the ass end of nowhere. And AJ was going to be here for six weeks, at least potentially. He'd told me the whole reason he came up with the theme park idea was because he wanted a break from all of it, in between the gigs. It was crucial that he stayed onsite and didn't go anywhere.

John: There was the car park, obviously, but Maggie explained that they'd ideally want somewhere that was in the park itself, within the gates, so people couldn't get to it. She said that otherwise the car park would be flooded with teenage girls for the duration of their stay. It was only then that I started to get a sense of just how famous this boy was. There was this big open space that people used for picnics or just to run around. Sometimes we put a circus tent there, or a birds of prey display. I thought that would probably be big enough for what they needed, so I said we'd head there first.

Maggie: There was enough space, and John showed me the access, how they could open up a big gate that was usually locked and the tour buses could drive right in. So that was the first tick in the box.

Danny: I think this was a real turning point for John. Like he says, he didn't have a sense of quite how big AJ Silver was before now. And I think everyone is seduced by fame and fortune, even someone like John. Sebastian was different, though.

Pea: Mum and I trailed along behind Dad's little tour, keen to be involved, but Sebastian stayed in the house.

Sebastian: No, I didn't go. I could see Dad was pissed off about that, but I just couldn't bring myself to care all that much.

Zak: When John asked where we wanted to go next, I said I wanted to see the biggest and best ride they had. AJ was a thrill-seeker and I knew he'd be disappointed if they didn't have a rollercoaster that did loops.

John: We had a couple of pretty great rollercoasters, but we didn't have one that fully inverted and I'd known for a while that we were going to have to get one if we wanted business to pick up. Alton Towers had had the Corkscrew for more than a decade and had fairly recently added the Thunder Looper, and there was talk in the industry of Thorpe Park coming up with something new and big. We'd never been able to compete with those parks, not really, but I was always keen to keep the distance between us as small as possible. I'd looked into the cost of getting a new, big rollercoaster designed and built, and we just couldn't afford it. Simple as that. I took them to Canyon. It was a few years old but it was a good rollercoaster.

Maggie: He asked whether we wanted a ride, but he was looking at Zak. I think I surprised him when I said I would. There were a handful of people in the queue and he led us to the front and ushered us into a carriage.

Pea: Dad went in after Maggie, which left me to sit next to Zak. I knew Mum wouldn't come on. She never went on the rides. I couldn't look at Zak. I felt like my face would catch on fire if I did. I'd been riding Canyon since the day we got it and I knew that near the end of the circuit, we'd be tipped on our sides and I would be pressed against his body for a second or two. I was dreading it and I couldn't wait.

Zak: Canyon was a pretty decent ride. It didn't loop but I knew AJ would like it. It was fast and smooth. Better than I expected.

Pea: It honestly felt like time stopped when we were coming up to that last bit of the ride. I held the bar tight and tried to stop myself from sliding against Zak, but it didn't work, of course. I could feel the heat of his body through our T-shirts.

Maggie: The minute the ride finished, John turned to me and asked what I thought. I said it was pretty good. But I was thinking if this was the best they had, then maybe we were done here.

Danny: This, from Maggie, is so telling. It could all so easily not have happened, or happened completely differently.

John: I wanted to keep the momentum going, so I took them straight from Canyon to the Wonder Wheel. You could see the whole park from the top, and whenever I went on there, I couldn't help but be impressed, looking down at all the people and the rides. This time, the four of us were in a carriage together. I remember my knees kept knocking against Zak's. We shouldn't have sat opposite each other. I don't think he said anything the whole time we were on there, but I kept Maggie chatting with questions about whether they were planning to see anything else while they were over in the UK. I wanted to know whether they had any other parks lined up to visit, and if so, who our competition was, but she kept her answers pretty vague. Said they only had a couple of nights and they'd see how well they got on today before deciding how to spend tomorrow.

Pea: I'd always had this dream of being kissed on the Wonder Wheel. I'd been thinking about it for years, since Alex had asked me about my ideal first kiss. Neither of us had kissed anyone at that point, which is funny to think of now, given how well known Alex is. We were misfits, weren't we? He rarely met anyone else who was gay, and I wasn't on anyone's radar. That ride on the Wonder Wheel with Zak, Maggie and Dad, I closed my eyes and tried to shut out Dad's ramblings, tried to imagine it was just me and Zak. It was a tight fit, four of us in one carriage, so my leg was up against his. It felt like my heart was beating a little too fast, and a little irregularly, and I thought everyone would know. But if they did, no one said anything.

Zak: It's so hard to remember when I first noticed that Pea was cute. But I do know that when we were on that wheel, I made eye contact with her for a second, and she smiled, kind of shy, and I just felt all the irritation I had inside me falling away. Like she released me from it or something.

Danny: So glad Zak's on the same page, or at least getting there.

Maggie: It was useful to get an overview of the whole site. It was a bit bigger than I'd thought. I tried to imagine what AJ would think, but it's hard to put yourself in the shoes of a sixteen-year-old boy when you're a thirty-eight-year-old woman. But that's where Zak came in. I'd quiz him later, in the hotel.

John: After that, I handed them a map and let them go where they wanted. I asked whether they'd like a guided tour of the whole place or to just explore on their own, and it was clear that they preferred the latter suggestion. So Cathy, Pea and I went back to the house and waited. Sebastian was up in his room, probably working. He was doing his A levels. When he came down for some lunch, he didn't ask how it had gone.

Cathy: I remember they were gone for hours. I couldn't settle to anything. John went back out to oversee things. He'd told all the staff about the visit, of course, and everyone knew to be on their best behaviour. So I was surprised when I heard about the incident on the Spinning Plates.

Pea: The Spinning Plates was like a high-tech roundabout, I suppose. There were three big plates, with space for ten people to sit in a circle on each one. The whole thing rotated and then each individual plate rotated in the opposite direction. It wasn't one of my favourites.

John: I was furious when I found out what had happened.

Pea: Kyle Lambert had been a couple of years above Sebastian at school and everyone knew who he was. The Lamberts were one of those families – four boys, all a few years apart. His brother Shane was in my year. Kyle had been working at the park for a few months – it was a common post-school or gap year job. He was operating the Spinning Plates when Maggie and Zak arrived, apparently. He must have realised who they were, given Zak's resemblance to his brother, and Maggie said later that he did a less than flattering rendition of one of AJ's songs – 'Baby Let's Go', I think – with accompanying dance moves while they were on the ride.

Zak: Yeah, some jumped-up kid was singing 'Baby Let's Go' and dancing. I kept sneaking looks at Maggie and the tension was radiating off her. I knew she'd get him fired.

John: Yes, I fired Kyle Lambert on the spot. And I made an example of him, too, by gathering all the staff who were onsite at closing time and doing it in front of them.

Pea: I knew Dad would fire Kyle over it, and I also knew it would cause me problems at school.

Maggie: John told us he'd fired the kid, and I was impressed by that. I'd started to think this wasn't our place, but that showed me he was serious.

Cathy: They finally returned to the house in the middle of the afternoon.

Maggie: My jetlag was catching up with me. I was desperate to lock myself in my room and have a bubble bath with a large glass of red. Zak didn't seem to be showing any signs of being tired, though, and I thought he'd probably want to go somewhere to eat. That's why I suggested Pea show him around.

Pea: There we were, all in the kitchen, which was too small for that many people, and Maggie said why didn't Zak and I go out for an early dinner. I didn't know what to say.

Zak: Yeah, it was Maggie's suggestion. I don't think it was a matchmaking thing, I think she was just tired and wanted to spend the evening by herself. I wanted a burger and I didn't have any objections to getting one with this pretty girl, so I shrugged and said it was fine by me, and we ended up agreeing to meet up at a diner near our hotel.

Danny: Clearly a matchmaking thing, I'd say.

Cathy: Pea didn't know what to do with herself after they'd gone. She'd never been out with a boy, other than Alex. I was a bit unsure about it, with him being three years older. I dragged John into the kitchen, but he said she was nearly sixteen and I had to stop being overprotective. Looking back, I'm pretty sure he just didn't want anything to get in the way of the deal being done.

Pea: I spent ages getting ready, choosing what to wear. Then Alex called to ask how it had all gone and I took the upstairs phone into my bedroom and lay on my back on the bed, filling him in.

Alex: I knew there was something she wasn't telling me. She sounded all distracted, and then she said she had to go and she'd tell me the rest at school. I asked her to wait, and she went quiet. Then I asked what the brother looked like and she did this sort of giggle that I'd never heard from her before. And I thought, 'Ah, so that's it. Pea fancies the brother.' I didn't think anything would actually come of it.

Pea: You have to understand, I'd never been on a date. Never had a coffee, let alone a dinner, with a boy other than Alex. The place we'd arranged to meet was somewhere I'd been with my parents and Sebastian once or twice, and once for Alex's birthday. As I approached it, I could see him standing outside, smoking a cigarette. He was leaning back against the building, wearing the same clothes he'd been wearing earlier that day. Baggy jeans, layered T-shirts with a faded band logo on. I couldn't quite make it out. Had I gone to too much effort, and would he know? I was wearing a short denim skirt and a fitted Blur T-shirt with Converse. He had Converse on too. When he saw me, he threw his cigarette on the floor and stepped on it, gave me a lazy sort of smile. It took all the concentration I could muster to keep putting one foot in front of the other and give him a smile.

Danny: Takes you right back, doesn't it? First dates and teenage hormones and feeling like you'll die if someone doesn't kiss you.

Zak: Pea's smile was like warm sunshine. You know those days when it's been a long winter and there's a break in the weather and you can go outside with nothing on your feet and feel the warmth of the sun on the sidewalk? Pea's smile felt like that.

Pea: We stood there for a bit, just looking at each other, and I allowed myself to believe maybe he felt something for me. And then he opened the door and gestured for me to go in underneath his arm. He smelled like spice and summer.

Zak: The place was an American diner, but it was kind of exaggerated American, you know? It didn't feel like a diner you'd actually get back at home. But the burgers looked good. Pea was quiet. I wondered whether her dad had told her to make sure she helped seal the deal.

Pea: We ordered burgers and fries and Cokes, I think. I had no appetite. My stomach was churning. I wanted to ask what they'd thought of the place, whether they'd made a decision. It had been a good three hours since they'd left our house, so I was sure they must have talked about it. In the end, I settled for asking if he'd had a good day.

Zak: I told her I was pretty beat. The burgers came and they tasted like crap. I mostly ate fries dipped in ketchup. I knew I was being a bit of a dick, but somehow I couldn't rouse myself to do better. I guess maybe I was just tired, like I said.

Pea: I felt like it was going really badly. Started wishing for it to be over. But then I thought of something to try. I asked him about the band on his T-shirt.

Zak: I was wearing a Pavement T-shirt. She hadn't heard of them. I had no idea whether they were big in England. She pointed to her T-shirt, asked if I'd heard of Blur. I shook my head. Then we started naming bands we liked until we hit on some we had in common. Nirvana and the Pixies. I started singing 'Smells Like Teen Spirit' and she joined in and she sort of lit up. Music did that to me, too. It was like magic. She said she was surprised I was into that kind of stuff, and I asked whether she'd assumed I just listened to my brother's stuff on repeat. She laughed, and there was something so incredible about the sound of it, the unrestrained joy. It wasn't until later, when I was in an unfamiliar bed and on the edge of sleep, that I realised that was the first time my brother had come up that evening.

Danny: Since these interviews, I've been listening to Pavement on and off. They passed me by in the nineties, a bit like Pea, but they're pretty good. Some music from that time sounds so old now, but I think their stuff holds up pretty well. Have a listen.

Pea: He said he'd run back to the hotel when we were finished and grab me a Pavement CD. I said I wished I'd brought a Blur CD, so we could swap. And he said he could borrow the Blur CD from me when he walked me home. I didn't even see Shane Lambert approaching. I was too busy falling in love, or lust, or whatever.

Zak: This kid came up to the table. Pea told me afterwards he was the younger brother of the kid her dad had fired that afternoon. He put both his hands on our table and looked from me to her, his eyes full of fury. He said her family would regret what they'd done, that if you mess with one Lambert, you mess with them all. Then he was gone. Out the door. He must have seen us in there from the street. Pea was a bit shaken. I could see she was close to tears. I said why didn't she go to the bathroom and I'd take care of the check and meet her outside.

Pea: I was so flustered. Zak was great. Sent me off to the toilets to sort myself out and paid the bill. I stared in the mirror for a minute or so, blinking back tears. What if Zak told Maggie about it and said it was all too much trouble? I knew Mum and Dad were counting on this. And what would it be like at school, when Shane got his mates involved?

Zak: When she appeared, her eyes were red. I put my arms around her and gave her a hug. I just wanted to touch her.

Pea: When he put his arms around me, I could hardly breathe.

Zak: I wanted her to feel better. And yes, I was kind of curious about her. She had this way of pushing her hair away from her face and hooking it behind her ears that made me smile. Back at home, at high school, it was all girls I'd known forever, and I was always second choice to AJ, even though I was the older one. But Pea was looking at me like I was someone interesting, and not because my brother was famous. I was a sucker for that, I guess.

Pea: We walked to his hotel and, as promised, he disappeared to get me the CD. It was called *Slanted and Enchanted*. I said thank you and turned to walk away. I thought he might have forgotten that he'd said he would walk me home. But he called after me and covered the distance between us in a couple of loping strides, and we fell into step. He asked whether I was trying to get rid of him, and I laughed and said no, that I thought he might be tired.

Zak: I was so tired, man. You know the kind of tired that feels a bit like being drunk? But I didn't want the evening to end. It didn't take us long to walk back to her place. Not long enough.

Pea: He asked what it was like, living in a theme park. I shrugged. It was all I'd ever known. He said he thought it was pretty cool. I didn't know what to say to that, so I told him to wait while I got his CD. *Parklife*. It was in my CD player. Mum called out from the lounge to ask how my evening had been and I said I'd be there in five minutes. I was a bit out of breath when I got back outside. He took the CD case from me and our fingers touched and I took a sharp breath in.

Zak: I leaned in and kissed her. It wasn't really like me, to move so fast, but I was worried the next time I saw this girl I'd have my brother with me and I wanted to stake my claim, I guess.

Pea: First kiss. Not on the Wonder Wheel but under a streetlamp by the park entrance. I remember he put his hands on my face as he leaned in. It was magical. It was over too quickly.

Zak: I thought maybe I'd got it wrong, that she hadn't wanted me to kiss her. And then she broke out in this huge grin, and I did too, and I said goodnight and turned to walk away.

Pea: I stood there for a minute or two, my body tingling all over, waiting to see if he'd look back. But he didn't.

Danny: So, that's it. First date. Shall we see how the next day panned out?

Maggie: I was awake at three the next morning. Zak and I had agreed to meet for breakfast at eight. So I lay there with my head on that lumpy hotel pillow, the room just a degree or two too warm, going over everything we'd seen the day before. Truth was, I wasn't sure I wanted to spend six weeks of my life in this one-horse town. But there was something about the family I liked. We hadn't spent much time with Cathy but I got a really good vibe from her. And Pea was sweet. I wondered how her dinner date with Zak had gone.

Zak: I must have been in a really deep sleep when my alarm went off because it took me a while to come round. Maggie had asked at reception for a wakeup call for me. It was seven forty-five. If I got out of bed straight away, there'd be time for a shower before our breakfast. But I didn't, and there wasn't. Pea flashed into my brain, once and then again, and I smiled to myself. I'd listened to her Blur CD on my Discman twice after walking back to the hotel the previous night. The first time, I wasn't sure about it, but by the second, I'd started to like some of the songs. They were catchy, and the lyrics were a bit unexpected. I was planning to listen to it once more before giving it back to her that day.

Maggie: I got to the hotel restaurant at three minutes to eight. Zak arrived at about twenty past, and by that time I was on my second bowl of fruit and my third coffee.

Zak: Maggie and I hadn't had much chance to catch up the day before, because she'd wanted to go to her room and call her husband when we got back to the hotel, and then I'd gone out with Pea. She got straight in there, asking me what I thought of the park. More specifically, what I thought AJ would think. I said I thought it was perfect. She looked surprised.

Maggie: He definitely hadn't thought it was perfect the day before. Something had changed.

Zak: She asked me whether something had happened with Pea, and I was back there for a moment, my hands on her warm skin and my lips on hers. My face must have given it away.

Maggie: I couldn't believe it. We'd been there less than twenty-four hours and he'd seduced the daughter! Sorry... I don't mean to laugh. It's not a joke, but, it did strike me as funny at the time!

Zak: I said I hadn't seduced her. That we'd got on well and we'd kissed.

Maggie: I'd known Zak for a long time and I hadn't seen him like that about a girl, all flustered and a bit embarrassed. Come to think of it, I hadn't really seen Zak with many girls, which was strange because he was a good-looking kid.

Zak: It's not exactly easy to meet someone when you're the brother of the most famous pop star in the world, you know?

Maggie: I ate toast and watched Zak put away a plate full of sausages, bacon, mushrooms and eggs washed down with a gallon of coffee. Then I asked if he was ready to go. He said he needed ten minutes, and I said I'd meet him outside, that I'd call the car.

Zak: Everyone knows ten minutes doesn't mean exactly ten minutes, don't they? But when I got out on the street, after a quick shower and change, the car was waiting and Maggie was inside it, looking pissed. We didn't speak on the way over to the park.

Pea: That second day was a Saturday, and Alex had turned up at nine, desperate to get in on the action. I didn't tell him about the kiss. I couldn't stop thinking about it, though. Zak's hands, and his lips, and the way my stomach had turned over when he leaned in. I thought Alex might know, just from looking at me. I thought it might show, on my face.

Alex: I didn't know about the kiss that day, no. I guess maybe Pea was acting a bit strangely but that was sort of to be expected, given that her family's theme park was being assessed for suitability for *the* AJ Silver. It's not every day something like that happens, and certainly not in our town. It wasn't long after I arrived that that massive fuck-off limo turned up and Maggie and Zak got out of it. Zak was hot, no doubt about it. He had that lazy, laidback American look, like that guy from *My So-Called Life* that Pea and I talked about endlessly. The one who leaned.

Pea: I could tell that Alex fancied Zak.

Zak: Alex was kind of annoying. Pea had mentioned him the night before, said that he was her best friend and that he'd probably be around that day, but all I was interested in was getting her on her own so we could make out again, and it seemed to me that that was pretty unlikely with him hanging out with us.

John: I asked them how they wanted to play it. Whether they wanted to wander around on their own again, or have more of a structured tour this time. Zak just shrugged. Maggie was clearly in charge, but I wasn't sure about who was going to make the final decision. Zak hadn't been brought over for nothing, had he?

Maggie: I said what about Pea and Alex showing us around. I didn't want John doing a hard sell on us, and I thought I'd probably get more of an insight into what AJ might think by spending the day with teenagers. John didn't look all that happy. He was a bit of a control freak, I think, and he wanted to make sure we saw what he wanted us to see. But I wanted to see it all, even the bits that weren't so sanitised and clean. Especially those. So that's what we did. John said if he wasn't needed he was going to go and oversee the powering up of the bigger rides. He pointed to the walkie talkie on his belt and told Pea to take one, in case we needed him. Cathy went off to the kitchen, and I think Sebastian was watching TV, not taking much interest in any of it.

Alex: I had all these questions I wanted to ask about AJ, like whether he was involved in writing the songs and how he spent all his money, but I didn't want them to think I wasn't cool. So I just asked how their flight had been and what they thought of Wildworld so far.

Zak: I tried to engineer it so Alex was a bit ahead, asking Maggie all his inane questions. It worked, too. I brushed my hand against Pea's and she looked over at me. I said hi. She said hi, then looked down at the floor. She was wearing another band T-shirt. Pulp. I asked her about them, and she started to say she'd lend me a CD but then I guess she remembered I was flying home the next day and she went quiet. I tried to get her talking again, asked if she'd listened to the Pavement album, but she said she'd fallen asleep straight after she got home.

Maggie: It was obvious there was something going on between the two of them, so I played my part. I chatted to Pea's friend Alex, who was obviously a bit fame-hungry and excited by my proximity to that life. He asked me what AJ eats for breakfast. I said that AJ was a teenage boy and ate pretty much everything he could get his hands on, but that I thought his ideal breakfast was probably chocolate Pop Tarts and about a loaf's worth of toast with peanut butter.

Alex: Maggie was cool. She was almost our parents' age but she seemed so different from them. I asked whether she had kids and she shook her head and looked away. I thought maybe it was having kids that made you boring.

Pea: I told Alex to head for the Pirate Ship, and he laughed and said, 'You and your pirate ship.' Zak asked why there, and I said it was my favourite ride. We got on the very back row, which is always my favourite place to sit, and when we got to the highest point I reached across and peeled Zak's hands off the metal bar and he laughed and put them in the air like mine. I snuck a look at Maggie, but she wasn't giving anything away.

Zak: I'd been on rides like that a hundred times. AJ had always been a theme park nut, and Dad had taken us to tons of parks with tons of rides. But there was something about it, sitting there next to Pea, my hands in the air and my heart in my throat. I felt like I was a kid again, and somehow like I was older, too, and more sure of what I wanted. When it stopped, I felt like something inside me had changed.

Maggie: A pirate ship's a pirate ship, am I right?

Pea: After we got off, Maggie asked where I'd go next, if it was just me and I could go anywhere. I almost laughed at that, because I *could* go anywhere. This place had always felt like my playground. I looked at Alex and he raised his eyebrows and we both said it at the same time. Wild Water Rapids. Sometimes, we'd go on that thing five times in a row. It was Alex's favourite, and I loved it too. You never knew how wet you'd get, or who in the boat would bear the brunt of it. I led them over, raised a hand to Jack, who was getting people on and off the boats, and he waved us through.

Zak: We all got in the boat, Maggie first, then me, then Pea and finally Alex. The seats were a bit wet and I felt the water seeping through my jeans. I looked over at Pea and she was smiling at Alex. It was like the two of them had this private, unspoken language. I didn't like it. And then I realised I was actually feeling jealous, of this guy who I was pretty sure was gay, because he was closer than I was to this girl I'd met literally one day before.

Maggie: I thought I'd got through it relatively unscathed but then right at the end this enormous wave crashed over the side of the boat, soaking me through. Luckily, my hair stayed dry, but my jeans were drenched. I said something about this being a great idea as we got off, and then I saw that Pea felt bad about it, so I gave her a quick smile and said it didn't matter, but I would need to head back to the hotel to get changed. Pea asked if she or her mum could lend me something, but she was a lot smaller than me and I'd seen the kind of clothes her mum wore, so I politely declined. Said I would just get the driver to take me back, do a quick change and meet them back near the gift shop in an hour.

Pea: I kept thinking that if this was what put them off the place, Dad would kill me.

Alex: It felt a bit strange after Maggie had gone. Pea and I had been roaming that park unsupervised for years, but somehow that day I felt like we were kids who'd escaped their adults and were going on the rampage. I asked Pea where we were going next, and she suggested getting an ice cream so that Maggie didn't miss any of the rides. So that's what we did.

Zak: I got the ice creams and we found a picnic table. It was getting warm and I was pressed up against Pea and I wished to God that Alex wasn't there.

Pea: I remember that Zak put a hand on my knee under the table and I felt like my heart would jump out of my body. Or stop altogether. One or the other. Alex was talking about school, how he'd never understood what the different year groups were called in America, what sophomore was, and junior, and freshman, and Zak was explaining it but all I could focus on was the pressure of his hand on my knee, the small, slow circles he was making with his index finger. I kept thinking that I couldn't wait to tell Alex all about it, and then remembering that Alex was right there, living through this moment with me, but not really.

Alex: Pea was definitely being more girly and giggly than I was used to. She obviously had a crush on Zak. Why wouldn't she? I certainly did. After we'd finished eating, Zak said he was going for a smoke and asked if either of us wanted one. We said we didn't smoke, and we both watched him amble away. The second he was out of earshot, Pea grabbed hold of my hands and told me that he'd kissed her. I had to tell her she was so high-pitched only bats could hear her. It felt like a kick in the teeth. It had always been me and her, hopeless romantics and hopeless at anything romantic. And what, now she was just kissing fit Americans? How the hell had that happened?

Pea: I'd thought Alex would be excited for me, but he seemed sort of pissed off.

Zak: There was an atmosphere between them when I got back. I tried to get a conversation about music going but it ended up with Alex asking me loads of questions about AJ, about our family background and how he'd got into the music business. I gave him chapter and verse – the singing and dancing lessons, the agent, *The Friday Show*, the family move from Georgia to LA which didn't include my dad. He looked a bit embarrassed at that bit, and then said he'd heard that divorce was much more common in the States, which sounded like bullshit to me. People fall out of love everywhere, don't they?

Pea: I couldn't wait for Maggie to get back. When it was just the three of us, it was all wrong. I couldn't quite put my finger on why.

Maggie: When I came back for round two, we covered a lot of the same ground Zak and I had covered the day before, but it was so much quicker with Pea in tow. Not because of bypassing the lines – John had given us a special ticket for that – but because she knew every cut-through and shortcut in the place. I was pretty sure that, by the end of the day, we'd seen everything that Wildworld had to offer. I was ready for an early night and a flight back to my husband.

Zak: I hadn't wanted to go, but now I didn't want to leave.

Pea: I mean, I knew he was leaving. I thought about films I'd watched, where one person would ask the other to stay. Thought about how little control I had over my own life. When they were going back to the hotel, he asked if I'd meet him for a walk later.

Danny: I don't know about you but I am right back in my teenage years, feeling all that incredible longing and heartache.

Alex: When they'd gone, Pea and I went up to her bedroom and I told her to tell me everything. Every last detail. But she was sort of coy about it. She kept saying that it felt like something really special and she felt like talking about it would take the shine off or something. I asked her whether she knew what a big deal this was, her being with AJ Silver's brother. She said they weren't together and reminded me that he lived in LA. I went home in the end. Sometimes she got like that and there was really no talking to her.

Pea: I was nervous about telling Mum and Dad I was meeting Zak again. I went downstairs. They were sitting at the kitchen table, heads together, no doubt talking about how the visit had gone. I said I was going to go out for a walk in a bit. I was hoping they'd just assume I meant with Alex, but Mum must have got the scent of something suspicious and she asked straight out if I was seeing Zak again. I said I was. Dad smiled, said he couldn't have come up with it himself but a romance was just the thing to make sure they chose us. Mum gave him a hard stare for that. She asked where we were going. I think she was worried we were going to go back to his hotel. I panicked a bit at the thought of that. Kissing was one thing, but I wasn't sure I was ready for anything else. And Zak was three years older, and he looked like *that*, so he was bound to have loads more experience than me. If I'd had a mobile phone back then, I might well have called the whole thing off, because of nerves. But I'd said I would meet him and I knew Dad would make sure I did. If a romance was enough to seal the deal, a no-show might be enough to break it.

Zak: I wanted to ask her to come up to my hotel room and lie on the bed with her with an earphone each and listen to music. And yes, of course I wanted to kiss her again. But I didn't know how she'd react to any of that, so we walked, as planned. I'm not sure whether it was something to do with walking and not looking at her as I spoke, but I found myself really opening up to her. I told her all about how AJ getting into music had been cool at first, but how it had taken on a life of its own and been a big factor in my parents' divorce. Dad had wanted AJ and me to be normal kids, but Mum was adamant that AJ was destined for greatness, and once he became a star, she was adamant that she'd been right all along. After we moved to LA, everything was about AJ and his career. I sometimes wished I'd stayed in Atlanta with Dad. Pea just listened. Sometimes, people try to tell you about things they've been through that are similar, but she didn't do that. I think we both knew that the turns my life had taken were pretty extreme. She just let me pour it all out, and said it must be hard. And just that acknowledgement, that his success had taken a toll on me, was all I needed, I think. I was so grateful for that. I wanted to hold her hand, but she kept reaching up to tuck her hair behind her ear. One time, when she did it, I grabbed it and wrapped it in mine, and when I snuck a glance at her, she looked happy.

Pea: When we'd done a loop of the town centre, walked along the side of the river for a bit and seen most of what the town had to offer, I led us back to his hotel. He hadn't kissed me, but we'd held hands for some of the walk and it had felt so natural. I wondered whether he might ask me to go to his room with him, and what I would say if he did.

Zak: We just stood there outside the hotel door for a minute or so. I was kicking at the ground with the toe of my sneaker. I was nervous, man. I was so young, and we'd only just met, but I had this feeling that this girl was it for me. And she lived on a different continent.

Pea: I just blurted it out into the silence in the end. Asked whether he thought they would choose us.

Zak: I said I would do everything in my power to make sure this was where we came for AJ's tour.

Pea: I believed him. It felt like it was really something, this thing between us. I went up on my tiptoes and put my hands on the sides of his face, the way he'd done to me the night before, and I kissed him. His stubble was scratchy and his lips were soft. I felt like I would do anything for him in that moment. When he pulled away, he grabbed my hand and pulled me behind him through the door. I couldn't look at him in the lift as we went past floors two, and three, and four. And then we were out in the hallway again and he was opening the key to a room and all I could see in there was this huge bed.

Zak: I was very conscious of the fact that she was fifteen. I just wanted to keep on kissing her. And not in the street, where everyone could see. But she was so nervous that her hands were shaking when I took them in mine. I said there was no pressure, that we weren't going to do anything she didn't want to do, and then I purposely didn't kiss her, so she'd believe what I was saying. I sat down on the bed, reached onto the bedside table for my Discman and CDs, and handed them to her to flick through. She chose Dinosaur Jr, and I handed her one of the earphones and we lay down, side by side. There was always something so powerful about listening to an album with someone in silence.

Pea: I liked the music, but I liked kissing him more. I was painfully aware that our time was short and we were wasting it. It seemed impossible that I'd spent all those days and months and years not touching him, not even knowing he existed. Would we keep in touch? Would he give me his address? He had mine, of course. We were on the last song when the phone rang and Zak leaned across me to get to it. I couldn't hear the person on the other end, but I saw his reaction. When he hung up, he said my parents were in the lobby and they were pissed. I knew, then, that this was my last opportunity to kiss him, possibly ever, so I did. He wasn't expecting it, but he kissed me back, just for a minute or so, and then he pulled away and said we had to go down to the lobby. I said that we call it reception, and he laughed and said he didn't care what we called it, he cared that my parents thought he was up here defiling their daughter.

Zak: We must have looked sheepish as hell, emerging from that elevator, even though we hadn't been doing anything. John didn't say anything, but Cathy asked me if I knew that Pea was only fifteen years old. I put both my hands up in surrender and said that there had been nothing going on in my room. Cathy laughed at that.

Pea: I said he was right, we'd just been listening to music, but Mum was really wound up. Did the whole 'Do you think we were born yesterday?' thing. I looked at Dad. Because in truth, he's the one I would have expected to get upset about something like this, but he was hanging back, quiet. And that's when I realised that the AJ Silver deal meant more to him than my innocence did. That he wasn't prepared to get aggro with Zak, in case it ruined the whole thing.

Cathy: Maggie appeared at some point, and she calmed me down. I was so angry that John wasn't backing me up. What father doesn't care that their fifteen-year-old daughter is spending time in a hotel room with an eighteen-year-old boy?

John: I believed them, that's all. Pea was a sensible girl. If she said they were just listening to music, then they were just listening to music.

Maggie: I was in my pyjamas when I got a call from the lobby saying there was some trouble with Zak. I pulled on my jeans and a vest top and went down there to find Cathy screaming at Zak and Pea. I told Zak to go upstairs and let me deal with it and Pea looked like she was going to cry.

Pea: We didn't get to say goodbye. I appreciated Maggie trying to calm things down, but in the months that followed, I replayed that night over and over and never got over the fact that we didn't get a goodbye kiss or even a hug.

Zak: I didn't want to go, but Maggie was in charge. I said goodbye to Pea without getting any closer to her and she bit her lip to stop herself from crying. I went back to my room, put my earphones in and turned the music up as loud as it would go. I didn't want to talk to Maggie about this afterwards. We had the whole journey home for that.

Cathy: Maggie kept saying that Zak was a good kid, and that she was sorry. We left in the end. There was nothing else to say and John was still doing a great impression of a mime artist, so I took hold of Pea's arm and marched out. As soon as we were on the pavement outside, she pulled away. She didn't talk to us on the walk home, and when we got to the house, she went straight up the stairs. What killed me was that she didn't seem angry, just desperately sad. And I remembered how it all felt, at that age. I lay awake that night wishing she could just have a crush on a boy at school, like everyone else.

John: I had no idea whether we'd blown the whole thing. No idea. I opened a beer when we got home and took it into the lounge, put the TV on. I chose something I knew Cathy wouldn't like. It was petty. Pea had stormed upstairs, and Sebastian was getting ready for bed. It was a quiet house that night.

Danny: So that's how the visit ended. Lots of tension and lust in the air. Life for the Hunters went back to normal while they waited to hear the verdict.

Pea: God, the wait. It had all ended so abruptly and none of us knew where we stood. Dad was wound so tightly for weeks.

Cathy: We didn't hear anything for a while. You have to remember, email and mobile phones were still in their infancy, so there was no way of sending a quick message. I thought Maggie might phone, a day or two after they left, and at least tell us when we could expect to hear from them with an answer, but nothing. John was awful to live with.

John: I was tense, yes. Who wouldn't be? This was make or break for us.

Pea: I didn't care about the money. I only cared about seeing Zak again. And everyone at school kept asking and asking about it. Shane Lambert had stayed true to his word and was trying to make my life difficult at every opportunity. In Science, he'd knock my test tube onto the floor and I'd have to get a dustpan and brush to clear up the broken glass. In PE, he'd call across from where the boys were playing football to where us girls were playing netball. Just little jibes, nothing that could get him in too much trouble. Once, when he knew I had Home Ec after lunch, he snuck into my things and cracked the egg I'd brought in for making scones all over my other ingredients. I only talked to Alex about it. I didn't tell anyone at home. What would have been the point?

Cathy: Problems at school? First I've heard of it. She was definitely down in the dumps for a while after that visit, but I thought she was just mooning over Zak.

Sebastian: God, it was tiresome. Everyone on tenterhooks. Every time the phone rang, they'd all jump. And it went on for so long.

John: It was about six weeks, I think.

Cathy: It was a good couple of months.

Pea: Zak's letter arrived fifty days after he left. Which felt like several lifetimes.

John: Cathy always put the post on the hall table, and then we'd each have a look and pick up anything addressed to us. I saw that airmail envelope and knew I'd have to wait for Pea to get back from school before I could find out whether it gave us any clues. Plus I knew that she could flatly refuse to tell us what he'd said.

Cathy: It killed John, having to wait to see what some boy had written to Pea. When she got home that day, she put her head around the office door and John just happened to be there. He was helping me with a spreadsheet. He told her there was a letter for her inside, that it was from America. She went bright red and turned to go. John followed her.

Pea: Dad followed me into the house, as if he expected me to open the letter and read it out loud to him there and then. I told him I was going upstairs. He put his hand over mine on the banister. I looked at him. His eyes were pleading. He asked me to tell him if there was any news about the tour. I think I realised then, for the first time, that we might really be in trouble if it didn't go ahead. I said I would tell him, and went upstairs.

Hey Pea

I'm so sorry about how it all went down that last night we were in England. Things have been crazy since we got back. AJ's got a new single out next month and he's starting the US leg of the tour in October. I'm trying to decide whether to leave high school and go with them. Mum's going, and she says it's up to me, but I know she wants me to come because then it won't feel like she's abandoning me. It was so good to talk to you about all that stuff, and I'm pretty sure I know what you'd say. Stay at home and finish high school, right? I know that's the sensible thing to do, but it's hard to always choose the sensible option when the alternative involves travel and music and being with your family. I talked to AJ about it last night. He said he'll always make sure I'm okay for money, so why am I bothering with high school anyway? I didn't know how to tell him that I didn't want to always be in his shadow, to always rely on him to pay my rent for me. There's this English teacher at school, and she says she thinks I would make a good journalist. And I know that's not the kind of thing that will make me rich and famous, like my brother, but when she said it, it made me really happy. It made me want to try.

Anyway, I know I should have written sooner. I've been thinking about you all the time. I can't wait until I see you again.

Love, Zak

Pea: I read it three times. It was frustratingly short. But at least I had his address now. I knew I'd write back immediately and then hold off on sending it so as not to seem too keen. But what the hell was I going to tell Dad? He hadn't really confirmed anything about whether or not they'd made a decision. He'd said he couldn't wait to see me again, but what did that mean? Did that mean he hoped we'd see each other again one day, or he knew we would?

John: I drank two cups of tea, waiting for her to come down and fill me in. When she did, she just shrugged and said he didn't say one way or the other. I felt like throwing my mug against the wall.

Cathy: I phoned Maggie, in the end. I just needed to know. I did it at a time when I knew I wouldn't be disturbed. The kids were at school and John was trying to repair the Ghost Train, which had one carriage that kept stopping and refusing to start up again, right in the middle of all the ghosts and cobwebs. I worked out the time difference. It was nine in the morning for me, so it would be five in the afternoon for her. I had an answerphone message ready, but she picked up. I said it was Cathy, from Wildworld, and she was quiet, as if trying to remember, and then I started babbling, saying the theme park in England, the one you visited. She interrupted, said, 'Cathy, I remember! I was just taking the phone somewhere quieter. AJ's rehearsing.' Then she apologised for the weeks of silence, said that as soon as they'd got back it had been full steam ahead for the US leg of the tour, and she'd put the arrangements for the UK leg to one side for a bit. I felt like she was about to let me down gently. But then she said they'd love to go ahead, and could we book them in? She told me the payment terms, but to be honest I didn't take anything in after she said they were coming.

John: Cathy radioed me and I knew, I just knew, that she'd heard.

Cathy: I was sitting there, in the office, this big, stupid grin on my face. And of course, I'd purposely done it when there was no one around, hadn't I? But now I had my answer, and I wanted someone to share the news with. So I radioed John.

John: I hotfooted it up to the office, and when I went in, I was all out of breath and I just raised my eyebrows at Cathy and she nodded with this huge smile on her face, and I went over to her and pulled her out of her chair and into my arms. We did a sort of dance, both shrieking and laughing.

Cathy: I didn't realise until he took my hand that it had been weeks since he'd touched me.

John: Something was finally going right. Maggie faxed over all the details. She gave me a phone number for a guy called Lou, who she said was AJ's money manager. We were going to get 10 per cent straight away, and then another 20 per cent when they arrived, and the remainder at the end of the visit. I was a bit concerned about that, about not seeing more of the money upfront, but when I tried to negotiate, Lou played hardball, and what was I going to do? Pull out of the whole thing? I don't think so.

Cathy: It wasn't until later, when we'd told the kids and had a celebratory Chinese takeaway for dinner, that I thought about Zak. I was lying in bed, John snoring next to me, and I swear even his snores sounded contented. And I thought about being in that hotel reception, the way I'd felt about my little girl being alone in a hotel room with someone who was more man than boy, and I wondered what would happen when they were here for so much longer. That was the only part of it I worried about. Looking back, I think maybe I was so focused on that that I didn't see the potential for anything worse.

Dear Zak

Mum just told me you guys are definitely coming over. I cannot wait. With the way it all ended, I've still got your Pavement CD. I've listened to it over and over. It took me a while to connect with it but I love it now. I miss Parklife though! There's nothing much to say about life here. Your visit was the most exciting thing to happen pretty much ever, and your next visit will go down in local history. Remember that boy who came over and threatened me when we were having dinner? He's still making my life hell at school. So when you wrote about having to choose between going on tour with AJ and finishing school, my first thought was that I'd leave school. But when I thought about it longer, you're right. I do think finishing school is the sensible thing to do. Then you have options. You can still travel with AJ if you want to, but if that all comes to an end, you're not left with nothing. It's nice that your brother said he'll always make sure you're okay, though. I can't imagine my brother saying that, even if he was rich and famous. Now thinking about what on earth Sebastian would be rich and famous for, and coming up blank. Him and Dad are arguing a lot about the future of the park. Dad wants him to take it over and he's just not interested. When things get really heated between them, I just shut myself in my room and put my headphones on, play music really loud.

We're trying to keep the news quiet for now. June feels like so long away. I'm sure it will come out long before you get here, but we're trying to put that off as long as possible. I've only told Alex, and he's a terrible gossip, but if you tell him to keep something secret, he does. I am imagining you rolling your eyes at that, but he honestly does.

This is hard to write. I know we didn't make anything official or make any promises to each other, but I'm hoping we might be able to pick up where we left off when you come over. I know, though, that that's months away, and I'm sure there will be other girls between now and then. I wouldn't expect there not to be.

Love, Pea

Hey Pea

I listen to Parklife whenever I think about you, which is a lot. Last night I tried to talk to Mum about my decision to stay behind when her and AJ go on tour, but she wasn't really listening because there's some problem with AJ's stylist and she and Maggie have to find a new one. I ended up telling her to forget it and walking out. Later, she came up to my room and said she was sorry and could we try again? So I told her everything, that I don't want to drop out of school and have no career prospects, that I want to have a go at writing for a career, that I don't want to live in AJ's shadow. She said, 'We all live in AJ's shadow, honey. Pretty much the whole world is in AJ's shadow.' I didn't say anything after that, but this morning she said she understood my decision and they would miss me. It's hard to explain but it just feels like she's chosen him over me. I would call Dad and ask to come and stay with him for a while, but I don't want to keep switching schools. It's a mess.

AJ gets it, though. He keeps telling me he knows what it's like to be pushed towards one thing when what you really want is something completely different. Mum got a bit stressed when he said that, and asked if he was still happy with doing all this touring, and he laughed and said that wasn't what he meant. I hope he'll tell me what he meant someday. It's not easy being his brother but I guess it can't be easy being him either.

Anyway, listen, there are no other girls. Okay? Only you.

Love, Zak

Danny: That seems like a fitting place to end today's show. Zak declaring his commitment to Pea like that. There's plenty more of that little romance to come, but next week we're going to tell you about an accident that happened at Wildworld six months before the one that killed AJ Silver, on the very same roller-coaster. It's pretty shocking.

Anthony_53
There's nothing like first love, is there? #WhatHappened-ThatSummer

EmmieGem
I love Pea and Zak! I hope they've stayed together! #What-HappenedThatSummer

BruceyBeans
I feel like Zak is going to break Pea's heart. Anyone else? #WhatHappenedThatSummer

MimiShepherd
It's so hard waiting a week for the next episode! I need to know about this accident! #WhatHappenedThatSummer

JDK443
My eyes are firmly fixed on Alex Robb. I don't know what I think he's done yet but there's something fishy going on. #WhatHappenedThatSummer

3

EPISODE 3 – ACCIDENT ON THE 360

Danny: Hello and welcome to the third episode of *What Happened That Summer?* I'm Danny Drake, and if you've listened to the first two episodes, you'll know that we're doing a deep-dive investigation into events surrounding the death of pop megastar AJ Silver at Wildworld theme park back in 1996. I've been talking to lots of people who were around at the time, with a forensic focus on the Hunter family, who owned and ran the park and were later found guilty of negligence.

As the podcast finds new listeners, AJ Silver's incredible revival is hitting new heights. Three of his singles have gone platinum – 'Island', 'Want You Back' and 'Last Love'.

Today's episode is an exciting one. Not many people know that, a few months prior to the accident that killed AJ Silver, there was another incident at Wildworld involving the same rollercoaster. So we're having a good look into that, and into who exactly was privy to the information about the rollercoaster's fault and how to fix it. Now, far be it from me to say that if you know how a fault was fixed, you might be in a position to unfix it, but, well, I guess I've said it, haven't I?

We left the Hunters at the end of Maggie McGee and Zak Campbell's visit to Wildworld. Pea Hunter and Zak had started a romance and Cathy, in particular, wasn't happy about it. So what happened in the months between that visit and AJ Silver's doomed stay at Wildworld?

Pea: Those months really dragged. Every day felt like a week. Zak and I kept writing to each other, and once Christmas was behind us we started to talk more and more in our letters about the summer. Making plans. In one letter, I asked him to send me some photos of him. I was starting to find it hard to picture him, but I didn't say that. He sent three. In one, he was standing with AJ, their arms around each other's shoulders. It sounds weird but it was a jolt to see them together like that. I'd thought and talked endlessly about the fact that he was AJ Silver's brother, but seeing them was a different thing. In the other two, it was just him. Jeans, band T-shirts, messy hair, Converse. I kept them in the top drawer of my desk and brought them out every time I read one of his letters, so I could imagine him saying the words.

Alex: Pea was obsessed with Zak. Obsessed. We hardly talked about anything else. I wanted to say that I thought she was going to get hurt. They might have a summer romance while AJ and co were over in England, staying at Wildworld, but where could it possibly go after that?

Pea: We never talked about afterwards. The trip itself felt like it was a long way away, so the time after just didn't come up.

Cathy: The airmail letters kept arriving. I was surprised, to be honest. I thought there might be one or two and then it would fizzle out, but no. It didn't make me any less worried.

John: I was working hard. We had to make sure everything was in tip top shape before they came. They paid us the first instalment of the cash, a sort of holding fee, and I used some of it to buy some new parts for various rides that had seen better days. It was all going pretty well. We were on track. Business was even picking up, for those cold early months of the year. I felt like 1996 was going to be our year.

Cathy: Maggie called in January. I hadn't spoken to her for a while but I knew it was her before she said her name. My heart started beating fast. Was she calling it off? Could she do that? We'd signed a contract but I knew they'd have better legal representation than us if anything went wrong. She must have picked up on the tension in my voice because she said it was nothing to worry about, and then she did a sort of nervous laugh, which didn't do much to put me at ease.

Maggie: Look, Zak had talked us all into using Wildworld so he could spend more time with his new girlfriend, and it worked for me because it meant I didn't have to do more research and make any more trips to England to check places out. Zak had told AJ the place had everything he wanted. But then one day, soon after Christmas, AJ came to see me, all serious, and asked whether Wildworld had a rollercoaster that did a full loop. They all seem to have them now, but back then, it wasn't a given. I stalled for time, trying to remember the two rollercoasters Zak and I had been on. One was really tame, a sort of runaway train thing for kids, and the other was faster and higher, but I didn't think it did a loop. I told him that. He reached out with his fist and punched the wall of my office. I didn't react. It was best not to react when he was in a mood like that. He just started to walk away, but he called back over his shoulder, 'I want a rollercoaster with a loop, Maggie!' Great, I thought. Just when it was all signed and sealed. So I called Cathy to double-check.

Cathy: John's philosophy, always, was to say yes, even when the answer was no, and then worry about it later. So when Maggie asked to confirm whether we had a rollercoaster with a loop, I almost said we did. But I can't lie convincingly. I said no, and there was this long pause, and I waited for her to say that it was a dealbreaker. But she didn't say that. Instead, she asked if I thought we could possibly get hold of one before they came. I told her to leave it with me.

John: When Cathy came to me with that particular request, I realised that we were dealing with a spoilt kid. They'd visited, checked the place out, it had all been agreed and signed, and now this. It's not like you can just conjure up rides out of nowhere.

Cathy: John asked me to call her back and ask whether it was a dealbreaker. We looked at the fine print of the contract. They'd paid us a deposit but they could walk away without paying the rest, if they wanted to. And the deposit was only 10 per cent. So I called her, and she said yes, it was. I hung up the phone and looked at John and said, 'We need to find a new rollercoaster.'

John: Rides do move between parks sometimes. It's like animals and zoos. Sometimes places close up and sell off all their rides, but I knew there wasn't anyone doing that at that time. I thought we were fucked, to be honest. But I had to try. So I got in touch with all the big parks and asked if we could rent or buy something from them. Most people I spoke to talked to me like I was insane, but I got lucky with Silvermead at the other side of Birmingham. They were bringing in a newer, better, faster rollercoaster and hadn't decided yet what to do with the existing one, which had a loop. Two loops, in fact. It was called 360. I asked how much they'd take for it, and they said they'd get someone to come back to me.

Cathy: It was a tense wait. I couldn't believe John had tracked one down. But rides like that didn't come cheap and I had a few sleepless nights imagining figures almost as outlandish as the one Maggie McGee had proposed to me.

John: They came back about a week later. Said they'd take a million.

Cathy: I didn't want to do it. It was half of the money we'd be getting from AJ Silver, most of which hadn't come in yet. I didn't see how we could do it. But John was adamant, said we had to do whatever it took to make this work, and that the ride would improve the park's revenue too, in the long term. Talked about speculating to accumulate. And in the end, I just let him deal with it. The park was his concern, for the most part. I did the admin and the payroll and answered the phone but he was the one with the head for business. Or so I believed at the time.

Pea: I remember there being a lot of stress and worry about a rollercoaster. AJ Silver had decided he wanted something we didn't have, which sent my parents into a spin. One night, I woke up at about one in the morning and went downstairs to get a glass of water. Dad was sitting at the kitchen table, his head in his hands. There was an almost empty whisky bottle beside him, and a completely empty glass. He was muttering something, and when I got close, it sounded like a string of numbers. I reached out, touched his shoulder, and he jumped as if terrified. When he saw that it was me, he put a shaky hand on his chest, where his heart was. I asked if he was okay, and he said he was just trying to work things out. I got a glass and ran the water from the kitchen tap until it was cold. I said something that I hadn't been thinking about, something that went against everything I wanted. I said that maybe we should just forget about the whole AJ Silver thing. He looked at me, horrified. He said we wouldn't be doing that. That he'd find a way to make it work. I said, 'What, are you going to just get a hammer and bash a loop in the runaway train track?' He wasn't in the mood for joking.

John: I don't remember talking to Pea about it at all.

Cathy: I didn't know where he got the money from, in all honesty. He didn't talk to me about it.

John: I went to a loan shark. It wasn't the first time. With a business, sometimes there are cashflow issues, and you know you'll have the money in a week but you need it now. I never told Cathy about those things, because I knew she'd worry. This was the most I'd ever borrowed, though. The guy whistled when I asked him, told me the interest would be high. I said I understood that, and we shook on it. I looked in his eyes, to see if there was any compassion there. I don't think there was. I'd never got on the wrong side of him, but I'd heard about what happened if you did. He had guys who worked for him, but I think he did a lot of the persuading himself. He was a big guy, and his eyes were dead. Like something had happened to take the life out of them and he no longer cared about anyone or anything. I kept looking at him until he blinked, and then I looked down. For less than a second, I wondered what I'd got myself into, but then he started pulling cash out of this bag in a desk drawer and I shook my head and started to count it. It was enough for the deposit. He was going to get the rest to me in a couple of days.

Pea: The new rollercoaster arrived from one of the other big parks. It takes a while, when they're moved like that, because they have to be dismantled and then put together again, and then they have to run loads of tests to check it's working correctly and it's safe. Dad was impatient to get it up and running. I guess it had cost a lot of money and he wanted to start making a return on it. He said that as well as sealing the AJ Silver deal, it would bring people to Wildworld from further afield.

It was a pretty cool ride, the 360. Half undercover, in darkness, and half out in the open. You had to go up some steps and through a door and get in the carriage in near darkness, and then when it started you shot out into the daylight and did various turns closely followed by two loops and then a slow ascent up to the highest point. The final drop took you back into the covered part, so you couldn't really see where it would end. Dad said he'd been thinking about getting a rollercoaster like this for a long time.

Cathy: I'd never heard him talking about getting a new rollercoaster. I thought we were focusing on the younger end of the market, but I didn't get involved. John had this way of making you feel small if you disagreed with him. He could argue with an empty chair, and even if you knew for a fact you were right, he was capable of twisting things around until you were no longer sure. I didn't want to get into that. We needed the roller-coaster to get AJ Silver there, so we got it. I phoned Maggie, told her it was in place and ready to go.

Maggie: I didn't ask about where the rollercoaster had come from. Cathy assured me it was there and up and running. That was good enough for me.

John: In order to fit the new rollercoaster in, we had to get rid of this tiny ride that barely got used. It had these cars and aeroplanes and buses and kids would sit in a vehicle and then it went round in a circle on a track. I didn't think twice about getting rid of it. But on the day, Pea appeared and she was flapping her arms and saying it had been her favourite ride when she was little. I shrugged, told her there was nothing I could do. There was nowhere else for the rollercoaster to go.

Pea: I told him he was putting it in completely the wrong place. All the biggest rides were in Adventure City, and he was about to get it set up in Fun City, where the little kids' rides were, just because there was a space. And he was planning to take out this ride I'd spent half my childhood on. I said there was room in Adventure City if he was just a bit creative. He folded his arms across his chest, and it was a challenge. He was inviting me to tell him something he hadn't been able to come up with himself. He didn't think I would, of course. I pulled a map out of my back pocket and opened it up, and he sighed as if he couldn't believe I was claiming to know best about his theme park. I said, 'Look, if we moved this ice cream stand over here, and got people to queue for the Gravity Spin on the other side, the new rollercoaster could go here.' I pointed. He shook his head. But I could see that he knew I was right. He said he would think about it. And next thing I knew, that old cars ride was safe and Dad was directing the people with the new rollercoaster to Adventure City.

John: It was a good idea. I admit that. And it made me realise how much Pea knew about the park. I'd always known she spent a lot of time there, but I hadn't realised she was paying so much attention. It was a lesson.

Pea: He never said thank you, or acknowledged that it had been a good idea. He didn't really go in for praise.

John: The first day the 360 was open, the queue stretched for miles. We used to have these markers that told you how long you could expect to queue for. Twenty minutes, or forty minutes, or an hour, sometimes. That queue went way past the hour marker. We didn't have a marker for an hour and a half, but I reckon people were queuing that long. And more than once, I saw kids get off and go straight back in the queue for another go. That was enough to convince me that I'd done the right thing. Yes, it was a lot of money, but it would pay for itself, I was sure of that.

Danny: Problem solved, right? Nobody could have predicted what happened next.

Pea: It was about two weeks after the new rollercoaster arrived, a few months before the AJ Silver visit. I was in the park with

Alex like usual. It was early March, still cold enough to freeze your fingertips off. We were wrapped up with hats and scarves, and I could feel the cold of the ground seeping into my boots, making my toes numb. I said we should go and get a hot chocolate. There were stands around the park that sold hot drinks in winter and cold drinks and ice cream in summer, but the only place you could sit inside was the huge food hall, which was a hellish place of kids screaming and running around everywhere. So we just bought our drinks at the stand near the go-karts and sat on a bench.

Alex: It was just a normal day. Freezing, so I guess February, or possibly the start of March. I was ready to suggest we give it up and go inside to watch a film or something when Pea said she'd buy me a hot chocolate. Still, I was about half an hour from actually freezing to death. I didn't have a good winter coat, because I could never find one I liked back then, but I had a hat and gloves on. We warmed our hands on the cups, and I asked her for the latest on Zak and she happily obliged.

Sebastian: I was at a friend's house. I didn't find out until later.

Cathy: I was in the office, just pottering about. I'll never forget, this woman came rushing in at about two in the afternoon, white as a sheet, and said there'd been an accident on the 360. I asked her what she meant by an accident and she said I had to call an ambulance, that someone was seriously hurt. I picked up the phone and dialled 999. First time I'd ever done that. The man on the other end of the phone asked me lots of questions and I clammed up, didn't know. I had to pass the phone to the other woman in the end. So I heard about it like that. A boy, she said, quite young, maybe ten. One carriage had gone into the back of another one and he was trapped. I felt sick.

John: I heard the shouting. I wasn't far away. I was at the Ghost Train and it was pretty close to the 360. I went straight over there to find out what was going on. The ride wasn't in operation and when I went into the covered part I could see that there were two carriages together, that one had gone into the back of the other. There were still people sitting in the carriages. Outside, I could hear a woman screaming. 'My boy, my boy!' I asked the ride operator whether anyone had called an ambulance and he said someone had gone to the office for that. I thought about Cathy, how she would react. And I turned and ran up to the office.

Pea: I can't describe it. We were nowhere near the 360, weren't even in Adventure City, but it was like the news spread through the park. A kind of unstoppable wave. I heard a couple of people walking past talk about the park closing, and I thought at first they meant the summer closure, for AJ Silver. Then I heard a mum rounding up her kids, saying the park was closing and they had to go home. I looked at my watch. It wasn't even three in the afternoon. I looked at Alex and he shrugged.

Alex: Pea wanted to go to the office and try to find out what was going on, so we headed that way. People were pouring out of the place, all heading for the exits. It was clear that something major had happened. Pea wasn't saying much, so I just kept walking with her. It took a while because the picnic bench where we'd been sitting was about as far from the exit as it was possible to be.

Cathy: John turned up, closely followed by Pea and Alex. I said an ambulance was on the way. I assumed they knew what had happened, but Pea didn't. Her eyes went really wide and she asked me to tell her what was going on. John was pacing, running his hands through his hair. He looked like he might explode at any minute. I told Pea there'd been an accident on the 360, that someone was trapped.

Pea: I didn't understand. I knew how rollercoasters worked. One carriage set off, and then when it was at the furthest point of the track, a second one went. It wasn't possible to send the second carriage going before the first one was at the right point. It was built into the mechanism that it wouldn't let you do that. I started to say some of this, but Dad looked up at me and told me to shut up. He'd never spoken to me like that before. I just stared at him.

Alex: I knew John pretty well, and I'd seen him angry, like the time Pea and I dyed our hair red and got dye all over the tiles and several towels. But that day was something else. The rage, or maybe the fear, was radiating off him. He couldn't keep still. And when he came close, I thought I caught a whiff of stale booze.

John: Drinking? It was three in the afternoon. Of course I hadn't been drinking.

Cathy: When the ambulance arrived, we all rushed over there. Me and John, Pea and Alex, and the paramedics, of course. The park was deserted by then, and it had the kind of hush you only heard after it was closed. But as we approached the 360, I could hear a woman crying.

Pea: It was the mother of the boy. She was crying. Wailing. She sounded completely deranged.

Alex: God, yes, I remember. There was a small crowd of people waiting just outside the entrance to the ride. Presumably friends and family of the people in the carriages. They'd ascertained that only one person was hurt, this young boy, and his mum was hysterical. Something felt off about it, and then I realised it was that I couldn't hear him crying. He was totally silent. I thought maybe he was dead.

Cathy: No, there was never any suggestion that it was a fatal accident.

John: All I kept thinking was what if someone had been killed? What if that little boy was dead? It would end us.

Terry: My name's Terry Blakely. I was one of the paramedics at the scene that day. We spoke to John Hunter, the owner, and he took us over to the little booth where the ride was operated from. It was inside and it was badly lit. I asked John if he could bring the carriages back in slowly and safely, and he said he could. He started the thing up and pushed a button to get the first carriage moving. My colleague had warned the people inside it what was going to happen. When the carriage was safely in the starting position, John released the safety bars. I held up both hands and asked the people in the carriage not to move. And then I went to them one by one, checking they weren't hurt or bleeding or in pain. There were a couple of teenagers in the back row who had some pain in their necks. I thought it was probably whiplash but I radioed for help just in case. We got them on stretchers so they could be checked over.

Then it was time for the second carriage to be brought in. John did the honours. I noticed that his hands were shaking.

Pea: God, I don't think anyone was breathing.

Alex: The carriage came in, painfully slowly. There were eight people sitting in it, in pairs. Their faces were white. We all looked at the little boy in the front row. Christ, he couldn't have been more than eight.

Terry: I repeated the instructions I'd given to the first carriage. Nobody move. I went to the boy first, since he was definitely injured. He was speaking, though. Conscious. His mum rushed over and I had to physically hold her back. I whispered to her that it wouldn't be long, but we had to do this properly. We got him out and onto a stretcher. His legs were spattered with blood but I was pretty sure they weren't broken. I told his mum she could come over, as long as she just held his hand and didn't try to move any parts of his body. After that, getting the others out was fairly quick and straightforward. And then we took those three to the hospital, the boy's mother holding his hand all the way.

John: It wasn't as bad as it had seemed at first. Thank Christ for that. The boy's legs were injured, but not seriously. And the paramedic claimed that another two people might need to be treated for whiplash, but I was pretty sure that was overkill. I breathed out, long and hard. Cathy reached for my hand.

Cathy: I didn't know what would happen with the park. I didn't care. I was just so glad that little boy was going to be all right.

Pea: I hate myself for it, but you can't help what your brain thinks, can you? One of the first things I thought was that this might mean that AJ and Zak's trip would be off.

Cathy: No one was thinking about the AJ Silver trip, no. That was the least of our worries, at that point.

John: It definitely entered my head, yes. Not at the time, when we were waiting to see that the boy was going to be okay, but a bit later. I remember thinking that we needed to keep this quiet, make sure the AJ Silver crew didn't get any wind of it. I wasn't prepared for a stupid accident to derail everything.

Pea: The police came when we were having tea. Shepherd's pie. None of us were really eating it, just pushing it around. They asked Mum and Dad some questions and said the ride would need to remain closed until it had been properly checked over and repaired if necessary. Dad was in a horrible mood after they left.

Cathy: I called the hospital that evening and was told the boy had been checked over and sent home. He had a few cuts and bruises on his legs, but he was fine. I stood in the hall for a long time after we ended the call. I didn't realise I was crying until Pea came out of the lounge and put her arms around me.

Pea: I was on my way to the kitchen to get a cup of tea, and Mum was in the hallway, weeping, the phone in her hand, but not connected to anyone. I took it from her gently and hung it up. I gave her a hug, asked what had happened. Was it the boy, I wondered? Was it worse than we'd thought? She just said,

'He's okay. He's fine.' Over and over. And I realised it was relief. That's why she was so moved.

John: Of course we made sure we knew the boy was fine first. That was our top priority. Once we knew that, Cathy visibly relaxed, and then she said she was going up to bed. That she was exhausted from it. Sebastian was already in bed. I waited for Pea to go up the stairs, and then I called Tony Hastings, at the local paper.

Tony: Tony Hastings. Yes, I was the editor of the local paper back then. I'd known John for years. I'd already heard about the accident when he called. He sounded shaken. Asked if I could possibly keep it out of the paper. I said it was too late, that we'd already gone to print. He got angry then. Asked how we'd done a story without any input from Wildworld. And I told him we'd been calling Wildworld's phone number for hours, hoping to ask if anyone would speak to us. He went quiet for a moment, and then he said there'd been no one in the office, that they had closed to visitors, and everyone left onsite had been dealing with the incident. I said I was sorry for him, but there was nothing I could do. The printing presses were running as we spoke. It wasn't as if I could halt circulation.

John: I thought Tony was a good guy, but he wasn't prepared to help me out.

Tony: He asked if it was about money. I said I didn't know what he meant. He said, very slowly and clearly, that he was asking whether I could make the story go away if he gave me enough money.

John: I didn't offer him money.

Tony: I asked how much we were talking about. I think he said a couple of grand. I laughed at him and ended the call.

Danny: Does anyone else have the feeling that someone's head is going to roll for this?

John: I didn't sleep at all that night. The next morning, I put the word out that there was a staff meeting first thing. Everyone knew about the accident, of course. I'd sent a few of them home early the previous day, because once we were waiting for the ambulance there was nothing much anyone could do. We met in the food hall, everyone sitting on green plastic chairs. I stood at the front, scanned their faces. Said that everyone was aware there had been an incident and I needed to get to the bottom of how it had happened.

Straight away, I saw that Tim Gooding was looking down at the ground. He was a student who did a few hours for us here and there. 'Who was manning the rollercoaster when it happened?' I asked. I had the rota in my hand, so I knew what the answer should be.

Tim: I'm Tim Gooding. I was down on the rota to man the rollercoaster all afternoon. From one until closing.

John: Tim looked up, met my eye. But didn't say anything. 'It says here, on the rota,' I continued, 'that Tim was on the 360 yesterday afternoon.'

Tim: I left for five minutes. I was bored shitless. It was about half two, and there was so much of the afternoon to go. I was dying for a fag. I saw Eddie walking past and called him over. Eddie did a bit of everything. Litter-picking, cleaning, maintenance. He wasn't officially trained to look after the rides.

Eddie: My name's Eddie Watson. Tim asked if I could cover him while he went for a cigarette. I wasn't sure. I didn't have training on rides. But he said he'd cleared it with Mr Hunter, and I believed him.

John: I asked Tim directly if he'd been there when it happened. He looked sheepish. Said he'd gone for a cigarette. I just about managed to stay calm. Asked who he'd left in charge. He said Eddie.

Eddie: Tim said to me it was just a case of getting everyone in their seats, lowering the safety bar and hitting a button to make the carriage go. Then when the button lit up, it was ready for the next one. It sounded simple enough.

John: Eddie wasn't trained on ride management. He did all sorts around the place, and he'd been with us for a couple of years, but he'd never asked to manage rides and I'd never thought to train him on it. I looked at him, then. He was in his thirties, and I knew he had a young family. His face was ashen. I asked why he'd agreed to look after the rollercoaster when he knew he didn't have the requisite training. He said Tim had asked him to and shown him what to do. I wasn't sure how much longer I could keep my cool. I dismissed everyone other than Eddie and Tim, told them to check the rota and get ready for the day, and then I sat down at a table with those two men. They were both wearing the uniform of black trousers and a green Wildworld polo shirt. I didn't know where to start with them.

Eddie: I said I was sorry. I genuinely was. After it happened, I'd stayed in the booth until Tim got back, and he'd said, 'Holy fuck, man. What the fuck are we going to do?' That boy's mum was shouting and crying, and I didn't know how serious it was, or how it had happened. I'm not proud of it, but we ran. We ran to the exit and didn't look back.

John: I said that what I didn't understand was how it had happened. Even with someone inexperienced at the controls, you simply can't send a second carriage until the first one is near the end of the track. The button lights up when the next one is ready to go, and if you press it before it lights up, nothing happens.

Eddie: I told him that the button lit up, and then I pressed it. It was the truth.

John: I was sure he was lying, but I couldn't work out what the truth was. I marched them over there, in the end. I took them into the hut and started it up. Then I sent an empty carriage round, and when it got to the furthest point, the light came on and I sent a second one. I looked at them both, as if to say 'See?'

Tim: I didn't know what he wanted us to say. We'd fucked up. But neither of us had done anything deliberately to cause that accident.

Eddie: I told him one last time. I didn't understand how, but I hadn't pressed the button until the light came on. He was muttering, face like thunder. Then he said we were both fired. Tim took it on the chin – it was all right for him, it was just a student job, he could probably get another one in a day or two – but this had been my livelihood for more than two years. I had two children at home, and my wife was pregnant. I wasn't too proud to plead for another chance.

Tim: When Eddie started laying on all the stuff about his family and their financial struggles, I wanted the ground to open up and swallow me. I was thinking about the festival my friends were going to, the one I'd turned down because of work. I was hoping there were still tickets available. I felt bad for Eddie, of course I did. It was me who'd asked him to cover. But he could have said no.

John: I told Eddie my decision was final, and I walked them out.

Cathy: I knew John would fire someone over it, but I was surprised he let Eddie go. He'd been a good worker. John told me what had happened afterwards, and I said it sounded like he'd made a stupid mistake and I wasn't sure the punishment fit the crime, and John looked at me like I was a stranger and said could I leave the hiring and firing to him. He stormed off then, saying something about how he needed to redo the rota now he'd lost two members of staff.

It was strange and quiet that day. When Pea got home from school, she walked into the office where I was faffing about pretending to catch up on admin and she put the local paper down on the desk in front of me. I gasped. Call me naïve, but I just hadn't thought about it being covered by the press. The headline read 'Boy, 8, injured at Wildworld'. There was a photo of him in his hospital bed, his legs all bloody and bruised. His mum had been quoted as saying she would never go back and she hoped other parents would learn from her experience. It was a disaster.

Pea: School was hideous that day. Everyone was talking about it. As usual, the rumours only contained a shred of truth. There were people saying the boy had broken a leg, lost a leg, lost both legs. Nicole Waddington sauntered over in Science, after lunch, and said she guessed AJ Silver wouldn't be coming to Wildworld any more, now that people were getting seriously injured there. As she walked away, she said, 'If he was ever coming in the first place, that is.' I was so over it by then. Alex was sitting next to me and he put a hand on my arm as if to calm me down. I don't know what made me do it, but I picked up my safety goggles and threw them at the back of her head. They were only light, just plastic. When they hit her, she stopped walking and spun around and asked me what the fuck I thought I was doing. Mrs Lane chose exactly that moment to walk in. It took her precisely two seconds to determine what was going on and she gave us both detention, said she didn't want to hear any more about it, and started the lesson.

Alex: Pea was so wound up over that accident. I mean, I can understand why. If that park went down, her family was sunk. And if news of this accident got back to AJ Silver's crew, I was pretty sure that whole thing would be off.

John: I told Cathy that we needed to focus on damage limitation. We couldn't let it ruin the AJ Silver visit. I was sure it wouldn't make the national news, some kid getting his knee scraped at a small theme park, and I was right, it didn't. It seemed very unlikely that Maggie and co would find out, unless someone told them.

Cathy: None of us were going to tell them, were we?

Pea: In the detention, Nicole didn't say a word to me. We had to copy out pages from our Science textbook for an hour. Usually, I walked home with Alex, but of course he was long gone by the time detention was over. It was just Nicole and me, no one else in sight. She lived in the same direction, too. I hung back and let her set off first, then made sure I stayed well behind her. We were almost at the turning for her road when she turned around and looked at me with pure hatred. 'You're going to regret doing that, Pea,' she said. I didn't really take it seriously. I mean, what was she going to do?

Danny: What was she going to do indeed? We'll find out pretty soon. But first, here's what happened to the rollercoaster after the accident. Pay close attention.

John: I called out an engineer who came to look at the ride the day after the accident. I wanted it open again as soon as possible. His name was Nigel Woods. He was familiar with Wildworld and all the rides, although this was his first time seeing the 360. He scratched his head and muttered a lot, and I told him everything I knew about what had happened. I had to leave him to it in the end. There was an issue with the food ordering, and a vast quantity of chicken nuggets had turned up that there was no freezer space for. I asked him to come and find me in the food hall when he was done. An hour or so later, he appeared. 'Loose connection,' he said. I raised my eyebrows, inviting him to go on. 'I'd better show you.' We strode over to the rollercoaster. Pea and Alex were sitting on a bench close by. Pea asked whether we knew what had happened yet, and I said Nigel was just about to show me. They both stood up and followed us to the hut. I don't really know why, though Pea did always take an interest in anything that was happening at the park. Sebastian appeared then, out of nowhere, said Cathy was looking for me. I held up a hand to tell him to wait.

Pea: I was just curious. I'd heard Dad talking about how he didn't understand what could have happened, and I didn't either. We crowded around Nigel, and he got out a screwdriver and started to dismantle the big green button you had to hit to send a carriage around the track.

Alex: When he'd got the casing off, he showed us two wires that had to be touching for the override to work. He said that they'd come loose, so that they were touching most of the time but could also come apart. He said that if those wires weren't touching each other, the light would come on and it would be possible to send a second carriage around the track. It seemed pretty simple. He'd put some kind of plastic tubing over them so they couldn't come apart again. He said he was confident it would fix it, but obviously John might want to send a few empty carriages around before opening it to the public again.

John: I was relieved it was such an easy fix, to be honest.

Sebastian: It made sense, what Nigel was saying. If anything about the park appealed to me, it was that side of things. The mechanics. It was clear that Dad was going to be tied up for a while, so I went back and told Mum he was busy.

Nigel: I'm Nigel, the engineer. I told John I'd fixed it temporarily, with that bit of plastic, but that the wires and really the whole mechanism could do with being replaced altogether in the next few months.

John: He didn't say anything about further work, no. I remember saying that I would see him in November because that's when he generally serviced all the rides.

Nigel: I mean, it was fixed, and I didn't see the fix breaking down any time soon, but if it was me, I would definitely have done the replacement. I told him it might be pricey.

Pea: There was something about Nigel coming back to do something more permanent, yes. I don't know whether that ever happened. It went straight out of my head.

John: After Nigel had left, I got the dummies we used to test rides when they were new or had been serviced, and I sent carriage after carriage around that track. One after another for a full hour. At one point I realised that Sebastian was beside me again. He told me to come home, that Cathy had sent him to get me, but I couldn't. I had to keep doing it, to prove something to myself. Every single time I sent those carriages around the track, the light came on exactly when it was supposed to and the carriages came nowhere near each other. So I was satisfied that it was resolved. We reopened the 360 the next day.

Cathy: John explained to me, later, about the loose connection. I asked whether Nigel had been able to fix it then and there. He said yes, he had. I asked whether he needed to come back for anything. He said no, he didn't. I left it at that. I handled the office stuff, the paperwork, and he handled the rides.

Danny: So the ride is fixed, but possibly not properly. But at least they've kept the news of the accident contained, right? Right?

Cathy: By the time Maggie called, it had all died down. The boy who'd been injured was fine, back at school. We'd sent flowers to his family. People were using the 360 again. It had been a slow start, with parents being overly cautious – understandably. But after they'd seen it in operation a few times, people seemed to relax a bit. So I was totally thrown when the phone rang and I heard Maggie's voice.

Maggie: Some kid called Nicole Waddington had sent me a letter telling me there'd been an accident at Wildworld. I had to admire the girl. I don't know how she found out my name and address and I don't know what her beef was with the Hunters. She said that a boy had been seriously injured and insinuated that he'd almost lost his leg. I didn't know what to make of it. But I called Cathy to ask her whether there was any truth in it. I half expected her to laugh it off, say she didn't know what I was talking about. I probably would have left it there, if she had. I wouldn't have gone digging for information. But that wasn't how Cathy reacted. She kept starting to speak and then pausing, starting from the beginning again. In the end, I said, 'Cathy, just level with me. Tell me what happened.' And she did. I was shocked. In the US, the kid's family would have sued, but she said it was all dealt with and the park was open as usual. 'Is that ride open?' I asked. She said it was. I sighed. I didn't really know how to play this. I couldn't risk AJ coming to any harm, but I knew he was still set on this theme park idea and it was a bit late to start scouting other options. I said, 'Cathy, do you swear to me that this issue is resolved?' She said it was. No hesitation. So I said I would talk to AJ and the rest of the team and we'd get back to her.

Zak: The first I heard of it was when Maggie called us all together, AJ and Mum and me, plus all of his crew – bodyguard, stylist, makeup artist, personal assistant. Everyone who'd be travelling to Europe, basically. She said there'd been an accident at Wildworld. I thought of Pea, imagined her hurt. I'd had a letter from her a few days ago. But something could have happened since then, couldn't it? I asked Maggie if Pea was okay. Couldn't help it.

Maggie: Zak was worried about Pea. I said she was fine. That everyone was fine. But a boy had been hurt on a rollercoaster. AJ looked bored. He said, 'Are you about to say we can't stay there?' I said no, I just wanted them to have all the information before we made the trip. He said, 'Cool, well, I don't care.' He was sixteen and invincible, of course. But his mum. Well, she was a mum. She asked me for more details, and I told her everything I knew, including the fact that Cathy had assured me the ride had been fixed since the incident and was open to the public again and there had been no further issues. She said she wasn't sure.

Grace: I didn't like the sound of it at all. I was ready to call the whole thing off. Who stayed in a frickin' theme park anyway? I wanted to go to a hotel and spend the money on some good security. Then we'd be able to sleep in comfort and have proper showers. AJ didn't care about any of that, though, and he was in charge. I held off for a couple of days but I knew he'd get what he wanted in the end. What I didn't expect was for it to be Zak who talked me round. He came to me late one night, when I was reading in bed and I thought he was playing video games, and he told me about Pea. Now, I knew when him and Maggie came back that there'd been something with a girl over there. Maggie had given me the lowdown. Zak had said nothing. Typical teenage boy. But that night, he lay on the empty side of my king-size bed and didn't look at me while he told me about this girl who he'd been exchanging letters with, and how he thought he might be in love with her.

Zak: Yeah, I begged Mom not to change the plans. I can't remember what I said, exactly, but it worked. The next day, I wrote Pea a letter to reassure her that it was all still on.

Pea,

It's been a weird few days. I thought the whole thing was going to be called off. I mean, not the tour, but the visit to Wildworld. AJ didn't care about the accident. Neither did I as soon as I'd heard you were okay. I mean, it's not that I don't care that someone was hurt, but it didn't make me not want to come. You know what moms can be like, though. I ended up telling her about you, about us, and how much I wanted to spend that time with you. She's a good listener, when she wants to be. She didn't say a single word. I kept looking over at her to check she hadn't fallen asleep. We were lying side by side on her bed. Then when I finally stopped talking, she said she appreciated me telling her all that and she would keep thinking about it. Then this morning, she came in while me and AJ were eating breakfast and said she was happy to leave things as they were, since we were both so keen to go. AJ high-fived me and walked off with a piece of toast in his mouth. Mom yelled after him to use a plate, but he didn't come back.

The US part of the tour is done now, and AJ's in rehearsals for the Europe leg. He can't just stand on the stage and sing, there have to be all these costume changes and special effects and dance routines. I go to watch him rehearse sometimes, although as soon as he notices me there he throws a towel or something at me and tells me to get out. They work him really hard. I suppose that's fair enough, with how much money he makes.

School is weird, too. I've got exams coming up and everyone's worried and serious. People are always asking what I'm going to do with my life, and whether I'm just going to follow my brother around like a puppy. It makes me want to hit something. That English teacher who said she thought I could be a journalist has been sort of coaching me, talking to me about colleges. I'm not going straight from high school to college, and I told her that. She said that was okay, but I might want to go in a year or two, or maybe in ten years.

It made me think about what things might be like in ten years. Will AJ still be famous? Will I be a journalist? Will I still be writing to you?

Love, Zak

Zak,

I was so relieved to get your letter and hear you're still coming. Mum has been talking to Maggie but it's felt like everything's quite up in the air. Not long to go, now. I don't *know whether it's okay to say this, but I forget, sometimes, what your voice sounds like or what precise colour your eyes are. I keep getting out the photos you sent. It doesn't feel real that we only spent a couple of days together, and now all these months have passed. It's going to be amazing to be together for six weeks.*

Exams here too. Everyone keeps going on and on about how they're the most important thing in the world, which doesn't help. I'm okay at Science and Maths but English and History, or anything where I have to write essays, are my worst nightmare. I'll never be a writer like you. I've been thinking, actually, about what I might do, when I'm finished with school. Mum wants me to go to university – no one in our family has ever gone. Is university in England the same as college in America? I'm not sure. Dad wants me to work at the park, but there's no way I'm going to do that unless I can be in charge. It's so sexist, the fact that Dad wants to give the park to his son and not his daughter.

Anyway, all of that is way in the future and I can't think much further ahead than your visit. Will you go to all the concerts with AJ, or will you stay behind with me when he travels?

Love, Pea

Zak: Something about writing to Pea calmed me. It was to do with the actual physicality of it, I think. The scratching of pen on paper. Forming those letters and words, knowing that they would travel across the world and end up in her hands, and that she would pore over them the way I did with her letters, folding and refolding. I told her that I would probably go to some of the concerts but most of the time I would stay at the park with her. There's only so many times you can watch your brother dancing around a stage in front of thousands of screaming girls singing the same songs before you go insane.

Cathy: By the end of March, things were settled. The visit was going ahead. John was so relieved. I mean, we both were, but him especially. The year had started off strong but there'd been a definite tailing off following the accident.

John: I just wanted to get it started. The sooner it started, the sooner it would be over, and we'd have the cash we needed to smarten up the place and reinvest.

Cathy: At night, sometimes, I dreamed about the amount of money they'd agreed to give us. It was enough to start a new life, if we wanted to. We could leave the park behind.

Pea: I never thought about the money, no. Just about Zak.

Sebastian: I felt like if I never heard the name AJ Silver again, it would be too soon. I'd never wanted to take over Wildworld, but I wanted it even less by then. But it didn't seem to matter what I said to Dad about it; it was like he couldn't compute it. I couldn't wait to get out of there, honestly.

Danny: So there you have it. The AJ Silver visit is back on, or still on. And next week we're jumping right in with that visit, and showing you that even before AJ Silver's death, everything that could go wrong did go wrong. Don't forget to tell us what you're thinking on socials at @WhatHappenedThatSummer. And if you're enjoying the podcast, leave us a review!

JanBee_6

I can't believe there was no real investigation into that poor kid's accident just because it didn't involve someone famous! The 90s were a wild time! #WhatHappenedThatSummer

MikeyBoy
I can't believe you can just buy a rollercoaster. Anyone else tempted to see whether they could fit one in the back garden? #WhatHappenedThatSummer

Alice_in_Wonderland
So, interesting that John, Pea, Alex and Sebastian all saw how the engineer fixed the loose connection. Do we think one of them could have sabotaged the ride when AJ died? I'm not sure why any of them would, though. What would the motive be? #WhatHappenedThatSummer

NotthatGina
I cannot wait for the next episode because I'm assuming that's when AJ Silver appears on the scene! #WhatHappenedThatSummer

86Ella86
I've had AJ Silver playing on repeat since the podcast started. Kid had some good songs. I was a metalhead at the time so didn't appreciate them. I think he would have gone on to do something great. Shame he didn't get the chance. No one should die at 17. #WhatHappenedThatSummer

4

EPISODE 4 – A CATALOGUE OF ERRORS

Danny: Welcome to episode four of *What Happened That Summer?* My name is Danny Drake. Thanks for coming on this wild ride with us. This week we hit 50,000 downloads and you may be aware that the new remix of AJ Silver's 'Ice Cream' is currently at number one in the download chart.

So, this is it, folks. The moment you've all been waiting for. AJ Silver is off the plane and on his way to Wildworld. I know you want to hear every detail of what happened when he got there.

As you'll hear shortly, a lot of things went wrong on this trip. Some of it was the fault of the Hunters, some of it was down to AJ Silver and his crew. He arrived with eight people in tow. His mum Grace, his brother Zak, his manager Maggie, his bodyguard Lucian, his stylist Trish, his hair and makeup artist Bree, his assistant India and his vocal coach Sammy.

So without further ado, here's what happened next.

Pea: The morning I woke up and knew they were coming that day, I felt like I'd explode.

John: I was exhausted. I'd been working every hour God sent, trying to make sure everything was as shipshape as it could possibly be. I'd been painting fences, cutting back trees, you name it. And of course the park had still been open to the public. We wanted to close it for the shortest possible amount of time. So I'd been doing everything I usually did with all this tarting up on top. I'd hoped Sebastian would step up and help me out, but he didn't lift a finger.

Cathy: John was drinking a lot. I think it was the nerves. Every time I tried to bring it up, he snapped at me. But he'd gone from drinking wine with dinner to sneaking beers and God knows what else at any time of the day.

John: I never drank when I was working. At the end of the day, yes. Who doesn't like to unwind with a glass of wine, especially at times of high stress?

Cathy: I didn't really think about the impact his drinking might have on his work. It wasn't like he was driving, I suppose. Maybe I was naïve. I knew it was something we needed to address, but the plan was to get these six weeks over and done with, collect the money, and then see if it continued. Part of me thought that once this was over, it would all go away.

Pea: I just assumed Mum and Dad would let us have the day off school, so I went down in my pyjamas that morning and grabbed a banana from the fruit bowl. Mum asked why I wasn't ready for school, and I said I wasn't going. That I wanted to be there when they arrived. Mum's mouth went all tight and she said she hoped I didn't think this was going to be one long holiday with my boyfriend. Then she went into her whole spiel about how important my GCSEs were. I couldn't listen to it. I walked off while she was still speaking, tears pricking at my eyes. I felt like she didn't understand anything.

Sebastian: I got ready for college as usual. I heard Pea stomping up the stairs and slamming her bedroom door and assumed she'd asked for the day off and been refused. They weren't even arriving until after lunch, so why she thought she needed to be at home all day is anyone's guess. People in town knew it was happening soon, but we'd kept the date pretty quiet because we knew they wanted to get in and settled before people found out they were here and started hanging around in the car park. At college, I'd get asked about it twenty times a day, and I always said I didn't know. What I did know was that if Pea didn't go into school, people would put two and two together. So I'm glad Mum didn't let her stay at home.

Pea: It was the longest day. Most of the teachers had given up on teaching us anything new by that point and we were just having revision sessions and working through past papers. I could totally have missed it. I still can't believe Mum didn't let me.

Alex: I think I was the only one at school who knew it was 'the day'. I kept giving Pea these little nudges and secret looks, and at lunch we went to the furthest point of the site, behind the pine trees where you only really went on cross-country runs, and talked about whether or not they might have arrived yet. I said, 'I can't believe that the actual AJ Silver might be in our town right now.' And Pea said, 'I can't believe that he might be in my actual house.' It never got any less surreal.

Pea: After lunch, I had double Maths. Normally I could get myself lost in the work, just solving one problem after another, lining up the answers, all neat and straight and right. That was what I liked about Maths, how it was straightforward. Not easy, but there was no debate about what was right and what was wrong. But that day, I made stupid mistakes. Careless errors. I couldn't concentrate on anything. I looked out of the window at one point, conjured up an image of Zak, imagined kissing him. Would I get to kiss him that day? How different would it all be, with AJ and the whole of their entourage there?

John: They arrived at around two o'clock. I'd had about six coffees and I was practically juddering. Cathy and I were in the office, neither of us doing anything productive, just waiting. It was eerie for the park to be closed, for there to be no sounds of kids or rides filtering through. I looked at Cathy and said, 'This is it,' and we went outside to greet them. I saw Maggie first. She put her hand up in a wave and Cathy and I both mirrored the gesture. Zak and another boy a bit younger than him were walking ahead of her. So this is him, I thought. The famous AJ Silver. He just looked like your average teenage boy to me. But then, what did I know about pop music and teenage girls? Like Zak, he had floppy, longish hair and was wearing baggy clothes. He was laughing at something his brother had said, and when they all came to a halt in front of us, he was still laughing.

Danny: I don't know about you, but I'm pretty keen to hear how it was when Cathy saw Zak again, after that hotel incident.

Cathy: John and I were just standing there and I didn't know what to do with my hands. The boys were in front, and there was a small crowd following them. I picked out the woman who I thought must be their mother, and I smiled at her, but she wasn't looking. She was saying something to Maggie, who looked up then and met my gaze. She put a hand on the other woman's arm and said something, and then she sped up so she was level with Zak and AJ. When they reached us, she broke into a warm smile and started doing the introductions.

John: AJ barely acknowledged us. I thought he was pretty rude.

Cathy: It was strange to see Zak again after the way it had all ended on his last visit. John and I had talked at length about him and Pea, what we would and wouldn't allow during this visit. I was planning to get them both on their own as soon as possible and explain our ground rules.

Maggie: It seems strange to say it, as only a few months had passed since Zak and I had visited, but John looked noticeably older. His eyes were a bit sunken and his skin was an unhealthy colour, bordering on grey. Cathy looked the same as ever. She was wearing a hideous orange dress and a pink cardigan. Did the woman own anything black?

Zak: I knew I needed to get Pea's parents on side if I was going to get to spend any time with her over the next few weeks. I smiled at them both, trying to convey my trustworthiness, but I'm not sure they were looking.

Cathy: Maggie did the introductions. I knew I wouldn't remember any of the names. There was the mum, plus a host of people who looked after everything from AJ's hair and clothing to his dietary requirements. I noticed AJ looking around, and I wondered what he made of it. What was it like, this life he lived that was so unlike anything I'd ever known?

Zak: AJ told me later that he thought the park looked like a shithole. He wasn't mad when he said it, just matter-of-fact. He said, 'Are we really only here because you want to bone the mad couple's daughter?' I wanted to hit him. I'd come all this way to scope the place out and he'd been here less than an hour and decided it wasn't up to scratch. I told him to give it a chance. Let the other stuff slide.

Maggie: After we'd introduced everyone and turned down the offer of coffee, John and I sorted out the gates so we could drive the tour buses in. He asked me when the shower and toilet units were arriving, and I realised I hadn't heard anything about that for a while. I said I would double check, but that it would definitely be that day.

John: She looked a bit panicked when I asked about the showers and toilets. But I still trusted she had it all in hand.

Danny: She did not have it in hand. Which is strange, because I had Maggie pegged as the super organised type. I guess everyone drops the ball every now and again.

Zak: Once the buses were in situ, I asked AJ if he wanted me to show him around a bit. I was on edge, wondering where Pea was. She must have gone to school. No one had mentioned it and I hadn't wanted to ask her parents outright. AJ shrugged and said he might have a nap, so I went to find Maggie. She was on a different bus, on her own, and she was shouting, 'Fuck, fuck, fucking fuck!' I laughed and she looked up. I asked her what was wrong. She said, 'The fucking showers and toilets aren't arriving for another two days.' This was a big problem. The buses had these tiny toilets that were barely useable, and obviously there were no showering facilities on them. AJ's first gig was in just over a week's time.

Maggie: It was totally my fault. I'd let the thing slip, and when I called the company, they said they'd been trying to get in touch to say there'd been a delay. They had a digit wrong in my number or something. I said that we needed those showers and toilets, and the man I was talking to said there was nothing he could do. I was freaking out about it when Zak arrived. He was always so level-headed. He was just a kid but he was great at calming me down. He said maybe we could ask John and Cathy if we could use their facilities for a couple of days. I said no way. We couldn't all be traipsing in and out of their house like that. That's when Zak looked like he'd had the best idea in the world and said, 'The park! There are toilets in the park!' I made a face. The thought of using portable toilets and showers for six weeks was bad enough without shitting where half the kids in England had left puddles of piss. Perhaps I could ask Cathy about cleaning one of the toilet blocks myself. I could bleach it to fuck and then maybe it would be just about acceptable. But what about showers? I felt grimy from the plane and my hair would be in need of a wash by the next day. I told him to keep thinking.

Zak: I didn't tell AJ. He could be volatile. By which I mean, he could be a dick. I didn't want him going off at Maggie over a mistake anyone could have made. We went for a walk around the park. There were five zones and we went through them, one by one. He didn't say much. He was soaking it all up. I couldn't tell whether he'd changed his opinion of the place, and mostly I didn't care. I kept looking at my watch. Pea would be back from school in an hour. Then in fifty minutes. Then in a half hour. AJ noticed what I was doing, of course. He said, 'You know you can't warp time to make your girl get here faster.' I didn't reply. Sometimes, I wanted to ask if he saw what all this madness was doing to him. He'd been a pretty regular kid before it all kicked off. And now, a few years in, he was cocky as hell, like he'd bought in to his own hype. I remember reading once that it's not good for anyone to be surrounded by people who never say no to them, and I thought about that a lot with AJ. I mean, who gets to demand a theme park and then walk around it deciding whether or not it's good enough? I wanted to change the subject. I asked how rehearsals had been going. He shrugged, said he was ready. Where did that attitude come from? I remember him being a little kid at football try-outs, nervous and hopeful. Sometimes it felt like this big, bad AJ had swallowed up my little brother.

Maggie: I thought about booking a few hotel rooms for those two days, so we could shower there, but there were no hotels that close by and we didn't want to take the buses in and out. Plus, we were trying to keep a low profile. Staying in the park, other than when we were travelling to the concerts, was part of the deal. When I thought I'd exhausted all other options, I went up to the house and knocked on the door.

Cathy: Maggie came to the door, told us about the problem with the showers. I said they could use the one in the house, no problem. John was pissed off, said afterwards that we should have held out for some extra money for the inconvenience and the hot water, but I told him he was being silly.

John: Cathy liked fixing problems. If someone came to her with an issue, whether it was a playground spat or a long-lost family member, she would wade in there and try to help. If I'd answered the door to Maggie, I would have held out a bit, seen what she was offering. These people had money, more money than we could ever dream of, and that's the bit I think Cathy never fully grasped. The money they were paying us for the park was a drop in the ocean to them, and a life-changer for us, so why not try for a bit more?

Maggie: Cathy was kind, said we could use the shower in the house. We agreed some timings, because there were going to be a lot of us trying to use one bathroom. We wouldn't go in until they were all up and ready for the day, that kind of thing. I was embarrassed about having to ask. It was unprofessional, but I didn't see a way around it. I knew John wasn't happy, but I didn't care all that much.

Danny: So this is pretty mad, isn't it? The world's most famous pop star and his entourage all sharing a bathroom with a lower-middle-class English family inside a theme park. You honestly couldn't make it up.

Zak: When Maggie came to find me and AJ to tell us about the situation, we were lying on the grass near this lake with pedal boats. It was a gorgeous early summer afternoon, no clouds. I knew from the way Maggie said AJ's name that she hadn't found a solution she was confident about. She filled us in, about using Pea's family's bathroom, and AJ just laughed. Said she'd better be joking. It was awkward, silent. Maggie asked what he suggested. He said she should get back to the company that were supplying the facilities and tell them they had an hour to get them to us or the whole deal was off. It was Maggie's turn to laugh. She said, 'But then we'll just have nothing for the whole time we're here. How will that help, exactly?' She knew how to handle AJ. Where his weak spots were and when you could get away with teasing versus when you had to leave him the fuck alone. It was coming up for four so I left them arguing about it. I wanted to be at the entrance when Pea got home from school. I'd said in my last letter that I would be.

Pea: Honestly, the day was the length of five, but when it was finally over, I shoved everything in my school bag. All I cared about was getting home and seeing Zak. I was curious about AJ, too, of course. Alex caught up with me when I was just going out of the gates. He asked if he could come with me. I hesitated. I didn't want him to, truthfully. I wanted to be alone with Zak. It had been months since I'd seen him. Surely he could understand that? I thought my silence probably spoke volumes, but he just laughed and said, 'Earth to Pea? Are you in there?' I was never very good at saying what I meant if I knew it would upset someone, so I just said yes, and he fell into step beside me.

Alex: I knew Pea didn't want me getting in the way of her and Zak, but I'm sorry, this was an opportunity I was not going to miss.

Zak: When I saw her approaching, I broke out in a grin, but then I saw Alex was with her and I was pissed with myself for not anticipating this. In my head, it had just been the two of us, walking around the park, sneaking off behind some trees to kiss and kiss and kiss. But this friend of hers was like an extra limb or something. Always around.

Pea: I said hello. I felt so shy. In our letters, we'd talked about all kinds of things. It was so much easier, when you were writing it down, to say what you really felt. But now he was in front of me and he looked even better than I remembered, his hair a little longer so that he kept having to brush it out of his eyes, and his skin tanned a golden brown. He said hi, and then went in for a hug, and it was amazing to feel his hard body against mine, but it was too chaste, like the kind of hug you'd give a grandparent. I felt it all slipping away. It might sound dramatic, but I'd put so much onto this. My expectations were sky high. I'd thought I would lose my virginity to this guy, and I'd been counting the days until his arrival, and now he was here and it was all wrong. Alex stood next to me, silent. I asked how their journey was and Zak said it was good. Then someone called his name and we all turned to look, and there was AJ Silver, this boy I'd seen on my TV screen and on magazine covers, and now he was walking over to where I was standing, a grimace on his pretty face.

Alex: AJ looked like a fucking angel or something. He had this aura, this glow. What was it? Fame? The weight of all that adoration? I watched him lumber over, couldn't have spoken if I'd wanted to. And I'm not known for keeping quiet. Zak introduced us and AJ said, 'So this is the famous Pea?' and Zak punched him playfully on the arm and I wanted to say, *You can't hit AJ Silver! You might bruise his perfect skin!* But of course I didn't. I stood there like a lemon, forgetting what words were and how conversation worked.

Pea: AJ was cute. He was. I mean, I knew what he looked like already, didn't I? But he definitely had something that drew you to him. Or maybe it just seemed like that, because we all knew he was this big star. I saw Zak noticing me noticing his brother. The thought of him being jealous made me smile this secret smile, because that would mean him thinking that something might actually happen between me and AJ Silver.

Zak: I hated it when girls I liked met AJ. For obvious reasons.

Pea: I hoped we'd get some time alone later. Alex would have to go home at some point. I would tell Zak that he was the only one I was interested in, and then hopefully he would kiss me, because I felt like if he didn't, I would go insane.

Zak: AJ started in on the shower situation, and Pea looked confused, so we filled her in.

Pea: Zak explained that they were going to be showering in the house for a couple of days. In our house. Alex gave me a look and I could read his mind exactly. He was saying, *Actual AJ Silver in your actual house! Naked!* But I wasn't thinking about AJ. I was thinking about Zak. About crossing on the landing wearing nothing more than a towel, about hair dripping onto shoulders, about sneaking into my room and him pressing me up against the door.

Zak: AJ was having a hissy fit about the whole thing but what could anyone do?

Pea: All day, I'd been willing time to move faster, and now I was standing here with the boy I'd been looking forward to seeing for months and I was still doing it, because it wasn't enough to stand this close to him, to feel the heat from his body. I needed to be alone with him, for our skin to touch.

Zak: I asked Pea if she wanted to go for a walk, and she smiled and tucked her hair behind her ear and said yes. I meant just her, but it was clear that AJ and Alex were going to come with us. I thought about all the times I'd left AJ alone with girls he liked, all the many, many girls there had been since the start of this journey, and then I thought about this one time that he wouldn't do the same for me.

Alex: Zak sort of steered Pea so they were in front, which left me walking beside AJ. I looked over and flashed him a quick smile, but he didn't return it. He was still going on about the shower thing, though Zak was largely ignoring him. I asked whether they'd thought about booking a room in a hotel in town, trying to be helpful. AJ looked at me then, and it was like he was noticing me for the first time. He said it was hard to be out in public, that they wanted to lie as low as possible, and I said of course, as if I knew what that was like.

Pea: It was so frustrating, that walk. At some point, Zak grabbed my hand and it calmed me. I knew, then, that the things he'd said in his letters were true and that when we got some time on our own, if we ever did, we'd be together.

Alex: I stayed as long as I reasonably could and then went home. It was a Friday so I said to Pea that I'd see her tomorrow. She didn't look thrilled.

Zak: Shortly after Alex left, Pea went home to eat dinner. I said I'd be over in an hour or so to wash the plane off me, and she smiled like she was kind of embarrassed, and I knew she was thinking about me showering. I liked that she was thinking about it.

Cathy: Over dinner, John and I told Pea what our rules were. No sneaking around, no visiting the tour buses after dinner, bedroom door to be kept open if Zak visited the house.

Pea: Oh my God, the rules. They were draconian. I couldn't believe it even as they were saying them. I was sixteen by then. I wanted to say that it was legal for me to do whatever I wanted with my boyfriend, but I didn't, because we'd never exactly been open about sex and I wasn't about to start.

Zak: Yeah, Pea told me about her parents' rules. Ironically, she told me that night after sneaking out to see me on the bus.

Pea: I hadn't thought much about the fact that there would be absolutely no privacy. I didn't want to take him to the house because I knew Mum would be watching us like a hawk and he was sharing the bus he was sleeping on with AJ. That first night, there was a lot of back and forth with everyone coming over to shower, and I stayed in my room for all of it, trying to work out the best way to see him. I waited until ten, when I heard Mum and Dad go to bed, and then I crept out. I'd never done anything like that before. Hadn't had a reason to, I suppose.

Zak: I was wondering why I hadn't seen her that evening when she knocked on the door of the bus a little after ten. I saw AJ rolling his eyes as I scrambled to let her in. We were both listening to music on our Discmans, lying on our beds, not talking. I pulled Pea inside and she gave me the lowdown, about the rules and her parents' obvious distrust of me, or her, or maybe both of us. She sat down on my fold-out bed and I lay down next to her, then pulled her down next to me. She looked at me funny, I guess because we weren't alone, but I kissed her anyway. I felt like I would die if I didn't.

Pea: That first kiss after they arrived was something I'd thought about for so long and it didn't measure up. It wasn't the kiss itself, more the fact that I couldn't relax into it, with his brother in the same small space as us. His brother, who was AJ Silver. I kept pulling away, and Zak told me we would work it out, that we'd find a way. I hoped he was right.

Zak: So that was the first day. Plans going awry, rules being broken. I remember thinking it could only get better. Yeah. Funny, huh?

Pea: I woke up at five in Zak's arms. I'd intended to go back home after an hour or so but we must have fallen asleep. I can laugh about it now, all these years later, but it was a definite 'oh fuck' moment. I knew that if Mum or Dad found out, they'd be locking me in my room to keep us apart. I sat up slowly, not wanting to wake Zak, and then I looked over at where AJ was sleeping. His mouth was open, his covers pushed off. He looked younger. It was astonishing, really, that all these people operated on the whims of this young boy. That he had our family's fate in his hands. I looked back at Zak, who looked impossibly peaceful, then I crept out and back to my house. I held my breath going up the stairs. Sometimes Mum prowled about in the early hours when she couldn't sleep, but I seemed to have got lucky. I peeled off my clothes and got into bed. But I didn't go back to sleep. My mind was racing.

Zak: Pea stayed over that first night. I don't think either of us were intending for her to. We just fell asleep. It was really innocent, actually, but I don't think her parents would have seen it that way.

Pea: Mum came into my room at seven and said I had to get up and have a shower if I wanted one, because 'AJ and co', that's actually what she called them, would be coming in from eight onwards. I asked if she knew it was Saturday, and she told me not to be rude, that she'd had to agree on a time schedule and she'd booked us in for seven until eight each morning. So I got up, bleary-eyed, only to find the bathroom door locked. Dad was in there.

John: That whole showering thing was ridiculous. I mean, I'm up early anyway, but I don't like to be told when I can and can't use my own bathroom.

Pea: I got back into bed for a bit, then got up when I heard the bathroom door lock click. But Sebastian beat me to it. I banged on the door, telling him I was next in the queue, but it stayed defiantly shut. I looked at Dad, who shrugged and said, 'You snooze, you lose.' I eventually got in the bathroom at ten to eight. When I came out, my towel just about covering my arse, Maggie was standing there with silk pyjamas on and a washbag in her hand. She said good morning, but I don't think I replied.

Alex: I usually turned up at about ten at the weekends, but that day I was there at nine. Pea was finishing off a bowl of cereal. She went over to the cupboard, held up a box of chocolate Pop Tarts and raised her eyebrows.

Zak: When I went over there to shower, Pea and Alex were eating Pop Tarts. I was starving. There was no food on the bus because no one had been out to get any yet. I asked if there was one for me and Pea stood up to put another one in the toaster. When she'd done it, I caught hold of her hands and pulled her towards me for a kiss. And that's when her mum walked in.

Alex: Oh God, Zak was standing there in a towel kissing Pea, and Cathy looked like she was ready to kill someone.

Cathy: I think I just said her name and they broke apart. Zak looked sheepish and disappeared upstairs to the bathroom, and I told Pea we needed to have a talk later.

Pea: The threat of that talk was hanging over me the whole day.

Alex: When Cathy left the kitchen, I burst out laughing. I thought Pea would do the same thing but she looked at me as if she didn't know who I was and then we just carried on eating our Pop Tarts in silence.

Zak: I showered in five minutes, and all the time I was cursing myself for letting that happen. I needed to get Cathy and John onside or I knew I could kiss my chances of spending time with Pea goodbye.

Alex: Every Saturday, without fail, we'd eat something and then head out into the park. So we did that, but when we went past the tour buses, Pea slowed down and asked if we should invite them to come along. I said, 'Who? Zak and AJ?' She nodded. I said I guessed we could.

Pea: It only struck me as I was knocking on the bus door that these guys had hired the entire park, and it should maybe be them asking us if we wanted to join them rather than the other way around. It was an odd realisation, because I'd tied my whole identity up with that place. Would they mind us still using it? I couldn't see why they would, and Mum and Dad hadn't said anything, but I wasn't sure.

Zak: I stuck my head out and said I'd be with them in five minutes. AJ was still asleep. There was a weird atmosphere between Pea and Alex, and I wished I could get rid of him somehow. Maybe when AJ woke up, he'd join us and then Pea and I could sneak off for a bit.

Pea: We headed for Adventure City. That's where we spent most of our time. It was where the Pirate Ship and Gravity

Spin and Canyon and, of course, the 360 were. Straight away, I could see there weren't many staff around. And when we got to the Pirate Ship, there was no one there to operate it. I looked around and noticed Guy, over at the Ghost Train. I waved and he jogged over. When I asked him what was going on, he said he guessed my dad had cut down on the number of staff because there weren't going to be many visitors. But he could operate any ride we wanted to go on, he said.

Zak: That staff issue was bullshit. I knew Maggie had paid Pea's parents a lot of money to hire the park, and that they'd expected it to come fully staffed.

John: Yes, I'd temporarily laid off some of the staff. It just didn't make sense for them to be standing around all day doing nothing. Even the mighty AJ Silver couldn't be in two places at once, could he? I kept on my most experienced ride operators and food servers and told them to make sure they were where they needed to be at all times. I don't see what's wrong with that. I mean, I still don't.

Danny: This is John all over. Always trying to avoid paying out for anything. Mind you, no one else knew about the debt, so I can kind of see it from his point of view.

Zak: I knew AJ would kick off about it.

Pea: I was a bit embarrassed, actually. It made Dad look like a cheapskate. I tried to cover it up and asked Guy to start up the pirate ship for us. I sat on the back row, in between Alex and Zak.

Alex: She didn't raise her arms in the air, like she usually did. She grabbed hold of Zak instead. Like she needed him to rescue her. I didn't like it. Didn't like who she seemed to be becoming when she was around him.

Maggie: I was trying to read a book when AJ came banging on the door of my bus. He stormed in, said he'd been over to Water City and none of the rides were going. He asked if I'd made sure that the rides were part of the deal I'd made. I went a bit cold. I mean, John and I had never discussed this. But who lets you rent a theme park and then doesn't have the rides up and running? I said I'd go up to the house, and he followed me there. It was Cathy who came to the door. She looked like she hadn't slept much. I told her what the problem was and she frowned and then retreated inside and called for John.

John: I told them there was at least one ride operator in each of the five cities and that operator would gladly walk about with them and start up any rides they wanted to go on. AJ had this grimace on his face, and it didn't change. Maggie didn't look very happy either.

Maggie: I said I thought it was pretty poor, him trying to save on staff when we'd paid them so much money.

John: But they hadn't paid the money at that stage, you see. Just the 10 per cent deposit and then the further 20 per cent on arrival. And what did she think the staff were going to do with themselves if we had them all here, with only a handful of people in the park?

Maggie: AJ spoke then. I remember because John stepped backwards with the force of it. AJ said he didn't give a fuck what the staff did or didn't do, but that John had better make sure they were here first thing in the morning to start up any rides he and his team wanted to go on. Then he stormed off. I looked at John, waiting for him to say he would do as AJ asked, but he didn't. He just held my eye contact until I blinked.

John: I wasn't going to be dictated to by a seventeen-year-old kid. I didn't care if he was AJ bloody Silver.

Cathy: I heard it all unfold from the lounge. I didn't want to get involved. The thing with John is, he's bloody stubborn. And he hates being told what to do by anyone. If I wanted him to do something, I usually started off by asking if he'd do the opposite.

Maggie: In the end, I said, 'Look, have the full staff back here tomorrow and we'll say no more about it.'

John: And I said, 'When are those showers and toilets arriving, again?'

Maggie: Yeah, touché. We'd both made mistakes. I was trying to fix mine. I was too mad to answer him.

Danny: Let's leave them all there and see what Sebastian is doing, shall we?

Sebastian: It was late morning, and I was the only one in the house. Everyone else was in the park trying to smooth things over or whatever. I was drawing. And then there was a knock on the door. I thought it must be someone needing to use the shower, and I was already annoyed with the impact this visit was having on everything, so I took my time going down the stairs and opening the door. I wasn't expecting to see AJ Silver standing there. He asked if he could come in, and I shrugged and said he could if he wanted to. He was in the hallway and I turned to go back upstairs, and he asked if I had ten minutes. We ended up drinking tea at the kitchen table. I found some Jammy Dodgers in the cupboard. I remember him saying they didn't have those in the States. The whole thing was kind of weird. I didn't know what he wanted. We didn't talk much, and not about anything important. Then he got up and left. I was a bit baffled, but I just went back to my room and put a film on.

Zak: It was almost lunchtime when I saw AJ. He was on his own, his expression furious. We were still in Adventure City, about to go on the 360. AJ was walking towards us, and when he got close, he broke into a jog. Asked me where I'd been. I said I'd just been around, with Pea and Alex. He looked at the two of them like he'd never seen them before. Said he'd been looking everywhere.

Pea: I said that maybe we should give them walkie talkies. The staff all used them, and since a lot of them weren't there, there would be a drawer full of them in the office. That way, they could keep track of each other.

Zak: Pea was just trying to be helpful, but AJ snapped at her. Said the staff would all be back in the morning. I wondered who had told him that. I asked if he wanted to hang with us now he'd found us, and I could see him trying to decide. He wanted to storm off, to make a big thing out of it, but he also wanted our company. That part won out, in the end.

Pea: I guess my first impressions of AJ were quite poor. But that Saturday, once he'd got over the fact of not being able to find his brother, I saw a different side to him. I remember being surprised by how funny he was. Not telling jokes, nothing obvious like that, but his responses to things we said were all so sharp and quick. I caught Zak looking annoyed a couple of times when I was laughing, and I tried to rein it in after that.

Alex: AJ and I got on really well. Something clicked with us. Neither of us took life very seriously, and we both liked to have fun. A few times that day, my brain reminded me that this guy I'd met and was getting on well with was one of the most famous people in the world, but after that I sort of forgot about it. He was just AJ.

Pea: We didn't go back to the house until late afternoon. We'd grabbed chicken and chips in the food hall for lunch, and then we'd gone over to Fun City and gone on all the kids' rides that I hadn't ridden for years. Zak and I had shared candy floss.

Zak: It was so great being around Pea, but all I wanted to do was touch her and it was hard with other people around. At one point, when AJ and Alex were swapping stories about music concerts they'd been to, I took her hand and led her around the back of the carousel. I put my hands on her waist and she tilted her head. Kissing her felt like diving into sun-warmed water. I was addicted to it. But after a couple of minutes, she pulled away. I asked her when we were going to get to spend some time alone, and she said she didn't know and left it at that.

Pea: I was scared. Not of Zak, obviously, but of his age and experience. I was scared that as soon as we were truly alone – if we ever were – he would be expecting me to sleep with him, and I didn't know whether I felt ready. I was embarrassed to tell him it was my first time.

Alex: Oh, those two kept sneaking off but I didn't really care. AJ had asked me if I wanted to go to the Manchester show next week, and I had tried to play it cool and failed spectacularly.

Zak: AJ was always inviting people to his shows. It was a thing he did, to make people like him, I guess. He knew those tickets were worth a lot – not necessarily a huge amount of money, but there were more people who wanted to go to his shows than there were tickets available – and he liked the power of offering them up casually, like it was nothing. I remember thinking, *I'm not sure how happy Maggie will be about that*, and before I'd even finished the thought, AJ had asked Pea if she wanted to come too. Now, I don't know why but the idea of Pea going to one of AJ's shows freaked me out. When she saw all the hysteria, and the spectacle of it, what if she decided that she liked him more than she liked me? Yes, I was insecure. I had a pop star for a brother. Who wouldn't be?

Pea: I was more into indie music, but when AJ asked if we'd like tickets for the Manchester show, I didn't hesitate. How many sixteen-year-olds got invited to a pop concert by the star themselves? How many got to travel with the band? A little voice told me that Mum might have a thing or two to say about it, particularly with the concert falling on a Monday night and almost certainly resulting in a late night, but I tried to ignore it. One thing at a time. I said yes. Zak dropped the hand he'd been holding. I turned to look at him, and he smiled, but his eyes were sad, or possibly angry. I hadn't worked out all his expressions yet.

Alex: I wanted to grab Pea and do a little dance, like I had when we'd heard Mrs Vine wasn't coming back to school after her cancer treatment or when I'd won second prize in a dressing up competition at school, but I held it all in. I didn't want AJ to think I was too much. Or that I was a loser.

Pea: AJ and Zak both smoked, and they'd offered the pack to Alex and me a few times, but stopped after we always said no. But for some reason I decided I wanted one. I asked Zak and he lit one for himself and another for me. That's when Sebastian turned up.

Sebastian: Pea was smoking and it was so fucking stupid. It was like she was changing who she was to try to be cool for this boy she liked. Anyway, I told her Mum and Dad wanted to talk to her. She asked what it was about, and I just shrugged. But I think we could both guess that it was about a certain American guy who was blowing smoke rings into the air at that exact moment.

Pea: I spent every weekend at the park, and I always returned at about six for dinner. It was four at this point. I wanted to know why I was being called in, like a child. But I knew things would be worse if I didn't go. I asked Alex if he was coming, and he said no, he'd stay with AJ and Zak if that was okay with them. They looked like they didn't much care either way. So Sebastian and I headed back to the house, with me frantically munching on a Polo mint to get rid of the smell of cigarettes.

Cathy: Pea came back reeking of smoke, so that wasn't a great start.

John: Sitting down with her for a talk was Cathy's idea, and I felt a bit uncomfortable with it. Every generation learns what they need to about relationships and sex, don't they? My parents certainly never sat me down for a chat like this.

Cathy: I made us all tea, but when I brought it into the lounge, Pea was tapping her foot as if she didn't have time for any of this.

Pea: I asked them what it was about and Mum looked a bit taken aback.

Cathy: I said we wanted to talk to her about Zak, and about what we thought was and wasn't acceptable while he was visiting.

Pea: I asked whether this was all about him kissing me in the kitchen this morning.

Cathy: I said that we understood she was sixteen now, and she was likely to start having boyfriends and going on dates, but that it was important to us that she respected us and herself and didn't move too fast with anyone. Particularly someone who usually lived thousands of miles away.

Pea: I get it, now. It's hard to imagine your children becoming adults. Often they're ready for this kind of thing before you are. Back then, I just thought they were being difficult for the sake of it. I said I thought I loved him. I actually said that.

Cathy: I scoffed when she said she loved him. She'd known him for such a short time, and for most of that time they'd been on opposite sides of the Atlantic. This wasn't love. It was hormones and lust and a bit of idolisation. And I said as much.

Pea: Idolisation? I mean, if it had been anything to do with the fact that AJ was famous, surely it would have been AJ I was interested in.

John: We were getting nowhere. I put my hands out and they both went quiet. I said that we were the parents and she was the child, and even though she might not like that, it meant that we made the rules.

Pea: They'd already told me the rules, the night before.

Cathy: We were entitled to come up with new rules at any point, weren't we? The kiss in the kitchen, with him practically naked, had shocked me. I didn't want Pea to end up pregnant. I said we needed to talk about contraception and Pea put her head in her hands and started rocking backwards and forwards.

Pea: I mean, who wants to talk to their parents about contraception? No one.

John: I hadn't known Cathy was going to bring that up. I asked later whether she thought they were actually sleeping together, and she said she thought if they weren't, they soon would be. That shook me up a bit, because even though I knew that Pea was sixteen, I still thought of her as a child, the way all parents do.

Cathy: I said I'd make an appointment at the doctors for her and we'd talk about her going on the pill.

Pea: I mean, it was hugely embarrassing, but I came out of the conversation thinking one thought over and over: *Even my parents think I'm having sex. So maybe I should be?*

Zak: After Pea left with her brother, I didn't feel like going on any more rides. I left AJ and Alex to it and went back to the bus for a sleep. When I woke up, it was a little after six and I knew I had to turn this thing around, with her parents. So I brushed my teeth and washed my face and went over there, to the house.

Cathy: We were eating. I invited him to come in and join us, because it seemed like the polite thing to do.

Zak: I was hungry, so I said sure. She led me into the dining room and brought me a bowl of some kind of chicken casserole. I looked at Pea and she looked down at the table. I couldn't work out whether she was mad at me or embarrassed. Sebastian was telling this long, involved story about something that had happened at college, involving his physics teacher and a battery tester. No one really seemed to be listening. But I waited until I was sure he was done to speak. I said I was wondering whether it would be all right to take Pea out on a date the following evening. I wanted to do this thing properly.

Pea: It was like something out of a film, like he was asking my father for my hand or something. Part of me wanted the ground to open up and swallow me, and part of me loved it. Mum and Dad looked at each other and I could see they were having a silent conversation but couldn't work out what was being said.

Cathy: Look, I remembered what it was like to be a teenager. And I knew that if we said no, they would sneak around and find a way to see each other anyway. I thought our best bet was to say yes, but I was conscious that John and I should probably discuss it first.

John: I said yes. I mean, she was sixteen, wasn't she? We couldn't lock her up.

Zak: I was a bit taken aback. It was like they'd had a change of heart with regards to me. I wasn't going to complain. After dinner, I said I was going to get an early night, thanked them for the food and gave them all a wave. Pea caught up with me outside. She was barefoot and kept squealing as she stepped over the gravel.

Pea: I wanted to thank him, for coming over like that and trying to make my parents like him. It meant a lot to me. But every way I thought of saying it sounded stupid. So I just stood there in front of him, looking at him.

Zak: She was so beautiful. And she had no idea of it. I kissed her, asked if she wanted to come to the bus, either now or later. I just wanted to be around her. I was high off it.

Pea: I wanted to go to the bus with him more than anything but I knew we had to play this carefully. Gain my parents' trust. I kissed him on the lips, just a peck, but he pulled me in and kissed me properly, his hands in my hair. When we came apart, I said I had revision to do, but I actually spent the entire evening lying on my bed reliving that kiss.

Zak: I was restless. I wanted to go see a movie, or get a coffee, or something other than sit in that bus. But I couldn't do any of those things with my brother, and Pea wasn't free, and who else was there? I ended up lying on my bed listening to music. AJ kept throwing things at me, a pair of socks and then a book, which hit me in the head. I pulled my headphones off, really mad. Asked what he wanted. He said, 'I'm bored, Zac-Man. I can't believe we got to stay in a theme park and I'm bored as shit.' I knew from experience that bored AJ wasn't a good thing. If nothing was happening, he had a tendency to make something happen. And it was never something good.

Pea: I don't know whether AJ snuck out or what. All I know is that when I woke up the next morning, I could hear this buzz. It was coming from outside. I opened my bedroom window and it got louder. It was girls, I realised. Teenage girls. I pulled some clothes on and went outside. Mum and Dad were a step ahead of me, and I caught them up, asked them what was happening. Mum shrugged and Dad didn't bother responding at all. The noise got louder and louder as we approached the locked gates. I'd never seen a crowd like it. Some of them were shouting AJ's name and others were just talking in groups and all of them were standing there as if they were going to be given access. Where had they come from? And how long had they been here? When we reached the gates, the sound died down. Did they think we were going to let them in? Dad made a sort of megaphone with his hands and asked what they were doing here. They started up a chant. AJ Silver, AJ Silver, AJ Silver, AJ Silver. Dad waved his arms around until they stopped. Then he did the megaphone again and said, 'The park is closed for the next six weeks. Please go home.'

Sebastian: I woke up and there was no one in the house. I remember thinking that everything was weird, and I just wanted it to go back to normal. I was eating cereal when they all came back in, dressed in pyjamas and flip flops. Dad was muttering about how they'd found out, and Mum was saying that people weren't stupid and could put two and two together after seeing that the park was closed. Pea was quiet. I asked what was up.

Cathy: Sebastian's always been in his own little world. He didn't seem bothered by the crowd the way the rest of us were. I was unsettled. Maggie had told us this would happen, but I'd sort of imagined a dozen or so pre-teen girls, and this was something quite different. There were hundreds of them. They must have come from all over the place. And they didn't look like they were going anywhere. We'd walked away after John's announcement but it was clear no one was getting ready to leave.

Sebastian: It was a bit later that I realised we couldn't use the car without opening the gates, and we clearly couldn't open the gates.

Cathy: We all felt trapped, and it struck me for the first time that we lived in a kind of cage. That we'd voluntarily set up our family inside these gates. It hadn't felt restrictive until we couldn't open them.

Pea: Once I was dressed, I went over to Zak and AJ's bus, asked them if they knew. They'd heard the buzz, of course. They didn't seem surprised, just weary. I remember Zak saying, 'I thought we might get a couple of days.' AJ said he was going to go to the gates and sign a few autographs, try to get them onside. Zak thought that was a terrible idea and that he should stay hidden. But AJ wasn't the kind to take advice. He went over there, to the gates. His bodyguard, Lucian, went with him. Zak and I followed. The way the noise rose when he came into view was inexplicable. The screaming, my God. He held up his hands, as if to say *I am but a man*, and I saw the showman in him for the first time. Suddenly he wasn't a teenager I'd been hanging out with but this thing, this star. I could see that the crowd was surging forward and it was so clear someone was going to get hurt. I turned to Zak, asked him what we should do. AJ was turning to go, as if he could just appear and rile everyone up and then disappear. Which I suppose he could. But the girls were in a frenzy, pushing and shoving. I saw this one girl with her face pressed up against the gates, and then I saw her fall.

Cathy: Pea came running into the house, saying we had to call 999. That people were getting hurt at the gates. I didn't find out until later that AJ had appeared there and caused a stampede of sorts where the people at the front couldn't move and ended up being trampled. Three girls were treated by paramedics in the end. None of them had serious injuries but it was a bit of a wakeup call.

Zak: AJ couldn't help himself. He was like two people, in a way. The one who hated all the attention, who wanted to play Pac-Man and listen to music and all of that, and then the other one, the famous one, who couldn't stop himself going to see the furore his very presence caused. Did he care that three girls got hurt? I mean, he said he did. But what's three girls in a crowd of several hundred? You start to think of them as numbers rather than people.

Pea: I didn't know AJ well, of course, but it was like he was on this path to self-destruction. It was too much, I suppose. All of it. The fame, the money, the isolation. He loved and hated it. Any dream come true is a nightmare when looked at from a different angle, right?

Maggie: It was Zak who came to tell me what had happened. I went straight to AJ and told him to stay away from the gates, from the crowd. Injured young girls were not a good look. I had flowers sent to the hospital for them, signed the cards from AJ. The showers still hadn't arrived so we had another morning of all going in and out of the Hunters' place. What with that and the issue with staff and the girls being hurt, it felt like everything was going wrong. But I was convinced it would get better when the tour started. The lead-up was always weird.

Pea: It was that same day, in the afternoon. We were all just hanging out again, and Zak and Alex wanted to go on Canyon for a third time. AJ and I stood back and watched them. It was strange to see the almost empty carriage going round, just the front two seats occupied. I was looking at Zak, thinking about being alone with him, when AJ spoke. He said, 'You know you're just his British girl, right?' I went cold. Couldn't look at him. I asked what he was talking about. 'When we get back home, you'll be this anecdote he brings out. "Yeah, I had a thing with this British girl." He won't even use your name.' I was shocked. It was so wilfully cruel. And I didn't know what to say. What could I say? The others were bounding over to us at that point and Zak put his arms around me and kissed my forehead and I wanted to turn to AJ and say, 'See? See?' But what did it prove, really? I spent the rest of that afternoon feeling sad, but in the evening, as I turned it over and over, the sadness turned to anger. How dare he?

Zak: I didn't know anything about what AJ had said to Pea until much later. Until after he was gone. So I never got to ask him. I have no idea why he did it. Just for something to do, would be my guess. It was all one big game to him, and he'd test out what might happen if he pushed this button, or that one. It was just like going to the gates to see the screaming fans. He wanted to see what would happen. When Pea eventually told me about that exchange, I was furious with him. And being furious with your dead brother is the worst.

Danny: Just before we leave them for today, let's have one last word from Sebastian. You're curious about that visit from AJ, right? I certainly was.

Sebastian: It became a bit of a thing, having tea with AJ. It happened most days while he was there. I don't think anyone else knew, because they were all out of the house. I think, looking back, that he liked the fact that I didn't treat him any differently to anyone else. I didn't care one iota about his fame. He was surrounded by people who treated him like he was some kind of God, and I think that wears thin after a while.

Danny: So that's it for today. Thanks for listening, and be sure to keep sharing your thoughts on your socials at @WhatHappenedThatSummer. Next week we'll be putting the spotlight on AJ's messy and complicated love life. Believe me, you won't want to miss it.

LeahLou
I was in that crush outside the gates! AJ Silver forever! #WhatHappenedThatSummer

MichelleOdin
Oh my god, me too. I was right at the front and saw the girls who went down. It was scary. But you don't think about getting hurt when you're a teenager, do you? #WhatHappenedThatSummer

Steve_O
I can't believe what AJ said to Pea – what a dick! #WhatHappenedThatSummer

56349Baz
Is anyone else thinking what I'm thinking? Pea and John both have a reason to dislike AJ now, right? #WhatHappenedThatSummer

BecksWilson

I don't care what anyone says, Ice Cream is a tune. #What-HappenedThatSummer

FreyatheFox

Imagine what he might have gone on to do, in later years, if he'd had the opportunity. #WhatHappenedThatSummer

DantheMan

Yeah, imagine. We might have had another three albums of mediocre pop music before he sunk without trace. #What-HappenedThatSummer

5

EPISODE 5 – TEENAGE KICKS

Danny: It's time for episode five of *What Happened That Summer?* with me, Danny Drake. Twenty-nine years after his death, AJ Silver is a streaming sensation. As of yesterday, 'Ice Cream' officially went triple platinum, and I don't know about you but I can't seem to go anywhere without hearing it.

As you surely know, AJ Silver took the world of pop music by storm in the early 1990s and his untimely death in 1996, when he was just seventeen, sent shockwaves all over the world. And despite being American as apple pie, AJ Silver died right here in the UK, at Wildworld theme park in West Wilding, near Birmingham.

At the end of the last episode, I promised you that we'd be looking into AJ Silver's love life. As you'd imagine for a teenage boy who was a household name the world over, AJ Silver had some complicated romantic entanglements. Over the years, there've been all sorts of rumours and speculations, including the infamous 'Was AJ Gay?' headline that led to AJ Silver's mother, Grace Campbell, suing tabloid newspaper *The Scoop* and winning an unspecified amount of money.

So, let's get right into it with not one but two people who claim to have had sexual relations with AJ Silver during that fateful UK trip.

Nicole: Yes, I had a thing with AJ.

Danny: So that's potential romance number one, Nicole Waddington. Sworn enemy of Pea Hunter and Alex. Want to hear from number two?

Alex: Stuff happened between me and AJ. I'll let you use your imagination.

Pea: I know nothing about that. Alex never said a word. I mean, I believe him, but I'm just surprised that he kept something like that quiet all these years.

Danny: I should point out here that all confirmed relationships AJ had in his short life were with girls. So perhaps he was bisexual, or perhaps someone is lying. Let's hear how it all allegedly played out.

Pea: They'd been there for a week, rehearsals had started, and the first gig was a few days away. AJ had a day off on the Sunday. He had this wild air about him, like he wanted to cause some trouble. Two more members of his team had just turned up. A guy called Lou who looked after his money and a private doctor called Haskins. I had no idea, up to that point, that some people had a doctor who would follow them around the world.

Zak: AJ was like a caged animal. He'd be fine once the tour started, I knew that from experience, but in the days leading up to the first concert he was always a nightmare. That Sunday, he looked like he wanted to tear shit up.

Alex: I went over again and it felt like there was something in the air. Pea was already in the park and I found her with AJ and Zak in Water City. They were about to go on the Wild Water Rapids and Pea called for me to join them, so I went over. Pea and Zak were holding hands, all loved up.

Zak: I couldn't decide whether Alex's presence was a good or a bad thing. Three was a tricky number, so maybe four was better. We got into the circular boat, Pea first, then me, then Alex and then AJ. It meant AJ was sitting opposite me. He had this look in his eyes that I'd seen before. I knew it meant trouble. Almost as soon as the ride started, this big wave crashed over the side and soaked Alex. We all laughed but he looked pissed. He was the kind of guy who spent a lot of time on his hair, you know? He started talking about having to go home and get changed, and AJ said it was just a T-shirt and we could lend him one. He cheered up a bit, then. I was starting to think he had a crush on AJ. Of course, it didn't cross my mind that AJ might have had a crush on him back. AJ and I had never talked about our sexuality – I don't think many brothers did. Back then, the assumption was that you were straight unless you told people otherwise.

Anyway, AJ and Alex went off to the bus to get Alex a dry T-shirt. I looked at Pea and she looked at me, and then I took hold of both of her hands and kissed her. We were round the back of a hut that sold ice creams and she pushed me gently back against it. I told her that I really wanted to get some time alone with her, and she blushed a furious red. It was then that I thought for the first time that maybe she didn't have much experience. It hadn't occurred to me before, because she was so fucking pretty. I asked whether she'd had a boyfriend before, and she looked down at her feet.

Pea: I'd known it was going to come out at some point, the fact that all of this was so new to me. I said no, I'd never had a boyfriend. He asked whether I'd had sex, and it was shocking to me, him asking straight out like that. But I knew I wasn't going to get a better chance to be totally honest with him, so I gathered my courage, looked up and said no. He said it was okay, that there was no rush for anything, and it put my mind at rest a bit. I kissed him again, and he put his hands on my waist and I understood why people do crazy things for this feeling. I thought, in that moment, that I would probably do anything to be with him.

Alex: Over the time they'd been there, AJ and I had hung out for the odd hour or so here and there. Zak was always trying to get Pea alone, which left the two of *us* alone too. So on that walk back to the bus, my hair and clothes dripping wet, I felt pretty comfortable with him. But when we got onto the bus, something changed. The air was charged, somehow. It felt kind of dangerous. AJ went to a suitcase and pulled out a T-shirt without really looking at it. He sat on his bed and looked at me while I changed. I was so aware of my body and his eyes on it as I peeled off my wet T-shirt. I asked if he had a towel, and he reached out and threw one at me. It smelled musty. I dried off, rubbed my hair, and then I was about to put the new T-shirt on when he stood up and came towards me. I thought he would stop when he was a few inches away, but he didn't. I didn't move, could hardly breathe. And then he stopped and reached out to touch my chest. His hand was cold and I pulled back, but then I tried to tell him with my eyes that I wasn't saying no. That I was hungrily, greedily, saying yes. We just looked at each other, no more than a few centimetres apart. Was this it? Was AJ Silver going to kiss me? Was my first ever kiss going to be with AJ Silver?

It was.

Zak: It was Pea who said they'd been gone ages. I didn't notice. I was completely lost in her, in this thing between us.

Alex: It was more than a kiss. It was pushing and pulling, touching and sliding, our hard, young bodies slamming against one another in something that felt strangely akin to fighting. And then it was over, as quickly as it had begun, and AJ was getting back into the top I'd pulled off him and saying nothing. I was so naïve. I thought it was the start of something. And it was, in a way. But not the way I imagined.

Pea: I did notice things were a bit weird when they came back. They were too quiet, too careful. But I didn't think much of it.

Zak: I thought maybe they'd had an argument or something. Like I said, AJ was in a funny mood that day. He lit a cigarette and said that he wanted to go out. 'Out where?' I asked. The girls were still there, at the gates. He asked Pea if there was another way out and she confirmed that there was another, smaller gate just behind their house. He said, 'Let's do it. I'll wear sunglasses and a hat.'

Alex: I didn't like it. I guess because I'd literally just spent some time alone with him, and I still couldn't believe it had happened, and it was bad enough going back to Pea and Zak. I didn't want to open the circle any wider, to risk other people seeing him.

Zak: I did feel sorry for him, sometimes. When we travelled, I could go for a walk or talk to people and it was just impossible for him. So I went along with it. I thought it would be okay if it was just this once, before the tour actually started. We all trudged back to the bus and I found a baseball cap and AJ dug out his sunnies. He piled his longish hair on top of his head and made sure it was covered by the hat, then turned to look at us.

Alex: It was a small town. Everyone knew everyone, pretty much. And people weren't stupid. I knew someone would recognise him.

Danny: This has got disaster written all over it, hasn't it?

Pea: We went up to the gate, the four of us. It was the one we used to get in and out on foot, to save us walking up the long driveway. I was kind of surprised the crowd hadn't found it yet, but I went ahead and there was no one around. We set out, and it was so strange, feeling like we had to sneak around in broad daylight. I got a tiny sense of what it must be like to be him, how restricting his life must be. Every time a car passed us, he put his head down. Zak was holding my hand, his fingers laced through mine, and I kept looking down at our hands, not quite able to believe it. Alex was quieter than usual. At one point, AJ told this awful joke. He said, 'How many gay guys does it take to screw in a lightbulb? No one knows, because they're all too busy screwing each other.'

Alex: He looked right at me when he said it. It was a message, clear as day. No one could find out about what had happened between us. But I wasn't going to be silenced like that.

Pea: It was really uncomfortable. I'd heard jokes like that before, of course, at school or even on TV. But since I'd known about Alex being gay, I'd felt this need to protect him from all that.

Zak: AJ was being a dick. Maybe he was testing Alex, seeing whether he would challenge him. I don't know. He was just stirring shit up.

Pea: I saw them first. Nicole and Kelly and Fay. Probably the worst people we could run into. I tried to get Alex's attention but he was looking straight ahead, his eyes set on a fixed point in the distance. I looked down at my hand again, in Zak's, and I knew they would notice and comment on it. They were sitting on a bench and we were heading straight for them, and it was like a car crash was going to happen and only I could see it.

Zak: Pea slipped her hand out of mine and I noticed that she was looking at these three girls. We were in front, AJ and Alex behind, and when we reached them, the girl in the middle called out. 'Who's your boyfriend, Pea?'

Pea: I froze. Nicole never spoke to me. Never. But I can imagine how surprised she was to see me walking down the street with a tall, handsome stranger. I knew that if he opened his mouth and spoke it was all over. But I didn't know whether it was best to ignore her completely or make something up. I muttered, 'He's just a friend.'

Zak: That hurt, man. It made me question this whole thing. If she didn't want her friends to know that there was something going on between us, then what was it, really?

Alex: I was barely aware of Nicole and her little gang of bitches. I was hearing that joke AJ had told, over and over. Feeling the warmth of his tongue in my mouth and his hands on my skin. What the fuck did any of it mean?

Zak: Before I knew what was happening, AJ had sat down on the edge of the bench and was talking to them.

Nicole: It was the maddest thing. I should have known as soon as I saw Pea Hunter with some guy who was really quite fit, but I didn't put two and two together until the other boy came and sat on the bench next to Kelly and asked how we were and I heard his American accent.

Kelly: I'm Kelly Cross. I almost screamed, I swear to God. AJ fucking Silver, sitting next to me on a bench in West Wilding town centre. Five minutes ago we'd been buying gum and cigarettes in Somerfield. It was like some mad dream.

Nicole: He asked what we were up to and whether we wanted to go with them. Kelly said, 'Go where?' As if we were going to say no! We all stood up and he asked our names and we said them, Kelly first, then me, then Fay. He said, 'Hey Fay, rhymes with AJ. I'm AJ, by the way.' We were all pissing ourselves laughing and I remember noticing how good he smelled, kind of woody and minty combined. He pulled out a pack of cigarettes and offered them around.

Pea: I wanted to go back. I looked up at Zak but he wouldn't meet my eye. Then he pushed forward a bit and introduced himself before taking one of the cigarettes from AJ's pack.

Kelly: The brother was a bit older and he had these intense eyes. If it was now, I'd definitely have gone for him. But we were totally blinded by fame. I mean, we were smoking a cigarette with a guy who we had posters of on our bedroom walls. Nothing in our lives had come close to this moment. And I knew from the way Nicole was giggling and reaching out to touch AJ's arm that the race was on for one of us to get off with him.

Nicole: No, I didn't think at that stage that anything would happen.

Fay: My name's Fay Johnstone. Nicole was definitely flirting. I mean, I think we all were but she was better at it. We all stood and started walking, following Pea and the brother, Zak, to God knows where. I'd known Pea since primary school. She wasn't our kind of person at all. Alex wasn't either.

Nicole: The whole time we were with them, part of me was experiencing it and part of me was working out how I'd frame it the next day at school. This was big. Bigger than the time Simon Watkins's dad was on *Blockbusters*. Bigger than Eve Anthony having a cousin who was in some indie band who'd toured with Oasis. In a different league from those things.

Pea: I didn't know where we were going. I just kept walking, down the High Street, past the shops. Nicole didn't say a word to me after that initial question. I don't think anyone else noticed AJ, but it didn't matter because now Nicole knew, it would be everywhere by tomorrow. I reached for Zak's hand but he pulled away, and I thought maybe he fancied one of those girls, like everyone at school did.

Zak: It felt like it was all going wrong, sort of slipping away. We'd been in this little bubble, away from the mania that came with being in AJ Silver's family, but now I could feel it creeping in. I wanted to go back to Wildworld, but I knew I had to stay with AJ, keep an eye on him. I didn't know, yet, what he was going to do.

Pea: We ended up going down to the river. There was this bit on the bank where you could sit and we all took our shoes off and paddled a bit. We were messing about, pushing each other. I don't know whether Zak and AJ noticed that Alex and I didn't talk to the girls and they didn't talk to us. At one point, AJ pulled a bag of weed and some papers out of his pocket and started rolling a joint. Zak said, 'Fuck, AJ, did you bring that through airport security?' AJ didn't answer, just pushed his hair out of his eyes and laughed, reached for his lighter.

Alex: I'd smoked weed a couple of times with my brother. Never with Pea. She was kind of innocent. Didn't drink, or smoke, or really anything like that. But that day, I wasn't sure what she'd do when the joint was offered to her. Nicole and her friends took their turns, but I passed. I wanted Pea to know that if she didn't want to do it, she didn't have to look like the only one.

Pea: When the joint was passed to me, I guess I just thought, *Why not?* Alex hadn't taken it and I saw his eyes on me as I inhaled, felt his silent judgement. For the first time, I thought that our friendship might not survive this. It was just a fleeting thought, but I remember acknowledging it, thinking, *Huh, I wonder where that came from.*

Zak: AJ and I smoked a bit back then, yeah. But I would never have attempted to take anything on a freakin' plane. That was AJ all over, though. It's common for teenagers to feel invincible, but with AJ it was massively exaggerated by the fame and the money. Nobody ever told him no, or put any limits in place for him.

Alex: It was a sunny day, and there was no one around but us. We all lay back in the grass and I felt like I might doze off, but Nicole and Fay kept asking AJ these inane questions and being all giggly. They pretended they were really stoned, but it was so over the top, they were sort of falling all over the place and shrieking with laughter. Pea was next to me and she didn't say anything, but I could tell she was hating it. But it didn't feel like it was our place to ask them to go. AJ had kind of picked them up and he didn't seem to mind how they were acting.

Zak: I could tell AJ had chosen Nicole long before they disappeared into the long grass. He was laughing at her stupid jokes, reaching out to touch her arm. Doing all the things that being AJ Silver meant he didn't really have to do. If he wanted, he could just point and say 'you' and teenage girls would follow him, hardly able to believe their luck. But he was like a cat toying with a mouse. He liked the chase. So I was not in the least bit surprised when things went a bit quiet and I opened my eyes and saw that they were kissing.

Fay: It was all I could do to stop myself from screaming. Nicole and AJ Silver! I could hardly wait for school.

Nicole: I guess I was a bit stoned and we were both flirting and one thing led to another. You know what horny teenagers are like.

Pea: I didn't know what was going on with me and Zak, so I was mostly thinking about that. I wanted him to put his arm around me, or kiss me, but since Nicole and her friends had joined us, it was like he didn't want to know me. And then AJ got off with Nicole. It shouldn't really have come as much of a surprise but it did, somehow. Yes, she was the most fancied girl in our year at school. But he was famous. Like, properly famous. I suppose, thinking about it now, he was just a teenage boy who was looking for a bit of fun. But then, I couldn't compute them being together like that. I also couldn't look away. I had sunglasses on so they wouldn't have known I was watching. He'd sort of pulled her onto his lap and they were really going for it, as if they were on their own, and then I heard AJ say, 'Shall we take this somewhere more private?' in this breathy voice. They stood up and disappeared off into the long grass and I looked at Alex, expecting him to be finding it hilarious. He looked like he was in pain. That's when I realised he definitely had a crush on AJ.

Alex: I mean, what can I say? I felt like an idiot. And I was angry, too.

Zak: I wanted to take him to one side and say, 'Dude, you can't just go around sleeping with girls like this, leaving a trail of broken hearts behind you.' But the truth was, he could. No one was going to stop him, and the girls were not in short supply. So what chance did I have of changing his mind? At the end of the day, he was a hot-blooded seventeen-year-old guy.

Nicole: No, we didn't sleep together. Not that day.

Fay: I don't think they had sex, but who knows? Nicole was on a high afterwards, kept talking about how she couldn't believe someone who could have anyone had chosen her, and I was thinking, *Yeah, he could have any girl he likes, but he's here, in this sleepy town of ours, so it might be more a case of who's around than anything else.*

Nicole: Fay was jealous, absolutely. A few months before that we'd both liked this boy at school and he'd chosen me over her. She acted like she was over it but I don't think she was.

Pea: When they came back, Nicole's shirt was buttoned up wrong and AJ's hair was wild, the hat gone. I looked away, didn't want them to catch me looking. When I turned to Zak, his expression was unreadable.

Alex: I'd had enough. I got up and said I was going home. I hoped Pea would come with me, but she didn't. I guess she didn't want to leave Zak alone with those girls. So I brushed myself off and started to walk away, and Pea called after me that she'd see me at school the next day. When I was out of earshot, I turned back to see whether AJ was watching me leave. But of course he wasn't.

Zak: AJ made another joint and passed it around. I was kind of bored. I wanted to be alone with Pea, to ask her what was going on between us, but something told me not to leave AJ with those girls, and the fact that that was my instinct made me feel really uneasy. So I was glad when AJ finally stood up and said we should get back.

Nicole: I wasn't stupid. I didn't think what had happened that afternoon meant anything to him. I didn't think I was going to be his girlfriend or anything like that. But when we got back to the bench where they'd found us and AJ said, 'See you, then,' without even looking at me, I did feel kind of... used, I suppose. I mean, I was sixteen and I hadn't had much shitty treatment up to that point. With boys at school, it was always me doing the dumping when I'd had enough.

Zak: AJ made it clear he didn't give a shit about her, and it was awkward as hell.

Fay: We watched them walk away, Pea Hunter in the middle of these two tall almost-men. Kelly said, 'Isn't he supposed to be going out with that actress who was in *Party of Five* for a bit?' And Nicole just glared at her, and we were silent after that. When I was at home later, and Mum was nagging me about my homework, it felt like something I'd dreamed up. On the wall opposite my bed, there was a poster of him, topless and moody, his hair covering half of his face, his thumbs in the belt loops of his jeans. I stared at him for twenty minutes or so, trying to tally the boy I'd met with this untouchable star. In real life, he'd been a bit more ordinary, his skin not quite so flawless and his hair a bit too long. But still, there'd been this sheen about him. Was it only because I knew about his fame, or was it just something he had?

Nicole: I went home and ate dinner and did some Maths revision. Quadratic equations, I think. No, I didn't tell anyone.

Pea: I breathed a bit easier as soon as we'd left those girls behind, but Zak was clearly agitated. He smoked two cigarettes back to back and didn't hold my hand. AJ walked ahead of us, whistling. When we got back to my house, I asked Zak if we were still going out later.

Zak: I shrugged and said we could if she still wanted to.

Pea: I definitely wanted to. I had to know what was happening, why he was being cold.

Zak: AJ said he was heading back to the bus to listen to some music and get his head in the right space for the morning. My gut told me to call off the date and stay with him, make sure he didn't get up to anything he shouldn't, but Pea looked sad and I wanted to try to get to the bottom of what was happening. I told her I'd pick her up at the house at seven.

Pea: He didn't kiss me and I felt sure that this date would be the end of things. I shut myself in my bedroom and cried until my eyes were sore. And then I had a shower, letting the water fall on my face until it was a little less puffy. When I was getting ready, the phone rang. I didn't go to answer it, but a few seconds later Mum called up the stairs that it was for me. I picked up the upstairs handset and waited for Mum to hang up the downstairs one. It was Alex.

Alex: Pea and I often spent hours on the phone, even if we'd been together mere hours before, but that day, she didn't have anything much to say. I asked her what I'd missed, and I wanted her to ask me why I'd left early, but she didn't. She just said they'd headed back soon after I went and now she was getting ready for her date with Zak. I asked what she thought had gone on between AJ and Nicole, even though bringing it up felt a bit like stabbing myself in the heart, and I remember that she laughed and said, 'I think that's pretty obvious.' I had to remind myself that she didn't know what had happened with me and AJ that morning. She didn't know how I felt. There was an awkward silence and then I said that my mum needed to use the phone and hung up. And I'd never felt so lonely.

Pea: Alex always liked to thoroughly analyse everything that happened in our lives and I just didn't have the time or inclination for it that day. Could I have been a better friend? Absolutely. Did I think he had something serious going on? Absolutely not.

Alex: Over the years, Mum always asked me who I'd spent time with at school, and I always said Pea. She would say, 'No one else?' She didn't like me putting all my eggs in one basket, friendship-wise. She was terrified that Pea's family would move away or she'd change schools or we'd fall out, and I'd have no one. And then, I got it.

Danny: But what of Sebastian and AJ? How was that little friendship developing?

Sebastian: In the afternoon, AJ came over and it was the same routine as ever. Tea, biscuits, low-key chat about this and that. It was the first time he'd brought Lou with him. Lou was probably in his late thirties, quite overweight and a bit dishevelled. AJ introduced him as his 'money manager'. It felt weird, having someone else there, but I wasn't going to ask Lou to leave.

Pea walked in just as we were finishing up. She stopped in the doorway and looked from me to AJ to Lou like she couldn't believe her eyes. She asked if everything was okay. AJ stood up, drained his mug and said everything was fine. And then he left, Lou following closely behind. She sat down where he'd been sitting and said, 'So are you and AJ friends now or what?' I didn't know how to answer. I didn't know what we were. I just shrugged and pushed my chair back and went up to my room.

Pea: Walking in on Sebastian, AJ and Lou having a cup of tea together was so weird. I couldn't imagine them having a single thing in common. But Sebastian clearly didn't want to talk about it, and I don't think it ever happened again, so I put it out of my mind.

Zak: I think that was the day that Mom went back to the States. There was something going on with the next album and either her or Maggie needed to go and sort it out. They decided Maggie should stay in England. I asked whether Lou could go, because I had this bad feeling about him, always had, but Mom insisted it had to be her, so we said goodbye. She said she'd be back in a few days.

When I walked over from the bus to Pea's house to pick her up that evening, my heart was in my throat. Earlier in the day, when we'd kissed against that ice cream stand, I'd been so happy. But it felt like weeks had passed since then, felt like Pea had somehow morphed back into a stranger. Her mum answered the door, and she gave me a look that left me in no doubt that she disapproved. In the hallway, she leaned in close and said, 'She is only just sixteen, Zak. Please remember that.' And then before I could answer, she turned and called up the stairs and Pea appeared, looking cute in combat trousers and a fitted tee. She didn't look at me as she walked down the stairs. And then we were outside, and it was still warm so I took off my sweater. We were quiet, in a way we'd never been. How had things got so messed up so quickly? I asked her what was going on with her, and she shrugged.

Pea: I couldn't believe he was going to make me say it. It was obvious he'd gone off me, that he'd seen there were other girls in our town and started being distant and cold. But when I said all that, he started laughing. I was so taken aback and so annoyed I shoved him in the side, and he almost went into the road. Then I asked him what was so funny. He said that the only reason he'd been acting like that was because I'd said to Nicole and co that we were just friends. He'd thought I was embarrassed. I couldn't work out what kind of world he lived in that he thought someone like me would be embarrassed to be seeing someone like him. We both ended up laughing about it, and I was so relieved I felt like I could cry, too.

Zak: Once we'd got that misunderstanding straightened out, we were back to the way things were before. Holding hands, sneaking kisses. I took her to the burger place we'd been to on my last visit. There weren't many restaurants in town, for one thing, and I thought it might be nice to relive that date, the one on which we'd really started to like each other. We both ordered cheese and bacon burgers, I think, and milkshakes. I liked that she liked food. Back home, the girls all seemed to be competing to see who could eat the least.

Pea: It was all going fine until he asked me what I thought about AJ. I stopped eating, my burger almost finished. I wondered, absently, whether I had any sesame seeds from the bun in my teeth. And I said I thought AJ was a bit spoilt.

Zak: She said AJ was a brat, or something like that. And listen, I know I shouldn't have asked. I knew better than anyone that AJ could be a handful, that people didn't always warm to him, because they saw the demanding, moody side of him and not the boy I grew up alongside. The one who liked playing stupid pranks and always shared his candy with me. What did I think she was going to say? That he was charming, all sweetness and light? He'd been restless and a bit obnoxious ever since we'd arrived. But you know how it's okay for you to criticise members of your family but no one else can, right? So it really stung when she said that. It was because she meant a lot to me, and I wanted her to see who he could be. Not pop star AJ. Not mega-rich, I-want-that-and-I-want-it-now AJ. I wanted her to see the kid who used to look at me like I was his hero, who'd only play basketball at the park if I went along too. The one who'd bring me a McDonalds cheeseburger back from any trip into town. But I hadn't seen much of that kid lately, and I knew Pea hadn't seen him at all. Anyway, it soured things a bit, and I was pissed with her for saying it, and pissed with myself for asking her.

Pea: It kind of ruined the whole evening.

Zak: So we'd started off badly but managed to pull it back, and then it had gone south again. I asked for the check without asking if she wanted dessert. And then we were back out on the street, but all the warmth had gone from the evening. Pea hadn't brought a jacket or anything and I could see the goose-flesh on her arms. I offered her my sweater, and she put it on. We both laughed because it looked ridiculous on her, and then she said that she was sorry for what she'd said about AJ, and I shrugged and pretended it didn't matter, even though it did.

Pea: Mum had told me to be back by ten thirty, and it was only nine. I wanted to go somewhere with him, somewhere we could be on our own, but I didn't know how to ask.

Zak: I couldn't take her back to the bus, because AJ would be there, but I didn't want the evening to end either. I asked if she wanted to go for a walk around the park. It was going dark and obviously there were no lights on because it was shut down, so we stumbled about a bit. There was this huge trampoline in the kids' play park, and we ended up there, and Pea took her shoes off and started jumping. I couldn't see her face but she was laughing, and it was infectious. I started laughing too, stooped down to take my own shoes off. I got onto the trampoline and took hold of both her hands and we jumped together. I hadn't been on a trampoline for years, and there was something about the pure joy of it, the childishness. I think I let go of some of the tension I'd been holding. And it sounds crazy, but I was sure I was falling in love with her.

Pea: We ended up lying back on the trampoline, holding hands. We were both looking up at the stars and he said he thought it was wild that he was thousands of miles from home but looking up at the same stars he could see from there. And then he rolled onto his side and I rolled onto mine and we were kissing, his lips on my lips, then my jaw, then my collarbone. I wanted to have sex with him, then. I'd been thinking and worrying about it so much but something raw and animal just took over and I wanted to be as close to him as I could be, skin to skin. I asked him where we could go, and he grinned at me. We went back to the bus to see if AJ was there. He wasn't, but I was conscious that he could walk in at any time. Zak told me he'd lock the door from the inside, and that way AJ would have to knock and we'd at least get some warning. It wasn't perfect, but it was the best we could do. I didn't think about where AJ was.

Alex: AJ was with me. I'm not proud of it. He'd treated me like shit, got off with someone else in front of me, but he called my house and asked me to come over. Half his team had gone out for dinner and drinks so there was a free bus. I said, 'What about your bus?' and he laughed and said he thought Pea and Zak would probably end up screwing in there at some point. I nearly picked him up on that. I didn't like the way he talked about Pea. But I didn't, because he said something else. 'Come over, please. I want you.' I practically ran there.

Pea: Zak led me over to his bed and we sat on the edge of it, kissing. At some point we fell back and he was on top of me and we were taking our clothes off. I kept thinking about all the things I'd ever heard about losing your virginity. That it hurts, that you bleed, that it's just something to get over and done with. But it didn't feel like that, for me. Zak was slow and gentle and I felt this connection to him, like we were caught in a web together or something like that. I mean, I was young. Naïve. But it felt like love.

Alex: On the walk over, I told myself I'd wait for him to apologise. But when I got there, he didn't even speak. He was waiting outside, in the dark, and he nodded his head to show which direction we were going in, and I followed him to the bus. Once we were inside, he didn't put a light on, he just grabbed me by my belt and started kissing me. It was rough and urgent. When he pushed me back on the bed, half of me liked it and half of me wanted to speak out, to say that I was a person, not a toy. I wouldn't have dreamed of telling him it was my first time. It was really clear that he was more experienced than me.

Pea: Afterwards, Zak kissed my eyelids, and I laughed. He asked why and I couldn't tell him. I was just so happy. He held me really tight and when I said I had to get dressed and go home, he wouldn't let me go for a minute or so. I didn't want to move, didn't want to break the spell.

Alex: Afterwards, I said I should get going and AJ said 'yeah', and I realised it was the first word he'd spoken in the whole time I'd been there. He didn't see me out. I walked home with tears stinging my eyes. Why was I letting him treat me like that? But I knew why. He was AJ Silver, wasn't he? Beautiful and almost magic. Known the world over but only touched by a few.

Danny: So Pea and Alex lost their virginities to brothers on the same night. It would be sweet if it wasn't all so messed up.

Pea: The next day, on the walk to school, I asked Alex why he'd left abruptly when we were all down by the river. He said he couldn't stand being around Nicole and her friends. I understood that. He asked how my date with Zak had gone, and I said it was nice. I didn't want to tell him what had happened. I felt like a different person, somehow, someone a bit more grown-up and knowledgeable about the world. I wasn't ready to dissect that.

Alex: Pea didn't say much about her date with Zak, and I certainly didn't tell her about my encounter with AJ. We talked about a History project we were doing instead, and it felt a bit like old times.

Zak: When Pea and Alex were at school, and AJ was in rehearsals for long days, I mostly walked around the park, thinking about what I was going to do with my life. Somehow, it felt like going on rides alone would be dumb, and it used to make me laugh that AJ had insisted on there being a full staff. There were people in green Wildworld T-shirts everywhere, just sitting around with nothing to do. At least the weather was good. Sometimes I'd go into town, and that would usually end up with people thinking I was AJ, then realising I wasn't. It doesn't do much for your self-confidence, when people get really excited thinking you might be your younger brother. I felt kind of sorry for myself, I think. I was so lost. I mean, I think a lot of teenagers don't really know what they're doing or where they're heading, but I had an extreme case of that. I had a place at college waiting for me and I still didn't know whether I was going to go. But I knew for sure I didn't want my whole life to be like this, waiting around for AJ to finish whatever he was doing. Travelling the world was a huge privilege, and I knew that, but it was his thing. It wasn't mine.

Pea: I had exams going on. I sometimes forget that. I'd done all right throughout school, and I'd worked hard on my revision, in between daydreaming about Zak, but I found it tough to concentrate knowing what was happening at home. I just wanted to be back there, all the time. And it was funny, because the real action was taking place elsewhere – the rehearsals and the concerts. When I was at the park or at home, it didn't feel different other than the fact that Zak and AJ were around and the park was empty. The crowd at the gate had more or less dispersed. Even adoring teenage fans can't stick around forever if you don't give them anything to live off. Sometimes there were a handful of them there, and they'd change. Like they were tag teaming or something. The concerts had started, and AJ's moods were all over the place. He always seemed to be on a massive high or really agitated. And he invited Nicole and her friends over a couple of times.

Alex: AJ and I were together on and off the whole time. Whenever there was an opportunity to be alone, we'd sneak off. I don't think anyone noticed, because they didn't expect it, and because Pea and Zak were so wrapped up in each other. But he was seeing Nicole too, and that was out in the open.

Nicole: I didn't think I'd ever hear from him again after that first day, but a couple of days later Mum called me to the phone and mouthed that it was 'someone American', and I felt like I was going to faint. He asked me if I wanted to hang out, and I hoped he meant do more of the stuff we'd done in that field. And he did. There was a lot of bus-hopping, because there were a few couples looking for somewhere to go. Two of his team, if I remember correctly, and then Pea and Zak, of course. I still couldn't get over that. I'd been hoping to set Zak up with Kelly or Fay, but it never happened. I think it was about the third or fourth time that we had sex. It wasn't my first time. And it wasn't that good, either, if I'm being totally honest. It was hurried and frantic – typical teenage sex, I suppose.

Alex: Every time I saw him and Nicole together, I'd promise myself that I'd say no next time he grabbed my hand or phoned me. But I never did. It's hard to explain, because when I look at photos of him now, he just looks like a teenage boy. I mean, he was hot, and he had this aura, but it was like I was under some kind of spell, and it would never happen to me now.

Sebastian: One afternoon, AJ asked if I wanted to come to the Manchester show. He said they were taking one of the buses and Pea and Alex and Nicole were going. I said no thanks. It wasn't my thing. He laughed at that, like no one had ever said no to him before.

Danny: Time for the show. Sebastian didn't want a ticket, but everyone else did.

Pea: When the Manchester show came around, there was a crowd of us going. Me, Alex, and Nicole were travelling there on the tour buses with AJ and his crew. Mum and Dad had let me take the day off school because they were leaving at lunchtime to get everything set up and sound checked. That had been a whole drama, with plenty of tears, but I didn't have an exam that day, so I really didn't need to be there. I felt anxious on the journey and I didn't know why. I never felt relaxed around Nicole, I suppose. Her and AJ were flirty and I often saw them kissing or sneaking off to an empty bus, but I never saw them holding hands or anything like that. It just felt sort of fake. And I hated watching Alex watch them. I had no idea, back then, that something was going on with Alex too. It's awful, looking back. Like Nicole was this front, because he didn't want people to question his sexuality. We arrived at the venue and there was nothing to do for a few hours. Zak and I sat in the empty stadium and watched AJ rehearse some of his costume changes. It was quite fascinating for me but I could tell that Zak was bored. I suppose he'd seen it all before. I said, 'It's hard to imagine that in a few hours' time, this place will be full of screaming girls.' He just shrugged.

After a while, we went to get something to eat. AJ was busy so Zak said he'd bring him back a burger. Alex and Nicole tagged along and we found a McDonalds and Zak ordered everyone's food. I tried to offer him money, but he said it would be covered on expenses. We found a table and when he brought the food over, there were bags and bags of it. He said he thought it was easier to just get a bit of everything. It made me laugh. Whenever I went to McDonald's with Alex, I'd have three pounds to spend on a value meal and that was it.

Nicole: That McDonald's trip was bad even before all hell broke loose. There was no love lost between me and Pea or Alex, and Zak was sort of oblivious and just tried to keep the conversation going. I think there was something going on with Pea and Alex too. They weren't the same as they'd always been before. It was like they were strangers.

Alex: Things with Pea had been weird ever since this whole escapade had started. She was secretive about her relationship with Zak, and it felt like she'd found him and ditched me. Nicole kept making little digs, saying things like she'd never envisaged doing something social with me and Pea and it was exactly as fun as she'd thought it would be.

Zak: Yeah, Nicole was a bitch. I didn't know why AJ was hanging out with her. She was kind of pretty, but it didn't make up for the way she spoke to people.

Alex: She was talking about AJ as if he was her husband or something. I said, 'You do know he won't remember your name in a month's time?'

Pea: It went so quiet after that. Then Nicole stood up and threw her milkshake in Alex's face. He did that comedy thing you see clowns do after getting hit in the face with a cream pie, wiping the gunk from his eyes. She stormed off.

Nicole: I probably shouldn't have done it, no. Would I do it again? Probably. Alex and Pea were nobodies. They weren't important. But I knew it would get back to AJ, through Zak if no one else. I walked back to the venue and the security guards wouldn't let me in. I said I was with AJ, and they just laughed. So I had to wait there until the others arrived.

Zak: We cleaned Alex up as well as we could in the toilets and then we headed back. There was loads of food left over so I put it all in my backpack for AJ and the crew. Nicole was standing outside the main entrance, looking sheepish. As we approached, she said, 'Will you tell them I'm with AJ?' The security guards looked at me. Pea squeezed my hand. I said, 'I'm sorry, I've never seen this girl before in my life.' We walked in with her screaming after us.

Alex: It was brilliant. Made it worth the milkshake thing. AJ wasn't on the stage so I went to his dressing room and knocked on the door. He was pacing, clearly tense. He asked what had happened to my hair and T-shirt, and I told him. He came over to me, kissed me hard like he was angry, started to unbutton my jeans. I reached across and locked the door. He said something, while we were undressing, something like 'You're better than her' or 'It's you I want to be with'. I can't quite go back to it, in my mind. There have been a fair few sexual encounters since then, but those early ones are so formative, especially if they're with someone enormously famous. It was enough, anyway, whatever he said. Enough for me to drop to my knees.

Nicole: I was furious. I went to a payphone to call AJ's mobile but I didn't have enough change. So there I was, in the middle of a city I didn't know, on my own. I didn't know what to do.

Alex: Afterwards, AJ said, 'Where's Nicole now?' I couldn't believe it. I said she was outside last time I saw her, that the security guards wouldn't let her in, and he looked furious and stormed out. When he came back, she was with him, looking all smug, so I walked out, went off in search of Pea.

Nicole: After AJ rescued me, I asked him how he was feeling about the show. It was obvious he was nervous but I knew he wouldn't admit it. He said he had twenty minutes before hair and makeup was starting, and I said, 'Well, what can we do in twenty minutes?' He was sitting on this chair in front of a huge mirror and I sat on his lap, facing him, and kissed him. I could feel him, hard against me. It was our last time.

Danny: Teenage lust, hey?

Zak: The show was fine. Everyone talks about it now, because it ended up being his last show, but obviously we didn't know that then. If you'd told me AJ would never play another show, that less than twenty-four hours later, he'd be dead, I would have laughed in your face. He was so alive, my brother. I never met someone who seemed so alive.

Pea: There was so much waiting around that day, but it was all worth it. The show was incredible. Like I've said, I wasn't a big fan of pop music and I'd never have gone to a concert like that in other circumstances, but this was a proper show, in every sense of the word. The costume changes, the choreography, the special effects. It was electric. And I just stared at AJ the whole time he was up there, unable to believe that this star was the same person I'd been spending time with for a couple of weeks. There was no trace whatsoever of the sullen, spoiled teenager I knew. It was like he came to life on stage.

Alex: I was pissed off with AJ so I wanted to hate the show, but really, it was impossible. I got so caught up in the atmosphere, and by the second song I was dancing and singing along like everyone else around us.

Nicole: It was a real rush seeing AJ up there and all these thousands of girls screaming his name and knowing that I was the one he was sleeping with. That I'd been naked with him just a couple of hours ago. I don't think I've ever topped that feeling, to be honest. And then of course it ended up being so famous, because it was the end. And it really seemed like he was just getting started.

Pea: He was on such a high afterwards. We all went backstage and he was bouncing off the walls. I wondered if he'd taken anything. Maybe he had, I don't know. I can't imagine what it's like, any of what he experienced, so I tried not to judge it. But it took a while for him to be calm enough for us to get back in the buses. And even though we left the venue more than an hour after the concert finished, there were still hundreds of girls waiting outside to catch a glimpse of him. I wondered whether he ever met them, whether anything ever happened between them. He was often in the papers with various girls, but they were always famous – models, pop stars, actresses. Never ordinary teenage girls. Anyway, he was with Nicole, at least kind of, that night, wasn't he?

Zak: The journey back from a show was always awful. AJ would come off stage on a huge high and then he'd crash at some point after and become very withdrawn. The others didn't know that, of course. They were talking about how good it had been, trying to engage him, and he said almost nothing. Nicole looked all put out about it, and Alex was quiet too. I sat with Pea and we talked about other stuff. It felt like it took twice as long to get back as it had taken to get there. When the bus finally pulled up, I had this overwhelming feeling of wanting Pea to stay with me. I knew she couldn't. It had been a big win getting her parents to agree to her coming at all, and I knew we shouldn't push it. But I kissed her and held her really tight, and I was scared to let go and I didn't know why. I don't know, maybe I'm imposing some of that with hindsight, but

I'm sure I remember a feeling of something ending, and I assumed it must be to do with me and Pea.

Alex: I fell asleep on the way back, or at least pretended to. I couldn't watch Nicole fawn all over AJ. Pea and Zak sat with their heads together, talking in low voices. They did that a lot, and I don't think they realised how excluded it made other people feel. They were just all wrapped up in each other. So I sat with my eyes closed and focused on not saying anything. I knew I could blow up whatever was going on with AJ and Nicole if I wanted to, by telling her what he'd been doing with me, but I also knew AJ would hate me if I did. You have to remember that this was my first experience of anything romantic. And it came after years of homophobic abuse at school. To be chosen like that, by someone like him, and for it to be a secret. Well, that really fucked with my mind for a long time.

Pea: Zak was strangely emotional when we parted that night. I wanted to stay with him. I always wanted to stay with him, but I knew my parents would be waiting up. They were in the kitchen with mugs of tea. They asked how it had been, and I said it was amazing, that AJ was a real superstar, that they would have loved it. Because I genuinely think they would have done. You didn't have to be an AJ Silver fan to appreciate the spectacle of it. Dad just grunted, and Mum got up and poured the rest of her tea into the sink. She told me I'd better get to bed, that it was gone midnight and I had school tomorrow. As if I didn't know those things. She looked so weary, like she'd been beaten down by something. I was worried about her and didn't know how to express it. I said, 'Mum, things will be back to normal soon, won't they?' Dad grunted again, but when I looked at him he just widened his eyes as if he didn't know what I was asking him. I remember Mum saying, 'I hope so, love.'

Cathy: Pea was off in her own little world. She was in love. I genuinely think she had no idea of the toll this visit was taking on her dad. He was jumpy, on edge. Forever meeting with Maggie to discuss something AJ wasn't happy about. I couldn't wait for it to be over, and I knew he felt the same. But I knew, too, that them leaving would break Pea's heart, and I was braced for that. I had no idea that something far worse was on the horizon.

Zak: After everyone was gone, it was just me and AJ. We went for a walk in the park and smoked a joint. I knew AJ wouldn't be able to sleep for hours. It was the intensity of the show, the extreme high followed by that awful crash. It made me wonder why he did it. I asked him, and he laughed. 'Money and fame, Zak-man,' he said. And then he said it again, but his voice was so sad I looked away. I often wonder what I would have seen in his eyes if I'd been brave enough to meet his gaze right then. After a bit of silence, he asked me about Pea, about whether it was as serious as it seemed. I said it was, that I was crazy about her, but I couldn't see a way to make it work. We were so young, and we lived so far apart. He nodded. I didn't ask about Nicole. It was clear she didn't mean anything to him. I don't think any of the girls did. They were just playthings, and I wonder whether that would have changed, if he'd lived. Whether he would have learned to care properly about people he was sleeping with. Because he was the brother with all the wealth and celebrity, but right then I felt like the lucky one. What I had with Pea was real, and he was locked out of that experience. I thought, then, that he'd perhaps never be able to trust anyone fully, enough to really fall in love with them, and that seemed like a terrible shame.

Danny: A sombre note to end on, which seems entirely fitting given that next week we'll be going over the day of AJ Silver's death. Now you know all the people who were around him, is there anyone you think is suspicious? Anyone you think might have hated him enough to have a hand in that terrible roller-coaster accident? Be sure to let us know on your socials at @WhatHappenedThatSummer. And I'll see you next week with some answers.

MickeynotMouse
This friendship that's blossoming between AJ and Sebastian is strange, isn't it? #WhatHappenedThatSummer

Heather421
Alex Robb needs to have a bit of self-respect. #WhatHappenedThatSummer

Alisha_Lea
I can't believe AJ was playing Nicole and Alex like that, and so brazenly #WhatHappenedThatSummer

KellyBlake4
How cute are Pea and Zak? #WhatHappenedThatSummer

J_oshAnd_erson
I have such a sense of impending doom. I know it's because we know what happened next, but I'm still on tenterhooks waiting to hear all the details. #WhatHappenedThatSummer

SarahSmith675

I was at that Manchester show! I was twelve years old and my mum took me. I cried for weeks when he died. #WhatHappenedThatSummer

LiisawithtwoIs

Gutted. I had tickets for one of the London dates which obviously never happened. #WhatHappenedThatSummer

KevKing9

Roll on next week! #WhatHappenedThatSummer

6

EPISODE 6 – 20 JUNE 1996

Danny: Welcome to episode six of *What Happened That Summer?* I'm Danny Drake, and this podcast is a forensic investigation into the circumstances surrounding the death of pop superstar AJ Silver in 1996. I just had confirmation that 'Ice Cream' is at the top of the download chart for 2025 and Silver's *Greatest Hits* album has gone double platinum.

AJ Silver died in a rollercoaster accident while staying at Wildworld theme park in West Wilding, near Birmingham, England, and the Hunter family, who owned and ran the park, were later fined £500,000. We've been talking to the Hunters and the Campbells (AJ's family), as well as AJ's manager and crew, about what happened in the run-up to the accident. And now we've arrived at that fateful day.

If you've come straight to this episode, it might be useful for you to know that sixteen-year-old Pea Hunter is in a relationship with AJ Silver's brother Zak, and AJ himself has allegedly been sleeping with both local girl Nicole Waddington and Alex Robb, Pea's best friend. Yes, *that* Alex

Robb. The stay itself has been fraught with issues, from late-arriving shower and toilet facilities to staffing issues to John Hunter's alleged drinking problem. It's also worth noting that AJ Silver hasn't made himself hugely popular with a number of people because of his behaviour.

So without further ado, let's look at what happened that day.

Cathy: I remember it was a glorious day. A Tuesday.

John: I was a bit under the weather.

Cathy: John was hungover. He was like a bear with a sore head.

John: I think I had the flu.

Pea: I went down for breakfast and Sebastian was eating peanut butter on toast. I asked him if he wanted to hear about the show the night before and he said, 'Not really.'

Sebastian: I really didn't care that Pea had been to the show. To be honest, I was surprised she'd gone at all. It wasn't her kind of thing. It felt like she was changing to cling on to Zak or something and I didn't like it.

John: The kids were arguing over breakfast. That wasn't really unusual. I made a pot of coffee and started to go through my day in my head. I had a lot of paperwork to do, so I was planning to base myself in the office with Cathy.

Cathy: John and me in the office together was always problematic. It was too small for two people, and we just worked totally differently. I was tidy and John was chaotic. So when he said he was going to base himself there for the day, I tried not to roll my eyes.

John: We were two weeks into AJ Silver's stay, and I was counting down the days until they were leaving. I knew it would be worth it, in the end, when we got the rest of the money, but it had been a pain in the arse.

Pea: I had a couple of exams coming up later that week, so I was heading into school to revise. I met Alex on the corner, as I always did. He looked tired. I probably did too. It had been a late night. But there was something else, too. He seemed touchy and off with me, and when I tried to broach the subject, he stopped walking and looked at me and said, 'Let's not pretend that things are the same as they used to be between us.' I was shocked by that. I knew me seeing Zak had had an impact on things, but I didn't think it was a serious problem. And then I made it worse by saying I knew he had a crush on AJ and that it must be hard to see him with Nicole of all people. He put one hand up, a few inches from my face, and told me that I didn't know what I was talking about. And then he stormed off, faster than I could walk. I walked on, alone, pulling my cardigan off and shoving it in my bag because it was warmer than I'd expected. Alex would calm down, I thought. By the time I saw him at break, he'd be back to normal.

John: I'd just set myself up when the phone started ringing. Cathy picked it up, and I guessed within about a minute that it was her sister, and she started filling her in on every last thing that had happened in our lives since they last spoke, the way she did. It was so bloody distracting. I was trying to work out some figures. I did a few sighs, hoping she'd get the message.

Cathy: John was being a total pain. Huffing and puffing while I talked to my sister on the phone, as if he wasn't the one who'd invaded my workspace.

Zak: AJ had the day off. Maggie knew how badly he slept after shows so she usually arranged for him to have the next day free if possible. We woke in the bus at about ten, and it stank of sweat and stale beer and smoke. I wanted to be at home, in a proper bed in a proper house, but as soon as I thought that, I felt guilty. Pea. I wanted to be with Pea, too. Someone from the crew went to get us some breakfast. I think we had bacon sandwiches. AJ was in a foul mood. I'd hoped he would have slept it off but it seemed not. He kept saying that the whole trip had been a shitshow and it was all down to John. He really had it in for the guy. And I get it, John had made some mistakes, but AJ was brutal. I think if it hadn't been John, it would have been someone else. AJ said he was going to go and find John and tell him that it needed to improve, if he wanted the rest of the money that had been promised to him. I said, 'Yeah, *promised*, AJ, you can't just threaten to take it away,' and he said, 'I can do whatever the fuck I like. Just because you've got this thing going with his daughter.' I told him it was nothing to do with that. He had this wild look in his eyes, and when he pulled open the door of the bus, I knew I should follow him.

John: AJ strode into the office, looking like death warmed up. Zak was a few steps behind him. I thought, *Here we go*. I wasn't in the mood for it, I really wasn't. He started jabbing the air with his finger, saying nothing had been good enough, that we needed to get our shit together.

Cathy: I was shocked, honestly. I'd thought things were back on a pretty even keel. Zak was looking sheepish, not making eye contact, and AJ was just ranting about everything that had apparently gone wrong since his arrival. When he brought up the delay with the showers, John was quick to point out that that was Maggie's error and not ours. But he wasn't really in a place to be reasoned with, I don't think. He was agitated and looking for someone to blame, and John and I were there.

Zak: It was embarrassing. First off, there had been a few small problems, but AJ was making out like everything had been terrible, blaming them for things they'd had nothing to do with. And remember, these were the parents of the girl I was falling in love with. The last thing I wanted to do was get on the wrong side of them. But I'd known AJ his whole life and I knew that when he was in this kind of mood, there was no changing it. You just had to ride it out. He knew he could get away with as much bad behaviour as he wanted to.

John: After a while, I said I wasn't listening to any more of it. I wasn't going to be told off like that by a jumped-up little kid. He lunged for me, then. I really think he would have punched me in the face if I hadn't ducked out of the way. He roared, 'Who are you calling a jumped-up little kid?' I folded my arms, said I would have thought that was obvious. Zak came forward then and caught AJ's arms, stopped him going for me again. Wise move. I was *this* close to throwing a few punches myself.

Cathy: John was so red in the face I thought he was going to have a heart attack.

John: Zak told AJ he needed to calm down and sort of manhandled him towards the door. But just as they were about to leave, AJ turned back and said, 'If you think you're getting all of the money, you're very much mistaken.' It's a good job he left then, I'm telling you, because I felt this rage start to build in me and I didn't feel in control of it. Everything we'd done, everything I'd sacrificed, for this. The loan shark was already on my back about the rollercoaster money, and I'd given him some of it when we'd got the second instalment, but honestly, there were a queue of people I owed money to and he wasn't at the front. The very idea of not getting the rest put the fear of God into me. It would be the end of everything. When they'd gone, I turned to Cathy and she said she thought we all needed a few minutes to calm down. I said I was going to speak to Maggie or Lou, and she said perhaps it would be best if she did that. I had to admit, she was calmer than I was. But I wanted to be there too, to make sure we got our points across.

Cathy: We found Maggie outside, striding up and down, looking at her mobile phone and muttering about the lack of reception. I touched John's arm, asked if we should maybe come back later, but he said no, we needed to get this sorted. I knew nothing good was going to come of it.

Maggie: The first I knew about the problem was John and Cathy waiting for me to finish my call. I was trying to talk to the Glasgow venue about merchandise sales, I think. Some supplier had messed up and they only had T-shirts with the latest album cover on in extra-large. I'd been trying to say that there weren't too many extra-large teenage girls and they needed to sort it before we got there in two weeks' time when I lost cell coverage. I was feeling all hot and bothered, and John started launching into a tirade about AJ and how he'd said they weren't getting all their money. Cathy shouted him down, reminded him he'd promised to let her do the talking, and I thought – though it was nothing to do with the matter in hand – that their marriage was in trouble. There was no fondness in either of their eyes when they looked at each other. I thought it would probably be over between them within a year or two. Cathy said, 'Look, we're sorry to bombard you like this, we're just a bit concerned because AJ's been in the office throwing accusations around and saying we won't get the amount that was agreed...' I cut her off. I said, 'You leave AJ to me.'

Zak: Maggie was not happy. She usually dealt with AJ quite well but I think she'd had enough. It can't have been easy, looking after him. He was always throwing tantrums, like some kind of oversized toddler. She started telling him he had no right to interfere in the business side of things, that he should have come to her if he had a problem. AJ just flipped, then. He said that she wouldn't have a job if it wasn't for him, that he could replace her 'like that'. He clicked his fingers. I was sick of all of it. I walked out.

Maggie: Christ knows what had gotten into AJ. He'd always had his moments but that day I really felt, for the first time, like he wasn't coping with all of it. Like maybe he was being pushed too hard, too fast. I thought that when this tour was over, we should probably sit down and talk about what he wanted and needed. Because he was just a kid, at the end of the day. He was a fucking nightmare, but he was a kid, too.

Zak: When I went back, the bus was empty. I walked around the park for a bit, looking for AJ. I smoked a couple of cigarettes, had a hotdog. I couldn't find him. I felt lost. What was I doing in the middle of an English theme park on my own? It just all felt wrong, like I'd mis-stepped and ended up in the wrong life, somehow. I thought about going to Mum and saying that I wanted to live with Dad for a while, but I knew she'd take it personally, see it as an abandonment. The only thing that made sense to me in my whole goddamned life was Pea. And she lived so damn far away.

John: I couldn't settle to anything in the office after that confrontation, so I went out into the park to check on a few things. As usual, all the staff were standing by the rides, doing precisely nothing. I hated to see that, but AJ had insisted, of course. I talked to a few of them, tried to get their spirits up a bit. It's disheartening, doing nothing. Even if you're being paid to do it. I distinctly remember going past the 360. It was being looked after by this guy, Simon, who'd been with us for about a year. He was a good worker, always where he was supposed to be when he was supposed to be there. He called me over as I went past.

Danny: Meet Simon.

Simon: I'd been stewing on something since arriving that morning. When we first heard about this whole AJ Silver thing, we all thought we were onto a good thing, that we'd be being paid for doing very little. Then John laid us all off temporarily, then he took us back on, and since then, we'd learned that days doing nothing are long as hell. My girlfriend was pregnant and her three-month scan was that day, and we'd got the date through too late for me to book leave. But it was hard to stand there doing fuck all when I knew she was on her own and needed my support. I even thought about sneaking off – I'm not sure anyone would have known. Some days AJ and his brother and Pea came down and went on a few rides, but some days they didn't. And then I saw John, and without thinking about it too much I called him over, and he came.

John: I could see he had a bee in his bonnet about something. That's what it's like, when you're the boss. There's always someone who's unhappy about something. But I was having enough trouble with AJ to deal with other people's concerns. He launched into this story, about how his girlfriend was having a baby, how she was having a scan that afternoon. He wanted the afternoon off, is the bottom line. But I just couldn't risk being understaffed when AJ was already on the warpath and he'd kicked off about that previously. I said I was sorry, but there was nothing I could do.

Simon: When he'd gone, I kicked the gate where people were supposed to queue up. Where precisely no one was queueing up, and probably no one would all day. I thought about Mary. We'd lost one baby, got to the scan and found that there was nothing there, no heartbeat. We'd been devastated, but after a few months we'd started trying again. The previous night, she'd reached for my hand in the dark and said she was scared. Said, 'What if it happens again?' What could I say? I couldn't tell her it wouldn't, could I? I looked at my watch, saw that it was coming up for midday. The scan was at two. I remember realising that I could walk out. It would be the end of my job, for sure, but I could get another one without too much trouble. At least, I thought I could. But then, it was a risk, wasn't it, with

the baby coming. What if I couldn't find something else? What
if I couldn't support them?

Sebastian: I was in the kitchen when Dad came in muttering
something about Simon wanting to take off for a hospital
appointment with zero notice. I asked what ride he was on,
and Dad said the 360. And I offered to look after it while
Simon went to the hospital. Dad did this sort of double take,
which I think was supposed to be funny, because I never
offered to help out in the park. But he'd insisted on training
me on all the rides, and I wasn't doing anything that day, so
why not? He asked whether I might be changing my mind
about taking over the place, and I told him for the thousandth
time that I wasn't. We didn't argue but I was fuming as I walked
away. He just didn't listen.

Danny: Why is Sebastian being so helpful all of a sudden?
And what were Zak and AJ up to at this point?

Zak: AJ found me and we went down to the lake. It was a real
stunner of a day, and we lay there with our hands clasped
beneath our heads, and I felt like I was falling asleep. When I
heard AJ's question, I couldn't quite work out how to answer it,
so there was a delay while I dragged myself back to conscious-
ness. He'd asked whether I ever thought about putting an end
to it all. I said, 'What, my life?' He didn't answer so I turned on
my side and propped myself up with one arm. 'What do you
mean, AJ?' He said, 'All of it. It's all just so much shit, it feels
like. Sometimes I just don't want to be here.' I shivered, and I
felt cold right to my bones. I said, 'AJ, you've got the whole
fucking world at your feet. If you don't like something about
your life, you can change it. You can stop doing the music

thing or you can take it in a different direction or you can do anything. There are literally no limits on you.' I meant it to sound supportive, but looking back, I worry that it might have sounded like a criticism. Like what the hell do you have to worry about? I know more about mental health, now. I know that having it all doesn't mean shit if you feel like you're drowning.

He was quiet for a bit and I asked if he wanted a smoke, or a walk, and it was clear that he didn't know what he wanted. He was lost. And I hadn't seen him quite like that before. Suddenly all the cocky front was gone and he was like a scared little boy. I had this memory of this time we'd lost him for a bit in a supermarket. He must have been about three or four. Mum and I had raced around the shop, holding hands, and when we'd found him, his feet were rooted to the spot and his eyes were full of fear. And that's exactly how he looked that day at Wildworld.

There were tears in my eyes, and I saw him noticing. He didn't say anything. It felt like we were standing on opposite sides of a train track, in full sight of each other but unable to touch.

The next show wasn't for a few days, but rehearsals were back on the next day. Maybe that's what he needed, I thought. Maybe he wasn't good with free time. I wasn't either, to be fair. It made me think too much about what I could or should have been doing instead. I thought he'd go back to rehearsals the next day and everything would be fine. I didn't know – I couldn't – that nothing would ever be fine again.

Pea: When school finished, I waited for Alex to appear under the tree where we always met. I hadn't seen him at break, but then I didn't always, depending on which classrooms we'd been in just before it. And at lunch I'd had rehearsals for this end-of-year show some of us were putting on. I was sure he would have calmed down by now. He could be hot-headed sometimes, but he never held a grudge. When he appeared, he was with a girl called Sophie who we weren't really friends with. I watched him kiss her on the cheek and then head in my direction.

Alex: I'd been thinking for a while that it was time Pea and I broadened our horizons a bit, when it came to friendship. I had French with Sophie and she was kind of funny. Things between Pea and me were so intense. This whole thing with Zak had shown me how precarious it was, putting all your faith in one other person for friendship. I was widening the net. But I wasn't looking to ruffle any feathers. Pea looked so ridiculously hurt, though.

Pea: I wasn't hurt, exactly, just surprised.

Alex: I said I was sorry for earlier and she forgave me. But then she asked me what it had all been about, and I said, 'Isn't that obvious? You've barely got time for me these days.'

Pea: It wasn't fair. One of us was bound to have a boyfriend at some point, weren't we? And it just happened to be me first. I was sure that if he'd fallen for someone, he would have done exactly the same as I had.

Alex: You see, that's where she was wrong. I had fallen for someone, hadn't I, and I hadn't cast the friendship aside for it. But I couldn't tell her that, because she didn't know about AJ and me, and I didn't want her to.

Pea: We ended up saying we'd put it to one side and come back to it another time, when things had calmed a bit. And on that walk home, it almost felt normal between us. It felt as close to normal as it had since AJ had arrived. We got back to the park and Alex said he thought he'd stay for an hour or two, like he always did, and we went off in search of Zak and AJ. I did ask if he'd prefer for it to be just the two of us that afternoon. I said I could catch up with Zak later and we could just stick together for the afternoon, but he said no, it was fine.

Danny: It feels a bit like Pea and Alex's friendship is falling apart in front of our eyes, doesn't it? They're not in touch now, by the way. Haven't been for years.

Alex: AJ and Zak weren't on their bus and they weren't in Adventure City, which were our first two ports of call. We had to go through Animal City to get to Water City, but we weren't expecting to find them there. Just as we went past the hut where all the exotic animals were kept, they came out of the door.

Zak: AJ had seemed like he needed a change of scene, and it was the one thing he couldn't really have, so I had taken him to Animal City, because we rarely spent time there. We'd looked at the rabbits and guinea pigs, the goats and the sheep, and then we went to look at the snakes and tarantulas and lizards. AJ liked animals. At home, we had a couple of dogs, and they always calmed him. This guy who worked there came into the building and asked if we wanted to handle any of the animals. AJ looked at me and shrugged, so next thing we knew we both had snakes around our necks. It was unexpected, and it seemed to do the trick, for AJ. When we walked out of there, he was in a much better mood. And then we saw Pea and Alex, and I gave Pea a hug and kissed her, and I sensed there was something a bit uncomfortable between AJ and Alex, but I didn't think much of it.

Alex: I looked at AJ and he looked at me. Pea and Zak were hugging and it didn't go on for that long, but it just served as a reminder of the healthy, functional relationship they had and the secretive shitshow that we had in comparison. At least Nicole wasn't there. That was something to be thankful for. Anyway, we set out with no real destination in mind, wandering. I guess all of us thought that eventually someone would find a ride they wanted to go on. At one point, Zak and Pea offered to get us all a cup of tea, and AJ and I sat down at a picnic table to wait for them to come back. Something hung in the air between us. I just looked at him, refusing to make things easier by looking down at the ground or at the table. There was a piece of splintered wood and he picked at it with his fingernail. And when he did start speaking, it was as if everything inside his brain was tumbling out. Like he'd removed a cork and then he couldn't get it back in again.

'Look, I know this isn't what you want. All this secretive shit.' I didn't answer. He didn't know what I wanted, because he'd never asked. He'd just taken what suited him, at his convenience, and left me to watch him being with someone else in public. 'But I can't offer you any more than that right now. Do you know what the press would do to me if they found out I was with a guy?' I shrugged. I mean, I knew there had been speculation in the past, and I knew there was an intense interest in who he was seeing, no matter who it was. There was so much I wanted to ask him, like whether he was gay and the thing with Nicole was just a front, or whether he was bi. Whether I meant anything to him. Whether we'd be together for real, if things were different.

'Fine, I get it. You don't want to talk. You're pissed. But this is my life, Alex.' Inside, I screamed, *And this is mine.* 'It's not going to happen again. I'm not gay. It was nothing. Okay?' As if he needed my agreement to call it off. I gave a curt nod, and I was biting back tears when Pea and Zak returned, each of them holding two steaming cups of tea. And they had Sebastian in tow, which was unusual, but I was too busy processing what had just happened to think anything of it.

AJ changed again, then. Started talking about getting the whole crew out, doing the biggest rides. Sebastian told them that there'd always been this thing, this challenge. None of us remembered how it had started. You were supposed to eat a giant hotdog and a cheeseburger from the food hall and then go straight on the Gravity Spin, the Twister and the Canyon, in that order. If you could do it without throwing up, you were some kind of hero. AJ grinned. 'What about the 360?' he asked. Pea said that that was new so it hadn't been part of the challenge. AJ said he would do all of it and then the 360, and asked if any of us felt like joining him. I certainly didn't. I felt fragile, like I was made of glass and I was waiting for someone to drop me. And I knew Pea wouldn't do it, because she never had in the past. Zak said he'd give it a try and AJ high-fived him, getting up from the bench. He said he was going to go back to the buses and see who else was around and up for the challenge.

Pea: We watched AJ jog off in the direction of the buses. I said to Zak that he didn't have to do it. I'd never got it, this challenge. I'd seen countless teenage boys being sick in bins while doing it. But some people just have to push at things, don't they? And AJ was one of them. I knew Zak was just doing it for his brother's sake. That's the kind of person he was. He shrugged and said he was game. 'AJ will totally hurl, though.' I laughed.

Alex: I felt like I was breaking and I couldn't tell my best friend about it.

Zak: When AJ came back, he had the whole gang with him. He said he'd found them all sitting around watching repeat episodes of *EastEnders* and they were glad of the interruption. We all went to the food hall to get the hotdogs and burgers, leaving Pea and Alex at the picnic table. They said they'd see us back at the starting point. All the rides were in Adventure City, so we could go right from one to the next. I do remember thinking that usually people would have the time spent in the queue between one ride and the next. But what the heck? I wasn't about to back out. Spirits were high and it was like the AJ of earlier in the day was a distant memory. Maybe I'd taken him too seriously, I thought. He had it easy, and he had it tough, in different ways. I would keep an eye on him and check he was okay.

AJ insisted on us all having mustard and ketchup on our hotdogs, and Sebastian took the order and went to get them. I can't stand mustard. I thought there was an outside chance that I'd spew before I even got on the first ride. But I went along with it because he seemed so lifted by the idea of this challenge and I didn't want to be the one to bring him crashing down again. I watched him, surrounded by his team, laughing and joking, and there was no sign of the vulnerable young man I'd seen earlier. No sign at all.

Bree, AJ's hair and makeup artist, was flirting with him.

She had at least five years on him, but I knew they had this on-off thing going on. The thing is, if you hook up with a celebrity, then if nothing else, it makes for a good story. It must have been hard, for AJ, to know who was genuine. I wondered idly where it would lead. Whether he'd bring Bree back to the bus later and I'd be asked to make myself disappear for an hour or two. And then we were done with the burgers and hotdogs and it was time to start the challenge. We all headed over to the Gravity Spin. I loved that one. You entered a circular metal cage and stood against the wall, and then it started spinning around, and the force pinned you back against the wall. I asked Pea if she wanted to go on it with us, and she shrugged and said she would. She and I stood next to each other, holding hands. AJ was directly opposite me, Bree next to him. The others were scattered around. The guy who was operating the ride looked pleased to have something to do. He checked our safety straps carefully, and then it started. Pea's hand squeezed mine as the spinning took hold, and I turned my face to her with some difficulty and smiled. But when I turned back, and looked across at AJ, I felt unmoored. He didn't look right. I can't put my finger on it, on what exactly was wrong, but something tugged at me. I felt like calling the whole thing off. And I tried to, when we got off that ride. I went to him and said, 'Let's just forget this whole thing.' He looked at me like I was crazy. He had an arm slung around Bree's neck and he was leading the way to the Twister. He dismissed me, right off the bat.

Bree: I'm Bree. I was AJ's hair and makeup artist on that tour. We had a little thing going. It was on and off. Both of us saw other people, but when we weren't seeing anyone else, sometimes we saw each other. It wasn't a big deal. But that day, when we were doing the challenge, he put an arm around me as we walked from one ride to another, and it felt different. It felt like he was leaning on me.

Pea: I went on the Gravity Spin but I wasn't intending to go on anything else. I don't think Alex was either. But we were all along for the ride, keen to see who would make it. Sebastian had disappeared again, as quietly as he'd arrived.

Alex: I hung around watching because I was infatuated with AJ. Simple as that. The fact that Pea was infatuated with Zak played into my hands at the time, because we both just wanted to be around them as much as possible.

Zak: Next up was the Twister. You sat in a row and then the whole thing was tilted left and right and up and down before being dropped from a height. I'd been on it a handful of times in the past couple of weeks, and it wasn't my favourite. It made me feel kind of sick. Pea and Alex said they would wait for us on the nearby picnic benches, and AJ shrugged. He pulled on Bree's hand. I was next to AJ on that one, with Bree on his other side, and she screamed the whole way through. AJ looked across at me and grinned, just before the final drop, and I had this impulse to reach across and take his hand. I felt like I was losing him. I couldn't have known what would happen, so I put it down to the fame thing. I'd been gradually losing him for a while, by then. But that day, the feeling was particularly strong. I wanted to go back to the bus and chill out. But I knew AJ would finish what he'd started. When we got off the Twister, Bree threw up in a bin and declared herself out. AJ called her a pussy, and she looked a bit hurt. Lucian, Trish, India and Sammy were still in, plus me and AJ.

Pea led the way to the Canyon, telling us it had been Wildworld's biggest and twistiest rollercoaster until they'd acquired the 360 especially for our visit. The Canyon was kind of tame but it did lurch you about a lot, and I wasn't feeling great by that point. I'm sure none of us were. There were a few green faces around. I got into the carriage next to Sammy, gritting my teeth. When we got off, I needed to go to the bathroom really bad. I said I was out and ran off to find one. I found out later that most of the others ducked out at that point, too. It was just AJ's bodyguard Lucian, and AJ himself who were left.

Simon: I was still stewing about the scan thing, thinking about my girlfriend on her own and scared, and how I might spend the entire day not doing anything anyway, because we were all subject to the whims of this jumped-up pop star, and I was *this* close to walking out. And then Sebastian appeared like some kind of knight in shining armour. To tell you the truth, I didn't even know he knew what he was doing, but he assured me that his dad had had a change of heart and sent him to cover me. I didn't wait around to ask questions. I had less than an hour to get to the hospital at that point. So I just went. Obviously I felt bad when I found out what happened, but it wasn't my fault. How could it be, when I wasn't even there? And I got to hear my daughter's heartbeat for the first time that day. No regrets.

Pea: When we got to the 360 and couldn't see a member of staff, I said the challenge was off, and Lucian looked sort of relieved but AJ just blew up. He was incandescent with rage. He started waving his arms around and saying that there'd been nothing but problems this whole trip and he was going to go and find my dad and tell him they were leaving, that they'd find somewhere else to stay. Zak tried to calm him down. And then Alex piped up. 'You know how to operate it, don't you, Pea?' Now, I knew how to operate all of the rides; it was the way Dad and I had bonded in the past few years. But I wasn't as experienced with the 360 as I was with all the others, of course, because we'd only had it for a matter of months. You had to go inside to get on the 360, because half of it was under-cover, but the ride operator always waited outside. I went inside the little building and over to the place where the ride operator sits, planning to look at the buttons and levers. And that's when I saw Sebastian, sitting there like it was totally normal. He'd disappeared after the first ride of the challenge and I hadn't known or cared where he'd gone. It was the weirdest thing, seeing him there. He never helped out. I asked what he was doing, and he shrugged and told me he was covering a staff absence. I glanced at the controls. It was straightforward, like I remembered. A button for go, a button for stop. And that override button the engineer had shown us after the accident. I told Sebastian that AJ and Lucian wanted to go on it, and he gave this bored little nod.

Alex: I'd followed Pea inside and to the little booth. It was so simple. I remember thinking a child could do it. But that didn't matter, because Sebastian was there to operate it.

John: I realised I hadn't even thanked Sebastian for stepping in, because I'd been so blindsided by him offering. So when I was passing the 360 after doing a bit of maintenance on the Ghost Train, I went to say something to him. AJ and his gang were hanging around near the ride, and when I went inside to the operator's hut, there were Sebastian, Pea and Alex. I asked what was going on.

Pea: Would I have done it if we hadn't found anyone who was trained? I've asked myself that a lot over the years. I'd like to think I wouldn't, but I don't know. I had that teenage invincibility. I was kind of buoyed up. It was that stupid challenge and those wild moods of AJ's. I told Dad it was nothing.

John: Pea kind of felt like a stranger in those weeks. It felt like she was slipping away from us, what with having a boyfriend and spending all her time with him and the rest of AJ's gang. The Pea I knew wouldn't have operated that ride without permission, but I wasn't sure about this new Pea.

Alex: It was crowded in the booth with the three of us in there and John just outside. But then John called to AJ and Lucian to get on the ride and Sebastian left the booth to strap them in.

John: AJ walked past me and said something so low that only I could hear it. I can hear him saying it now, clear as day. He said, 'You're a lame little guy with a lame little theme park. As soon as my brother is done with her, I'm going to fuck your daughter and break her heart. And you're not going to see another dollar of the money Maggie promised you.' I just froze. I knew what he was like by then, but that was another level.

Sebastian: They got into different carriages. I guess just because they could. Lucian in the front seat of the first one and AJ in the front seat of the second.

Zak: I was talking to Bree. She was planning to stay on in England after the tour was over and I was asking her about that. I could see what AJ liked about her. She was a cool girl. But yeah, we were chatting. So I didn't see any of it.

John: Sebastian did the checks, told them to keep their arms and legs inside the carriage. I was thinking that this is what it could be like, me and him, if he wasn't so stubborn. I was thinking about what AJ had said, too. I was hot with anger.

Pea: No, I didn't know he said that to Dad. I mean, he was a dick, so I can believe it. But why would he say that about me, when I was seeing his brother? It doesn't make any sense.

John: I wanted to hurt him. I did. I admit that. I walked away, back towards the booth, because if I'd stayed there I would have hit him.

Pea: I could see Dad was worked up. I asked if he was okay and he snapped at me. And that was when AJ called out to me. 'Hey, Pea, you might want to keep an eye on my brother. Looks like he's getting pretty cosy with Bree over there. I mean, it's my dick she's sucking right now, but I heard he's looking for someone who knows how to do the job properly too.' I couldn't look at Dad or Alex. I felt my face catch fire. And then the ride started up.

Alex: It wasn't enough for him to rub my nose in the Nicole thing. Now there was Bree too. And on top of all that he was trying to humiliate Pea? Hell no. I felt as furious as John looked. I think it was John who said something like, 'I wish I'd never heard that prick's name.'

John: Pea said she wished she'd never heard his name. I think she even called him a prick. She wasn't going to get any argument on that from me.

Pea: I didn't call him a prick. Alex did. He said he wished he'd never heard the name AJ Silver.

Alex: Believe me, the way I felt, if there'd been time to unscrew that 'go' button and pull those wires apart to make the carriages crash, I would have done it.

John: I started the ride up. Sebastian came over and started talking to me about the possibility of him coming to work in the park after all, and I was so bloody pleased. I set off back to the office. I was planning to find Maggie and get her to sign something about the money. I left Pea and Alex heading over towards Zak and that makeup girl. What had AJ called her, Bree? His words kept going over and over in my head, and I wasn't sure what I was most cross about – Pea or the money.

Alex: That fury I felt for AJ had reminded me how much Pea meant to me. When her dad had disappeared, I pulled her into me for a hug, and we were still standing like that, bodies close, when it happened. The noise was like nothing I've ever heard before. The scream of metal. We sprang apart as if we'd been caught doing something we shouldn't and looked over to where the noise had come from. But there was nothing to see. It was in the undercover part. I was pretty sure the two carriages had collided, though. Time slowed to a near stand-still. Zak was on his feet, Bree too. John had already turned around and was rushing back over. I couldn't make out the expression on his face. But I could make out the expression on

Pea's. She looked terrified. Zak called his brother's name in a strangled voice. And then that doctor of AJ's appeared, Dr Haskins, I think it was, and he rushed up the steps and into the little building.

Pea: It was weird, like I sort of left my body for a bit. I could hear Zak shouting AJ's name, but I sort of felt like I wasn't there. Sebastian came out of the booth, said that AJ's doctor was checking them both over and he'd already called a private ambulance. I was like, 'Don't we just need to call 999?' but it was like everything was done differently in AJ's world. I guess he couldn't just rock up at the local A&E the way I would have done. And then Dad was back, his face white, asking if anyone knew what the hell had happened.

Zak: It's hard to go back there, even now. One minute Bree was telling me about the list of things she wanted to do in London after the tour, and the next, that sound. That crunching of metal on metal.

Lucian: I'm Lucian Valenza. AJ's bodyguard and the only other person on that rollercoaster with him that day. Man, it felt like the longest wait. I knew there was something seriously wrong with AJ, because that kid was never quiet for a single second and I hadn't heard a sound from him since we'd collided.

Zak: I knew it was bad, that it was something that was going to derail things. Not just one of those stories you tell after drinking for years and years. More a story that you never tell, because it hurts too much.

Pea: The time between the collision and the ambulance arriving felt like hours and hours, time unspooling like ribbon, but then pulled taut, because it felt like almost no time, too. I can't explain it. If you've ever been in an emergency like that, a fire or an earthquake or a car crash or something, you might understand. Everything warps. Zak tried to go inside but Lou was at the doorway – I'm not sure when he'd appeared – and he said it wasn't a good idea. I took that to mean that AJ didn't look good. I remember Dad coming to stand by me, wrapping his arms around me from behind. It was the first time he'd touched me for a long time. He kept muttering the word 'no', over and over, under his breath. Nononononononononononono. Alex grabbed hold of my hand. It was like we all needed to feel each other's body heat, needed that reassurance that we were all okay. I could see Zak from where I was standing, and I knew that his world was falling apart, but I didn't go to him. I don't know why. Then Maggie was there. I don't know how she heard. She raced over to Zak, and they hugged awkwardly, and Zak let out a wail that sounded unholy.

Lucian: Dr Haskins checked me over but I knew I was fine. Going out of that building, though, when I knew everyone outside was gathered waiting to see whether AJ was going to make it, that was really tough.

Maggie: I knew in my bones that he was gone, I think. I didn't say it. I held Zak's hand and we just... waited for the verdict. When Lucian came out, he looked broken. His face full of guilt, like he couldn't believe he got to be the one who was okay. It's a bit like that, sometimes, with a celebrity. They seem so much larger than life. It's a shock when you realise they're mortal.

Zak: It seemed to take forever, but eventually Dr Haskins came over and said it was bad, but Lou was arranging for a private jet to take him back to the States immediately. I said I wanted to see him, go with him, but he just shook his head, asked us to trust him.

John: Earlier, I'd wanted him to die, but just then, I really wanted him to live. He was just a boy. An arrogant boy with his head up his own arse, but still a boy. I'd hated him. Those last few days, my hatred for him had been palpable. I'd let it take over everything.

Pea: Mum appeared at some point. She just joined us silently, didn't ask anything. Didn't need to. Because right at that moment, the ambulance arrived and two paramedics jumped out of it with a stretcher.

Cathy: I was a mother, and I put myself in his mother's shoes. Forget that he was a pop star, that he had this legion of adoring fans. He was a boy, with a mother, and she could be on the verge of losing him, and she didn't even know.

John: I remember thinking that's it. It's all over. The park, all of it. We would never come back from something like this.

Pea: I can't imagine anyone was thinking about the park. We were looking death right in the eye. It was horrifying.

Lucian: I couldn't look at any of them. It wasn't my fault, I knew that, but I'd been on that ride with him and I'd got out. Not a bump or a scratch on me. I would have switched places, I think. Because AJ was a cocky little shit sometimes but he was really something. He was seventeen and already as big as Michael Jackson and Madonna. I felt like I knew, that he wasn't going to live, that we'd never see what he would go on to do. It can be hard to be the one who survived.

Pea: Suddenly, I was aware of there being a lot of people who hadn't been there before. I was used to the park being crowded, of course, so at first it didn't register. But then I looked around, a bit dazed, and saw that there were loads of girls, and they were all crying. Hysterical.

John: I'd opened the gates to let the private ambulance in. The crowd of girls that had been outside early on hoping for a glimpse of AJ had dispersed by then, so I hadn't given it a second thought. There were more pressing things on my mind, weren't there? But somehow, someone must have heard. And it was like those girls had telepathic powers to contact one another. There was a swarm of them, all of a sudden, crying and screaming. I shouted at them to get out. Said they were on private property and I'd have them arrested. They scattered a bit, but they didn't go.

Zak: Oh yeah, the fans. I still don't know how that all works. Anywhere we'd go, they'd be there, no matter how much we kept the plans under wraps. And they were there within minutes of the accident, gaining access through the gates that had been opened for the medical team. Vultures.

John: I knew we had minimal time before the press got wind of it. I went into damage limitation mode. What had caused the crash? I went back to those minutes in the booth with Sebastian, Pea and Alex. There was nothing. I closed my eyes, thought carefully. Had one of them messed with that override button? Could they have done? I was 99 per cent sure no one had.

Cathy: No one was thinking straight. You don't, do you, when you're in the middle of something like that? I went to the food hall and ordered a tea, put plenty of sugar in it and took it to Zak. He didn't look up at me. That was the first inkling that there was a question of blame here. I said how sorry I was, how much I hoped he would be all right. It's what you say, isn't it? I wasn't apologising for doing anything wrong.

Pea: Time carried on moving strangely, warping and weaving. His body was taken away. At some point, the police arrived and started to ask everyone questions. The press came, camera flashes and microphones shoved in faces. Zak punched one of the photographers in the face when he wouldn't back away. I remember that. The pure fury in his eyes. It was scary. But I understood it, too. His whole world was crashing down.

Zak: I called Mom and Dad. Maggie offered to do it but I knew it had to be me. The press were somehow already swarming like ants. I didn't want them to hear from someone else. I went to the office to make the calls from the landline. Mom sounded relaxed and happy, and I thought about the fact that I was going to take that away from her. I said I had to tell her something, and she must have known from my voice. She was hysterical. I tried to tell her that there was still some hope, but I didn't want to make it seem less serious than it was. After I put the phone down, I called Dad straight away. I knew if I paused for a second I wouldn't be able to do it. When I said something had happened, he said 'What? Is it your mum?' I wondered, fleetingly, whether he still loved her. Whether there was any hope for them. Whether this might be the thing that brought them back together. I said, 'It's AJ, Dad. There was an accident.' He went silent for about twenty seconds and then he started asking questions, rapid fire. His voice broke on some of them. I told him what I knew and promised to call him again later. After I ended the call, I thought about him, dealing with it on his own. Or maybe he wasn't on his own; maybe there was a woman in his life, or at least a friend.

Maggie: After the initial shock, we headed back to the buses. I knew I had to get us all out of there. We'd fly back to the States in the morning, but I got us a hotel for that night. We had to get away from the place where it had happened.

Cathy: I wasn't surprised when Maggie came and said they were leaving.

John: It was Cathy that Maggie spoke to. When she told me, afterwards, I asked her where we stood with the remaining money, and she gave me this withering look. And look, I know that boy was fighting for his life. But the money those people owed us was not insignificant. And if I didn't get some of it to the loan shark, I was going to be in serious trouble.

Cathy: I said we'd do whatever we could to help. I mean, of course I did. You'd have to be inhuman to ask about money at a time like that, wouldn't you?

Pea: I walked around for a bit, shellshocked. The police had come and were asking my parents questions, and AJ's crew had all disappeared. I couldn't work out what it might mean. Could my parents get the blame for this? Could they shut us down? And would Zak ever want to talk to me again? And then I saw him. Zak. A world of hurt in his eyes, jogging towards me. He grabbed me gently by the wrists and pulled me in close. Said they were leaving. I asked what he meant. He shrugged and said they couldn't stay here. They were going to a hotel. I asked what he wanted, but he didn't answer. I guess he thought there were more important things.

Zak: I can't remember what I told Pea, really. After it happened, it was all blurry, like a smudged lens.

Pea: I made him promise not to leave the country without seeing me again, and he did. But it felt empty, like he was just saying it.

Alex: I went home. It felt ghoulish to stay. And also, I was totally broken and couldn't explain why to anyone. God, it hit me hard. I know it had only been a fling and it had only been a couple of weeks, but you have to understand that he was my first everything. First kiss, first fuck… first love. I shut myself up in my bedroom and howled, shoving a pillow in my mouth to stifle the sound. And I felt like the loneliest person in the world. Who could I tell? Who would possibly understand? Who would even believe me? I cried myself to sleep in the end. Woke at eight in the evening with my mum in the doorway asking if I wanted anything to eat. She took one look at me with my puffy eyes and asked what had happened. Had I had an argument with Pea? I nearly laughed at that. Out of nowhere, I asked her whether she knew I was gay. She bristled, turned the colour of a phone box. We didn't talk about sex in our house. When I'd got to thirteen or so, she'd left a book titled *Growing Up* on my desk and we'd never mentioned it again, though I'd devoured it for information about whether the way I was feeling was normal. I asked her again. I said, 'What are you so afraid of?' And I'll always remember what she answered. She said, 'I'm afraid of losing you.' After a minute or so of silence, she retreated and I went back to sleep.

Pea: They were gone so quickly. There wasn't much to pack up, I suppose. Everything was in those buses, and once they'd driven off the site, past the news crews that were gathering, it was almost like they'd never been there. Like they hadn't come in and upended everything, changed all our lives.

Zak: We got the call during the night. I was with Maggie in her room. Neither of us had any inclination to sleep. It was Lou. He said AJ hadn't made it. Hadn't survived the flight.

Cathy: We found out the next morning on the news that he'd died. AJ's face was plastered over all the newspapers, with headlines like 'AJ Silver plummets to his death' and 'Silver: Dead at seventeen'.

John: At least it wasn't *my* face on those newspaper covers. That was something.

Pea: I walked to the newsagents in the morning and looked at all those papers. They'd all used the same photo of AJ. It was an official one; I'd seen it before. I peered at it. He was all shiny and clean, the ultimate boy next door. I could barely see a trace of the boy I'd known. Those last words he'd said to me, about Zak and Bree, went through my head again and I felt a twinge of shame, a twist of rage. Was I glad he'd died? I'll tell you this: I wasn't not glad.

Danny: Wow. So what are you thinking – was anyone involved? John. Pea. Alex. Sebastian. They all had the opportunity and most of them had a motive. That's where we have to leave it for today, but next week we'll be dragging you from the 90s back to the present and taking a look at where all the key players are today. And I know you won't want to miss the moment when Zak and Pea saw each other after AJ's death was confirmed.

Bea_Happy
WOW! Who messed with the override button? I'm sure as shit someone did! #WhatHappenedThatSummer

Ferney229
My money's on John. I've thought he was dodgy right from the start. Reckon the police will reinvestigate? #WhatHappenedThatSummer

AliAliAli
Shame on you, dragging up old news for social media likes. This incident was a tragedy, but it was fully investigated at the time and people were held to account. There's no need to rake over it all again. #WhatHappenedThatSummer

SianTurner4
I can't believe what a nasty piece of shit AJ actually was. #WhatHappenedThatSummer

ClaireBear

Right? This podcast has really opened my eyes. To think I was an AJ Silver fan! #WhatHappenedThatSummer

Sam_the_Man
I hope we're going to find out what they're all doing now – there's one episode left, right? #WhatHappenedThatSummer

Frances_caDean
I can't believe next week's is the final episode. I've never been so gripped! #WhatHappenedThatSummer

7

EPISODE 7 – FROM THAT DAY TO THIS

Danny: I'm Danny Drake. Welcome to the final episode of *What Happened That Summer?* Now, I've been keeping you up to speed with AJ Silver's current resurgence in the world of pop music, and today I can tell you that another two of his songs have gone platinum – 'Tell Me True' and 'Going Out'.

If you've listened to last week's episode, 20 June 1996, you'll have all the facts – or, at least, all the conflicting accounts – at your disposal. So where do we go from here? Well, it won't have escaped your notice that all this happened nearly three decades ago, so today we're looking at everything that's happened since, bringing you right up to date. We'll drag you, kicking and screaming, out of the 90s and deposit you back in 2025, where you belong.

You might have followed the news story in the aftermath of the accident. It's possible that you already know the Hunter family were fined £500,000 and that Wildworld shut down with immediate effect. But what toll did that take on everyone involved? How did the Hunter family, and AJ's family, cope with what they'd witnessed and had to live with? And where are they all now? Let's find out.

Cathy: There were police swarming round for days. They brought someone in to inspect the rollercoaster, and they interviewed us all separately. It was necessary, I understand that. There had been a life lost, and they had to work out what had caused that. Meanwhile, the story was everywhere and the press were hounding us. We couldn't leave the park – I had to ask friends to bring us food. I guess we got a bit of a taste of what life was like for AJ Silver, didn't we?

John: The day after it happened, I made my way through the press and got in my car. They were all over it like a swarm of bees. Scattered pretty quickly when I started revving the engine, though. I went to see the loan shark, told him where I was. He shook his head. Said, 'Dear oh dear oh dear.' Thing is with people like that, they don't make allowances. They don't care what your excuse is. They break legs first and ask questions later. He said I had until the end of the following day to get him ten grand. There was just no way. On the drive home, I turned it over and over. But there was no solution. I was going to have to tell Cathy.

Cathy: John sat me down when both the kids were in their rooms and I could see he needed to tell me something big. It's almost funny now, but I'd convinced myself he was going to say the marriage was over. If only it had been something like that. He told me about borrowing the money for the roller-coaster, about using a loan shark, about how much he owed and how he had just over twenty-four hours to raise ten thousand pounds. I was incredulous. As if the accident wasn't enough to be dealing with. I asked him how he could have been so stupid, and he said he'd done it for us, for the family, for the park.

John: Cathy didn't even try to understand, to see it from my side. If you want the truth, I think she had one foot out of the door with our marriage back then, and she wasn't interested in being my support system. But I was desperate, so I asked if she could go to her parents. She laughed drily and said she would call them but she didn't hold out much hope.

Cathy: I called my parents. They'd heard what had happened, of course, and they thought I was phoning about that. When I said we were in some trouble and we needed ten thousand pounds urgently, my dad went quiet. He said he didn't have that sort of money lying around. And I said I thought that was the case but I'd wanted to ask just in case. And then I hung up.

John: She didn't even push them on it. When I challenged her, she asked whether I'd asked *my* dad. Which was hardly fair. My dad was fairly close to having lost all his marbles. I was frantic, pacing. I went to the kitchen and poured a measure of vodka. Tipped it back, poured another.

Cathy: He was shaking, and it was hard to know whether it was the drink or the fear. He started mumbling, saying they were going to come for him. That's when I realised how dangerous these people were that he'd got himself involved with. I asked if they knew where we lived.

John: I told her of course they knew where we bloody lived. Everyone knew where we lived, didn't they? We were like sitting ducks in that stupid house my grandfather had built right on the site of Wildworld.

Cathy: I said that I was leaving, that I was taking the kids. I couldn't risk them witnessing anything, or actually being hurt themselves. John looked at me with pure hatred. Said we were supposed to be a family. I said he'd lost the right to call us that the day he'd put us all at risk of harm.

Pea: Mum burst into my room and told me to pack a bag. Said we were leaving. It had come out of nowhere. I thought she meant the police had said we had to leave. I thought Dad was coming with us. Sebastian came in after she'd gone and asked what I was taking. He had his toothbrush in his hand and looked totally bewildered. I said we should pack clothes for two or three days, but I was only guessing. We were in totally unchartered territory.

Sebastian: It wasn't until we were ready to go that Mum made it clear it was just the three of us leaving the house. I thought her and Dad must have argued about the accident, that it would all be resolved in a day or two. I could hear him in the kitchen, slamming things around. And to be honest, a part of me was glad. Fuck him and his stupid theme park.

Cathy: I had some money in an account that John didn't know about. I'd come close, earlier that evening, to offering it to him to get us out of this hole. But it wasn't enough to cover his debt, so what was the point? It was enough for the kids and me to stay in a hotel until I got something else sorted out. So we went into town and checked in at the Ace Hotel.

Pea: We went to the hotel where Zak and Maggie had stayed on their first visit over, which felt like several lifetimes ago. I wondered briefly whether they were staying there that night but dismissed the thought. Surely they'd have travelled further away?

Zak: I was lying on my bed when I heard Pea's voice in the corridor. I thought I was going nuts at first, but I got up and opened the door and there she was, with her brother and her mum, dragging a suitcase behind her.

Cathy: There he was, this young man who'd just lost his brother, looking lost. The mother in me wanted to gather him up in my arms and tell him it would all be all right, but that wasn't something I had any right to tell him, was it? And there was a part of me, too, that hated him for taking my daughter away from me. She'd changed from girl to woman in the past few weeks, and even if she was ready for that, I wasn't.

Pea: We just looked at each other for about a minute, and then Mum pulled on my arm and we carried on down the corridor to our room.

Zak: I didn't sleep that night. I didn't sleep properly for a long time.

John: After they'd gone, I got blind drunk. I'm not ashamed to admit it. I stayed drunk, too, all the next day. There was no point dashing around looking for impossible ways to get the money together. I knew it wasn't going to happen. The loan shark was as good as his word. His men came looking for me at midnight on the deadline he'd imposed, threatening to break my legs. I let them take what they wanted from the house – it wasn't much but it was something. They told me they'd be back. As if I didn't know.

Danny: Now, I don't know what I was expecting, but I was shocked to learn that the Hunter family literally imploded within a day of the accident.

Sebastian: We stayed in that hotel for a week, and by the end of it Mum had rented us a tiny two-bedroom flat in the next town. She and Pea had to share. It was a dive but that didn't really matter. I just didn't quite understand how my family had fallen apart in a matter of days. When Pea and I questioned her, Mum said she couldn't cope with Dad's drinking any longer. A few days after we moved in, I went back to the house to see Dad. I was so angry with him, with the way he was trying to control my future, but he was my dad, too. He was in a real state, his face bruised and bloody. For a horrible minute, I thought he didn't recognise me. But then he broke down, practically fell into my arms. I asked what had happened and he told me the whole story. The debt, the loan shark, the financial ruin. And I remember so clearly what I thought. I thought, *Fuck AJ Silver.*

Pea: I didn't sit my last few exams. My life had gone to shit, after all. Alex tried to be supportive but things were strained between us. Every time we met up, I felt like he couldn't wait to leave. Was the park really the only thing that had held us together? Now we didn't have anywhere to hang out, it was as if we were lost.

Alex: The divide between me and Pea was nothing to do with her moving away from Wildworld. Of course it wasn't. What do you take me for? It was just all so broken. I was grieving for AJ and no one knew. I felt like I'd gone too far down the secretive route to backtrack and tell Pea about it then. Those few weeks made us grow up fast, and in the process, it was like we grew apart, too.

Cathy: For a long time, I thought there was a chance that John could go to prison. I would have done anything to avoid that, despite our differences. The day we found out it was just going to be a fine for negligence, I was so relieved. Wildworld had never reopened and John declared himself bankrupt and that was pretty much the end of it. Some of the rides were sold to pay off debts, but most weren't, because most people aren't in the market for theme park rides. They're not that easy to sell. AJ's family had gone back to the States, and I knew Pea was pining for Zak, but that was hardly the most important thing. The world had moved on, too. There's always a new star to take the helm, isn't there? No matter how shocking or sudden the demise, there's always someone waiting in the wings to take over.

John: I lost everything. Everything. My family, my park, my home, my dignity. I longed for a prison sentence, some days. At least it would be somewhere warm to rest my head. So when I heard, about the fine, I felt oddly cheated. I was bankrupt;

there was no way I was ever going to be able to pay it. So it was over, or as over as it ever would be. The lawyers had decided I was negligent, that I hadn't taken the necessary measures to ensure AJ Silver's safety. I didn't agree, but no one was asking what I thought.

Cathy: I got a job. Two jobs. Days I worked in a care home, bathing and feeding and chatting to old people who couldn't cope on their own. Nights I served pints in a local pub, making conversation with men sitting alone at the bar. In some ways, the jobs were different. But really, it all came down to loneliness. To helping people through their loneliness. I was lonely too, but I didn't have a chance to feel it too often. I was dead on my feet, shattered from trying to keep a roof over our heads. John didn't manage it. He ended up on the streets. It broke my heart when I found that out. I didn't want to be married to him any more, and I hated the danger he'd put us all in, but I didn't want him to have nothing, either.

Sebastian: I think I was probably the least affected, of the four of us. Pea was heartbroken. I'd never been in love, so I didn't know how that felt. Mum and Dad lost each other, and Dad lost a lot more than that. A few months after it all happened, I saw Dad on the street. I'd finished college and I was doing some temp work, trying to get into graphic design, and I was on my way to the office. It was before nine in the morning and he was clearly drunk. I asked him what he was doing, where he was staying, and he gestured to the shop doorway behind us. I was horrified. I thought about all the arguments we'd had over Wildworld. How much I'd hated him at times. And there he was, reduced to this. I told him to come to the flat we were renting. He said Mum didn't want him there. But I thought he must have been wrong about that. I told him to come for dinner that night, said I'd make spaghetti Bolognese. But then I got caught up at work and by the time I got home, it was past the time I'd told him. I thought maybe he'd forgotten, or spent all day drinking and thought better of it, but as soon as I saw Mum's face, I knew he'd turned up.

Cathy: John came to the flat one day, reeking of booze, swaying on his feet. Said Sebastian had invited him for dinner. Sebastian wasn't home from work yet and I didn't want to let him in. How had it come to this? I had loved this man, had married him, and now I didn't want to be alone with him for a single minute. Pea came out of her room and saw us standing there, on either side of the door. Her eyes were full of pain. I told him I didn't think it was a good idea for him to stay, and I was expecting a battle, but he just slunk off. There was no fight left in him.

Pea: It was worst for Dad, yeah. He really went off the rails. People talk about teenagers going off the rails, don't they, but I think it's an apt description of what happened to him. His life just went off track. That night he came over was the saddest. It was clear that Mum didn't want him anywhere near her and when she sent him away, it was like she'd kicked a puppy.

Sebastian: I was too late. She'd sent him away. I stood in the kitchen with my back to her, my knuckles digging into the worktop. I asked her if she knew he was living on the street. I heard footsteps and turned to see Pea had walked into the room.

Pea: That was how I found out he was homeless, yeah. Once I knew that, Mum turning him away seemed pretty unforgiveable. How do you go from loving someone to that, so fast?

Cathy: The thing was, it had been a gradual demise, our relationship. I hadn't loved him for a long time. And if he'd got sober, maybe it would have been different. Maybe I could have helped him get back on his feet. But the way he was drinking, I didn't want him around any of us. I knew no good would come from that.

Pea: I kept waiting for a letter from Zak. For weeks, months even, I believed he would write. And then one day, I came home from school – I was repeating my GCSE year – and for the first time, checking the post wasn't the first thing I did. I got an apple and a cup of tea instead, and that's when I knew I'd stopped hoping for it. There was this boy in the sixth form at school who'd moved from a different school and didn't know anything about my involvement with AJ Silver. His name was Thomas. He made it clear that he liked me, and we went on a few dates and sort of fell into a relationship that lasted three years. It was nice, it really was, but it was nothing like it had been with Zak.

John: I was on the street for two years, on and off. Sometimes I slept on friends' sofas, but it's amazing how fast friends disappear when you really need them. I didn't keep in touch with Sebastian or Pea. It was clear that Cathy wanted me out of their lives and I was low enough to believe she was right. And then one day, this young guy crouched down in front of me where I was sitting in a doorway, a blanket around me for warmth, and he asked me if I wanted some real help to get out of this situation. I thought he was going to start talking about God, but he just handed me a leaflet and it was for a treatment centre for addicts. I threw it away, but it planted a seed. Two months later, I woke up one morning in a pool of my own piss and I decided enough was enough. And I remembered the name of the treatment centre. I waited for someone to come along who looked kind. It took more than half an hour, but then there was a woman, about my age, and I asked her if she would do me a favour. She looked a bit shellshocked, a bit frightened, but I assured her it wasn't anything improper. I asked her to look this place up on her phone and tell me where it was. Turned out, it was three streets away from the doorway I'd been sleeping in. I went there right then and marched in, said I wanted some help. They had these spon-sored places, and they gave one to me. In there, no one knew who I was or how far I'd fallen. No one really cared. It was all about battling your own demons, and I did a good job of that, I think. It wasn't a straight line to sobriety but I've been sober now for over twenty years. Every day, I wake up and think, *I won't drink today*, and that's as much pressure as I put on myself.

Danny: Wow.

Cathy: A year or so after it all happened, Sebastian came to me and said he didn't want me running myself into the ground. I was doing two jobs, like I said, and he was doing graphic design. He was bringing in a bit of money, and he contributed what he could, but that day he said he could give me money to cover the rent for the next two years, but I wasn't allowed to ask any questions about where it had come from. Well, as a mother, you can't just accept something like that, can you? I thought he must have got himself mixed up with drugs or something. But he assured me it was nothing like that. I said I didn't want the money if I didn't know where it had come from, in case it was dirty, and he just laughed and walked out of the room. In the early hours of the next morning, I woke up, my heart pounding. I thought, *He's sold a story to the press.* I went to his room and woke him up, there and then. Asked him if he'd been talking to journalists about Wildworld and AJ Silver. But he said no, it wasn't that. He kept offering me that money week in and week out, and eventually I took it. I gave up the bar job but stayed at the care home. I'd become attached to some of the residents there. I felt like I was doing some good, making people's lives a little bit better. Whereas at the bar I was just helping them to get into a state like the one John was in.

Pea: Mum never told me about Sebastian's money. Sebastian didn't either. But I knew about it somehow. How he'd got it was a total mystery to me. I didn't think he could possibly be earning enough to have that sort of money. But sometimes you just accept something even though you know there must be something a bit fishy about it, don't you? Never look a gift horse in the mouth and all that.

John: Once I'd got sober, in 2005, I went to the flat again. I had no idea if they even still lived there, but Cathy opened the door. She looked different, older. I suppose I did too. It was as if her edges had been sanded, her colour dulled. She always wore these crazy outfits in bright colours and she didn't care what anyone thought, but that day she was wearing a pair of jeans and a pale green jumper. She'd grown her hair longer, and she'd got new glasses. It's a strange thing, to try to find familiarity in a face that you once knew as well as your own. She put a hand to her mouth and said my name, like I was a ghost come back to haunt her or something. I asked if I could come in, and she stepped aside to let me. We had a coffee together, talked things through. I said I was sorry about the way things had ended, about the person I'd been. Part of my recovery was about making up for the things I'd done wrong. I told her I had ninety days of sobriety, and there were tears in her eyes when she said she was proud of me.

When I got up to go, there was a sound in the hallway, and Pea appeared. My little girl, now a woman. She gave me a hug and said I was looking well, and I couldn't believe that we'd got to this point when we'd once been a family. When I was drinking, I pushed all thoughts of them out because I couldn't bear it, but since I'd been sober, they'd been crowding in. I asked after Sebastian, and Cathy said he was doing well, working as a graphic designer. That he was engaged, getting married the following year. They asked me to come back the next night, for dinner. I said maybe Sebastian could make me that spaghetti Bolognese he'd promised me years before. No one laughed. It wasn't funny, I suppose.

Sebastian: I have to admit, it was good to see Dad again, to see him well. It took a bit of getting used to, the four of us in the same room and interacting again. It was like we'd forgotten what our roles were, and we kept getting our lines wrong, but he came once a week and we settled into it. I even thought I saw a spark there between him and Mum on occasion, and allowed myself to entertain a fantasy in which they found their way back to one another. I introduced him to Gemma, my fiancée, who I'd met through work. We invited him to the wedding. It felt like things were coming good. We never mentioned the name AJ Silver. I wondered whether, without Wildworld to fall out over, we could have a more normal father-son relationship.

Danny: So that's the Hunters, and I don't know about you but I found John's story quite moving. We don't always see the ripple effects of big events, just the people at the very centre. Are you ready to hear about Alex? You'll know some of his story, of course.

Alex: AJ's death threw me off course in a major way. Think about it. I was sixteen, thought I was in love with this major celebrity, no one knew we were sleeping with each other, and then he died. At my best friend's theme park. I didn't know what to do with myself. And Pea was caught up in everything that was going on with her family. We didn't have a big argument or anything. We just drifted. Within six months, we rarely spoke and I was using any drug I could get my hands on. I remember how bewildered my mum was about it all. She had no idea what was going on. And I couldn't tell her.

It's interesting to hear that John ended up in rehab. We could have been there together, except it sounds like it took me a lot longer than him to get there. My twenties are a blur. Everything I can remember is bad. I did a lot of mistaking sex for love. I know, such a bloody cliché. But I did eventually get it together and I've been clean for over six years and I'm so fucking proud of that.

The TV work came as a surprise. I met this guy in rehab and for two months I didn't know what he did for a living. I'd done a bit of everything up to that point – always just trying to earn enough to feed my various habits. On the day he was leaving, he told me he ran a big TV company and he thought

I'd make a great presenter if I could stay on the straight and narrow. He told me to look him up when I got out. He even posted me his business card once he was home. It wasn't a career I'd ever considered, but it gives me something I'm pretty ashamed of needing. It makes me feel adored, in a way. And it's healthier than throwing back pills and sleeping around.

Danny: I don't know about you but I can't imagine my Saturday evenings without Alex Robb. But let's go now to the other side of the Atlantic and find out what happened next for AJ's nearest and dearest.

Zak: What do you do when your brother is the centre of the family, the centre of many people's worlds, and he's suddenly not around any more? Well, if you're me, you set your life on fire. I had a college place waiting for me and I didn't show up. Didn't let them know or anything. I left home because I couldn't bear to be around Mum's sadness. It felt like we would both drown in it if I stayed. I went to my dad's for a while, wasted a few weeks doing nothing. One day, he came into my room at eight in the morning and told me I was going to work with him. I pulled the duvet over my head, but he just turned the light on and opened the blinds. Dad was a labourer on a building site, and he said they were a man down and he'd volunteered me. He had to practically drag me out of bed, but I went.

And it's going to sound trite, but I think he saved me, that day. I'd been festering in that room, rarely showering, eating crap, and my thoughts had been taking darker and darker turns. If I'd been left to my own devices, I truly believe I might not be here now. An honest day's work was exactly what I needed, it turned out. The autumn sun on my face, an ache in my muscles from lifting heavy things and climbing up and down ladders. At the end of the day, Dad took me to meet the foreman and he said the job was mine if I wanted it. There would be a two-week trial and then I'd be on the team, as long as I didn't do anything stupid. I said thank you, that I'd see him the next day. That evening, Dad said he was grilling steaks, and for the first time since I'd arrived, I sat with him at the table. We talked about AJ. I'd avoided talking about him for so long, and it wasn't helping. I thought it was time to try a different way.

Dad asked me to tell him all about the trip. Not the accident, not the way it ended, but his last weeks. I kept stopping and starting. Because there was so much that I didn't think he'd want to hear, about AJ playing different girls off against each other and acting like an entitled little shit. I laughed, thinking about him that way. He'd become a sort of martyr. Everyone who dies young does, don't they? But he'd been far from perfect, and I knew that better than anyone. He'd behaved quite badly on that trip, and I wasn't sure what I could take from it to give to our dad.

In the end, I told him about Pea. About falling in love. He asked whether I was going to get in touch, and I said I didn't know. I'd thought about calling or writing to Pea every day since I'd seen her in that hotel corridor. What had happened hadn't changed the way I felt about her, not in the least. But now we were pitted against one another, in a way, our families at war. One of ours lost and one of hers potentially responsible. I didn't see how we could get through that, get past it. I told Dad I was going to have an early night ready for work the next day. And he smiled and said, 'That's my boy.'

Ken: I have to say, right back when AJ started getting into singing and dancing and Grace was encouraging him and driving him all over the place for competitions, I had this feeling it would end badly. We weren't the sort of family who knows how to handle fame. I was a labourer and Grace was a receptionist at a dental surgery. And then suddenly people were telling us that AJ could go all the way to the top, that he was a star. And they were right, weren't they? But it didn't sit right with me. When the money started flooding in, I didn't want to have anything to do with it. I kept saying to Grace that nothing comes for free and she would say it wasn't coming for free, that he was working hard for it. He was putting in the hours, I'll give him that, but we're talking about crazy sums of money. More money than any seventeen-year-old should have at his disposal.

If you look at stars who've made it big, especially young ones, their personal lives are almost always a mess. Failed relationships, drugs, arrests, alcohol abuse, you name it. I didn't want that for AJ. I wanted him to have a normal life. But Grace had stars in her eyes.

Anyway, you know what happened, how it all came crashing down. When I saw Grace at the funeral, for the first time in more than a year, there was a part of me that wanted to say I told you so. But it would have been cruel. We'd both wanted the best for him, we just hadn't been able to see eye to eye on what that was. So when Zak turned up shortly after, I was pleased to see him, though I did wonder how Grace was getting on without either of her sons. I let Zak wallow for a while, because we were all grieving, weren't we? And he was just a kid, really. Just trying to work out what life's all about. I gave him ten weeks. And then I got him up and out of bed and on the building site, where I could keep an eye on him.

Zak: I worked with Dad for a year. It went by so fast. I'd intended to take stock after a couple of months, but before I knew it, fall was there again. I sat Dad down over dinner. This time I grilled the steaks. We were learning how to live without him. I guess Dad had already learned it, when we'd moved away from him. But now it was different, now it was permanent. I said I was going to go to college. They'd chased me for a while the year before, and when I'd explained the situation, and they'd made the connection with AJ, they'd offered to defer my place. I'd been weighing it up for months, while I was learning to lay bricks and mixing cement and carrying window frames.

Ken: Grace and I had saved up over the years in case they wanted to go to college. I told him there was money for him, and I saw his eyes fill with tears.

Zak: Money had kind of lost its meaning in those final years with AJ. When you can buy anything you want, you sort of lose interest after a while. Working with Dad had brought me back to reality, taught me about an honest day's work. Part of my decision-making process about going to college had been about the debt I'd have to get myself into, but now here was Dad, telling me he'd put some money aside for exactly this purpose. But I guess you're probably wondering what had happened to AJ's money.

Danny: I'm so glad he brought this up without me having to ask.

Zak: He'd had a will drawn up with Lou. The fact that he'd done it made me think a lot about whether he was really considering suicide. Anyway, he asked for a fair chunk of money to go to Mom and Dad and me and the rest to go to this company him and Lou had set up for charitable causes. I was pretty surprised when I heard that, I can tell you. But it reminded me that he wasn't a bad person, not really, not deep down. And the money he'd left for me, I don't know why, but I didn't want to touch it. At least not at that point. I think Dad understood that without me having to tell him. I wanted to make my own way in the world. It was something I'd been grappling with in the last few weeks of his life and that crystallised for me in the months after his death. I didn't want to be carried. I swore to Dad that any money of his I used for college, I would pay back. And I did.

I went to college to study Journalism. I worked with Dad in the holidays, and again when I graduated for a while, sending out résumés for anything remotely writing-related. After a little less than a year, I got a job at the local newspaper I'd grown up stuffing through people's letterboxes. It felt like a nice cycle. Long days, some shitty tasks, but I learned my trade there over the next few years. I worked my way up from coffee boy to respected reporter. Nobody at work knew I was AJ Silver's brother. I had a different name, because Silver was a stage name, and our likeness wasn't enough for people to make the connection, especially since fashions and haircuts had changed along the way. So when that news story broke in 2009, nobody pussyfooted around me. They didn't know they had to.

Ken: I think that news story, all those years down the line, wasn't helpful to anyone. It dragged it all back up again. And I felt for Zak. He'd really fought to make a life for himself after such a blow. He was working hard, had just bought his own apartment, and he had a girlfriend who he seemed like he was getting serious about. I remember thinking, no more than a week before it broke, that despite what had happened to AJ, I was blessed to have a son who was doing so well for himself.

Zak: The story was that someone had come out of the woodwork and claimed they'd heard John Hunter threatening to kill AJ shortly before the accident. Now, there'd been an investigation at the time and the outcome was that the owners of Wildworld had been negligent. There was a fault with the rollercoaster and it should have been sorted properly after the first accident. But this was something different again. Could John have caused the crash deliberately? I felt sick. I went to the office bathroom and locked myself in a cubicle. Lowered the lid of the toilet and sat on it for a full five minutes, taking deep breaths. I still thought about AJ every day, but I had a life now. A life I'd built, bit by bit. When I went back into the newsroom, my editor called me over. He said, 'I want you to go over there, to England. Find out what's going on with this whole AJ Silver thing. He was from round here originally, you know?'

Maggie: I hadn't talked to anyone connected to AJ Silver for a long time when Zak called me. I'd seen the news story and it had brought it all back, but I hadn't given it a huge amount of thought. But one evening, when I was clearing up the kitchen after dinner, my work cell phone rang and Zak said, 'It's me, Zak. They want me to go back there.' I had to get him to go back to the beginning. I didn't even know he'd become a journalist. The irony of it, of him of all people being asked to cover this story. I asked how he felt about it. I was still wondering why I was the one he'd called. He said, 'I don't know, Maggie. It was bad enough when it was an accident. I'm not sure I can face finding out that it wasn't.' I thought about him back then, him and Pea. That was love, I thought. That thing they had, it wasn't just kids' stuff. It was real love. I'd lost and found it myself over the years in between, and I knew a thing or two I hadn't known then.

Zak: That evening, after I'd talked it all through with Maggie, who was always such a calming influence, I booked a flight for the following afternoon. I packed my things and I tried to get some sleep. The next morning, I wheeled my case into the office and I asked my editor if I could speak to him and went into his office and closed the door behind me. He looked surprised. His door was always open unless he was in there with one of the interns or doing lines of coke off his desk. He was a dick, and I didn't feel like I owed him anything, but I was ready to come clean about who I was. When I told him, his eyes went so wide I thought they were going to fall out. He said, 'No fucking way.' Then he smiled, and it looked insincere. He said, 'Surely this means you're the perfect person to cover it?' I felt like punching him in the face. I'd basically just told him that my brother had died, and he was reacting like this? I turned to leave his office, but he grabbed my arm. Said, 'Wait, weren't you there when it happened? Didn't I read that?' I said I was. He said I should do a huge feature, four pages, with all the background and then an update based on what was happening now. Asked me to get it to him in two days' time. I said, 'You understand what I'm saying, right? That AJ was my brother?' He still didn't seem to get why I was upset, so I just walked out of there without looking back. I grabbed my case as I went by my desk and wheeled it on out. Jumped in a cab to the airport. I could hear him calling my name as I walked away, and it felt so good to ignore him. I'd never dared before. But what was he going to do now, fire his reporter who had an inside scoop on the biggest celebrity news story of the year?

I was at the airport way too early for my flight, on account of having walked out of my office, so I grabbed a coffee and started jotting down notes. Just words at first. Wildworld. John Hunter. Rollercoaster. AJ. It was a thing I did, sometimes, to get my brain working. I found it helped me to make associations, to link things together, but I'd never worked on a story about someone I loved before, someone I'd lost. When I wrote 'Pea', I had to jam my teeth together to stop myself from letting out a sob.

Ken: Zak messaged me from the airport, said he was going to England for a few days for work. I asked him straight out if he was working on the story about AJ, and he said he was.

Zak: I had this urge, when we were talking, to ask him if he'd come with me.

Ken: I almost asked if he wanted me to come.

Zak: He told me to take care of myself, which is something he always said when I travelled anywhere, but it was different that day. I knew he wasn't only saying that I should keep myself safe. I knew he was talking about my heart.

I flew into Birmingham, just like we had before. First for the visit with Maggie and then with the whole crew. But this time, it was quieter. Nobody staring as I made my way through passport control. It was a long time since I'd been AJ Silver's brother. For years by then, I'd just been Zak. But that day I felt the loss of it, and I thought about what my life might be like if he'd lived. I wouldn't be doing this job, probably. Would I still have been following my kid brother around the world? Would he still have been travelling the world, singing his songs to those girls who loved him?

I freshened up at the hotel I'd booked. It was the one I'd stayed in before, the Ace, but it was unrecognisable. The whole place had had a refurb. Still, while I was in the shower, I thought about lying on a bed in this very building with Pea Hunter, one earphone in my ear and one in hers, swapping songs we liked. It almost brought me to my knees.

I had never looked her up. Never dared to, in case I found what I didn't want to. That she was married, settled. A mother. It wasn't that I didn't want those things for her, it was just too painful to imagine her having them with someone else. I realised with a jolt. Bonnie, my girlfriend. I hadn't told her I was going away. I sent her a text saying I was in England and she replied immediately with a string of question marks, then followed that up with another message that read 'What the fuck?' It wasn't like I'd never travelled for work before, but a trip this fast and this far was quite unusual, and me forgetting to tell her until I'd arrived was unheard of. But I couldn't face explaining it to her then. I needed to find John Hunter.

John: The story came out of nowhere and it knocked me for six, if I'm being honest with you. I'd put it all behind me, what had happened, and I never thought I'd have to see my face on the front cover of a newspaper again. But I suppose there's always someone who'll say something for a bit of money or attention, and those gutter tabloids will always listen and try to make something sordid out of it. My money was on Alex. I hadn't seen or heard from him in years, but it seemed like the kind of thing he might do. And he wasn't yet a TV star by this point. My reaction to it was to lay low, so I called in sick at work – I'd trained as a drugs counsellor – and spent a couple of days in my flat, just waiting for it to blow over. I didn't turn on the radio or the TV. I didn't want to hear anything about the bloody story. How could I know it had been reported on both sides of the Atlantic?

Zak: John Hunter was fairly easy to find. He hadn't travelled far from Wildworld. He was in the next town over in a dingy apartment. I took a deep breath before knocking on the door.

John: I thought about not answering, but I was waiting on a parcel and I thought it might be that. You could have knocked me down with a bloody feather when I saw Zak standing there. I recognised him straight off. He was older, of course, like we all were, but I'd have known him anywhere. Those weeks in 1996 were crystal clear to me, much clearer than some of the years since. He opened his mouth to speak and I closed the door in his face.

Zak: Yeah, he opened the door, took one look at me and slammed it shut. I knocked again, waited. I was used to having to talk people round. I said his name, knowing he was on the other side of the door, listening. I said I was a reporter now, and I'd come to find out whether there was any truth in what people were saying about him. I said I wanted to hear his side. I knew he'd open up eventually. People like him never pass up the opportunity to get their story out there. By the time he did, though, I was sitting with my back against his door, and I pretty much fell inside. He said, 'You'd better come in, then.'

John: He told me he liked his coffee strong and I made it weak. It was childish, but I wanted to have some form of control over this situation. And that was all I had.

Zak: I don't know whether English coffee is shit or whether that family just made shit coffee. I should have asked for water. I got straight down to it, asked if he knew who'd said they'd heard him threaten to kill AJ. He looked at me long and hard. Said he thought I was the reporter. I laughed at that. The last time we'd seen each other, I'd still been a kid. But now we were two men, going back over something that had shaped both of our lives. And I found that I sort of liked him. I sort of admired the way he held himself, all ease and confidence. He was a different man to the one I'd met before. I wondered what had changed, other than him losing his livelihood.

John: Neither of us knew where the story had come from. I didn't say anything about suspecting Alex. I needed to keep my wits about me. There was no telling what he'd say in that paper of his. I asked which one it was, and he said a name I didn't recognise. It wasn't the *New York Times*, I'll tell you that much.

Zak: He told me a bit about what he'd been through. How he'd lost the business, and Cathy and the kids, how he'd ended up on the streets. And all I could think was, *There but for the grace of God*. It could have wrecked all of our lives, that accident. It was a miracle, in a way, that the two of us were still there, still standing.

Danny: I'm waiting for him to ask about Pea.

John: I was waiting for him to ask about Pea. When he did, his voice was casual but he kept touching his hair and his face, like he couldn't quite work out what he needed to do. I said Pea was well, that she was living nearby. He said he would like to see her, to ask her about the story, and I said I would call her to ask whether it was okay to give him her address.

Pea: When Dad called, I was giving the dog a bath. Our relationship was pretty good by then, probably better than it had been when I was a teenager. He was sober and we talked roughly every week, so the call itself didn't come as a surprise. I put him on speaker, said it wasn't a good time but I could call him back later if that was any good. Then he dropped it, like a bomb. Said he was with Zak, and he was asking about me. Now, I didn't know any other Zak. Never had. And I was pretty sure Dad didn't either. I tried to keep my voice level when I said, 'Zak Campbell?' He confirmed it. I felt dizzy, let go of the shower attachment and let it spray up to the ceiling, Sidney jumping up to try to catch the water as if it was all part of some elaborate game. Zak. After all these years. In my dad's flat.

Danny: This is quite a moment, huh?

John: She said I could give him the address, so I did. And then he left, promising me he'd do what he could to get to the bottom of this whole thing. I thought about Pea after he'd gone, knowing how much my call had thrown her. Right then, I was sure she'd be getting changed and trying to sort her hair out while that stupid dog of hers dripped onto the carpets.

Pea: It sounds so silly, but while I waited for him to come, I felt like I was sixteen again. I hadn't seen Zak for thirteen years, but I felt like I'd sloughed off all that time, all those disappointments, all those men who were not him. I stood by the door, my heart jumping, and when he knocked, I reached out and touched it, knowing I was inches away from him. Knowing that even that distance was perhaps too much to bear. I opened the door and he said my name, soft and sweet, like he always had when we'd lain beside one another that summer, and I burst into tears.

Zak: Yeah, she cried, man. I wasn't expecting that. That was some reaction. I just stood there for a minute or so, not knowing whether it was okay to hug her, but then she reached out and pulled me inside and we were standing there in her hallway, inches apart, and I knew in that instant that I would end things with Bonnie the next time we spoke because all my life I'd been chasing this feeling, and I hadn't felt it since the last time I'd been in the same room as this girl in front of me.

Pea: He held out a battered CD case, and I saw that it was the Blur album I'd given him all those years ago. I took it from him, pulled out the sleeve notes. Because part of me thought he'd just picked up a new copy of it somewhere, which would have been sweet enough, but no, it was mine. I'd put a star next to my favourite songs. 'To the End' and 'End of a Century'. And I thought, he's kept this for years and years. That has to mean something, doesn't it?

I made him a coffee and we sat down and he started filling me in. Not only on what he was doing here, but on the years I'd missed, and I did the same, like we'd planned in advance to plug those gaps. When he said he was a journalist, I felt tears prick my eyes. He'd done it. Despite everything. And then I realised that he was here to poke around, to cover that new story that had come out of the woodwork, and I felt hurt. He wasn't here for me at all.

Zak: I saw her face fall when she realised why I'd come. And I wanted to tell her that I should have come earlier. That I'd wanted to come every day since I'd seen her in that hotel corridor with her mum and Sebastian. That I didn't blame her for anything. That it was all such a long time ago. But it's hard to know where to start when you haven't seen someone for so many years and the last time you did, your brother had just died.

Pea: Sidney came into the room and stood by my knees, looking from me to Zak. Basically asking if this guy was okay, if he needed to step in. He was the softest, sweetest animal I'd ever met, but he was protective of me, and I knew he'd rustle up a snarl or a growl if I gave him the nod. Instead, I gave his belly a good rub, to show him everything was all right. Zak said, 'Cute dog,' and reached across to let Sidney sniff his hand. Then he said, 'So is it just the two of you?' I knew what he was asking. I was nearing thirty, so it was perfectly feasible that I'd have a partner and kids. That I'd have a family. I nodded. 'Just the two of us.' And I saw him smile, and I knew.

Zak: She asked me the same question, and I didn't want to lie, so I told her about Bonnie. That we'd been together for almost a year but we didn't live together. She kept looking at me, waiting for more, so I said, 'No kids.' We'd talked about kids, that summer, me and Pea. We hadn't questioned whether we might want them. It was like it was a given. Pea had said she wanted three, all close together in age. That she wanted a chaotic, messy family home. I'd said that three sounded good.

And here we were, no longer those innocent kids, and neither of us had had a family. I wanted to ask her why she hadn't. I wanted to tell her why I hadn't – because I'd never met anyone who fit together with me the way she did.

Pea: It was tough to hear that he was with someone, I won't lie. Which is ridiculous. I still thought about him a lot but that morning if you'd told me I would be sitting here with him, I would have laughed. I had no claim on him. He was my first love. Hardly anyone gets to keep that first love forever, do they?

Zak: Long after the coffee she'd made me had gone cold, I asked her about her family. I'd gathered that her parents were no longer together, but I was shocked when she said they'd split up immediately after the accident. She told me about John's battles with alcohol, about his homelessness. It was a lot to take in. I'd thought so much about her, but I hadn't given much thought to the rest of them. It was good to hear that they'd sort of found a way back to each other, in the past few years. She said even Sebastian and her dad were on fairly good terms.

And then finally, we got onto the story. Did she know where it had come from? She said straight away that she thought Nicole Waddington was behind it. That name brought back a host of memories. That night of the Manchester show, the last show, that thrown milkshake. That afternoon by the river when AJ had taken her off into the long grass and I'd thought things with Pea were falling apart. It fitted, that she would have done something like this. Probably sleeping with my brother was the most exciting thing that had ever happened in her life, and now she was bored and restless and trying to bring it back, in a way. I asked Pea if she knew where I could find her, and miraculously, she did. She said she worked in a fish and chip shop in West Wilding. That I'd probably find her there the next day, if I went to look. I realised then that I didn't know about her, about Pea. What she did. So I asked her, and she looked down and I saw it was a mistake, that she was sad or somehow ashamed of how her life had turned out, and I wished I could unask the question.

Pea: I didn't want to say that I ran a dog shelter. I don't know why. I knew him well enough to know he wouldn't judge me for it. It's just, we'd shared our dreams when we were teenagers. His had been to become a journalist, and he'd done it. Mine had been to run Wildworld.

Zak: The dog shelter thing seemed perfect to me. Once she said it, I couldn't imagine her doing anything else. Other than being at Wildworld, of course. I asked her what had happened to it, hoping it wasn't too sore a subject.

Pea: I told him it was still there, that by some miracle the land hadn't been bought by developers. He looked pretty shocked. Over the years, it had nearly been sold a couple of times but the deal had never quite come off. It was the location – not close enough to the town centre. And perhaps it was down to what had happened there, too. Some of the rides had been sold off to pay Dad's debts, but a lot of them hadn't. The 360 hadn't. It was like it was tainted by what had happened. I said I could take him there if he wanted, and he nodded eagerly, and I wondered how much of it was about the story and how much was about going back in time. He asked when I finished work the next day, and we arranged it – I'd pick him up shortly after five in the afternoon, and we'd drive to Wildworld. I'd driven past it plenty of times but I hadn't stopped for many years. I wasn't anxious about it. It felt right, to go there with Zak.

Zak: The next morning, I woke up with a smile on my face. I looked up the fish and chip shop where Pea had said Nicole worked and found that it wasn't open until lunchtime, so I spent the morning drinking coffee and dealing with work emails on my laptop in the hotel room. At twelve, I walked over there. It was less than five minutes from where I was staying. I recognised her immediately. She was heavier, her dark hair a little greasy and scraped back into a ponytail. She asked what I wanted without looking up, but when she heard my accent, she froze. I asked if she had five minutes to talk to me, and she looked at the guy standing beside her who was obviously her boss. He looked from her to me and back again, then eventually said, 'Five minutes. No more.'

We went outside, but standing in front of the shop felt weird so she suggested we start walking. I got it. Sometimes it's easier to talk to someone when you're walking beside them or next to them in a car. I asked her straight out if the story had come from her, and she crumbled. Said she'd needed the money, that she was a single mum.

I asked if there was any truth to it, the story about John threatening to kill AJ. She was quiet. I reckoned we were probably two minutes into our five. I didn't want to push her, but I also didn't want to go back to my boss and say I had nothing. In the end, she spoke just as I was about to prod her.

'Look, you don't know what it's like for me, living here. Just me and my son and a crappy job and bills that there's never quite enough money to cover. Things were really hard last month. And my friend Fay, remember her? She said that she thought the press would still lap up any story I went to them with about AJ Silver. We laugh about it sometimes, about how that was the peak and everything since has been downhill. Why didn't I cash it in, she asked? So I found a phone number for *The Scoop*, called and asked who I could speak to if I had a story. It was so easy; they were so hungry for it. It's mad, isn't it, after all these years? No one gives a shit about me, despite me still living and breathing, but they're all dying for a new piece of gossip about him.'

She sounded so bitter. And that was it, I guessed. I'd flown over to chase a story that didn't exist. A story that had been fabricated by this woman whose life hadn't gone the way she planned, and who was holding on for dear life to the fact that, as a teenager, she'd slept with a celebrity. I wanted to be angry about it, but it was more sad than anything. And, if I hadn't come, I wouldn't have seen Pea.

We walked back to the shop in quiet contemplation. At the door, she asked whether I lived here in England, and I realised that I hadn't even told her I was there in my capacity as a reporter. That she didn't know I was. She just thought I was there as his brother. I said no, that I lived in Atlanta. It meant nothing to her. I added that it was in Georgia, and she nodded. We were from different worlds. We always had been, but it had never been so stark as it was then. I thanked her for her time. As I was walking away, she called after me. 'How long are you going to be around?' It was a good question, one I didn't know the answer to. I said probably a few more days. And then she said, 'I might see you around.'

I went back to my hotel room and called my boss, told him the story was dead. That there was nothing in it. He was frustrated but not angry. It went like that, sometimes. He told me to get a flight back the next day, if I could. I thought about going back, about going into my office and having dinner with

Bonnie, and it just felt like a different life. I'd been away for two days, and I felt sure that I didn't fit there any more. But I booked a return flight all the same. I had about twenty hours of my visit left.

Pea picked me up as promised and we drove the mile or so to Wildworld. As she pulled into the car park, there was so much stuff coming back to me and I didn't know what to do with the emotions. It looked shabby, which wasn't surprising given that it had been abandoned for so long, but I wondered whether it had ever been the way I'd remembered it. Shiny and special. I couldn't ask Pea. We stood side by side in front of the gates, her old house to our left. We didn't say anything for the longest time.

Pea: It was some weird shit, standing there with Zak after all that time had passed. It was almost too painful to look at the house, so I focused on the turnstiles and what I knew was beyond them. Then, without even knowing I was going to do it, I turned to Zak and asked if he remembered that smaller gate we'd gone through that day AJ had wanted an adventure, and found one with Nicole. He followed me there and we just pushed the gate open. It was kind of hidden away so I guess no one had ever thought to lock it. And just like that, we were back inside. I felt like Alex should be with us, but I hadn't seen or heard from him for a long time. It was deathly quiet. We just made our way around the five cities, saying very little, avoiding the 360 by silent mutual consent.

Zak: It was like being in a dream. It was like being young again. We couldn't go on any of the rides, of course, but just being there was almost magical. And at the same time, it was where we'd lost AJ, so it was as painful as it was nostalgic.

When we looped back around to the gate where we'd come in, I told her I was flying back the next day. I didn't say home. I didn't say I was going home. She nodded, said nothing.

Pea: It wasn't until we were back in the car that he said, 'I could come back.' I didn't know what he meant by it. Did he mean he could visit again, so we could rake over old ground? Or was he hinting at something more, something bigger? It had knocked me off my feet, seeing him. I wasn't sure how long it would take me to get back to normal.

Zak: It was hard to know what she felt, and I didn't want to push anything, so when I got out of the car at the hotel, I just thanked her. I meant for everything. I said she was right about the story coming from Nicole. That there was no substance to it. I asked her to tell her dad it was over, that I didn't think anyone would be coming to hassle him again. And she thanked me. We left it like that.

Danny: This should be the end of this episode, the end of the series. I started to trawl through all the interviews with a view to putting some final words in from everyone involved, but then, as I was finishing off the edits, something struck me. It was about those secret chats AJ and Sebastian and sometimes Lou had in the Hunters' kitchen, one of which Pea walked in on. There had to be something more to them, didn't there? I'd heard about them from Sebastian, but Lou didn't want to be involved in the podcast. However, I emailed him one more time, just on the off-chance that he'd let something slip.

Lou replied within twenty-four hours, and his reply was three words long. *Talk to Sebastian.* So I gave Sebastian a call, told him I'd been talking to Lou. And he went really quiet, and then he sighed, and he came out with the absolute last thing I would have expected him to say.

Sebastian: It's hard to know how to say this, after all this time. But AJ Silver didn't die on that rollercoaster. I know because I helped him stage it. And as far as I know, he's still alive.

Danny: How's that for a bombshell? There's only one thing for it. Bonus episode, out next week. Thanks for listening today.

SeanySean
WHAT THE ACTUAL FUCK? #WhatHappenedThatSummer

LisaintheClouds
No way. It's got to be a ploy to get people listening. #WhatHappenedThatSummer

OntheCasey
I mean, if it is, it's going to work! #WhatHappenedThatSummer

Mark48Edmunds
AJ Silver, still alive? How can that possibly be true? What about the police and ambulance staff who came out to the accident? What about the funeral? It's bollocks. #WhatHappenedThatSummer

EmmaJones64
You know, there's a guy who lives in the next town from me who looks a lot like AJ Silver. I've always thought it. #WhatHappenedThatSummer

BeaBaby

I can't believe what I just heard. #WhatHappened-
ThatSummer

AlisonONeill621

I mean, I know we're all reeling from that news, but how cute
are Pea and Zak? I so want them to get back together.
#WhatHappenedThatSummer

EPISODE 8 – PHOENIX

Danny: Hello and welcome to the episode of *What Happened That Summer?* that was never meant to be. My name is Danny Drake. If you've listened to episode seven of this series, or really if you've seen or read any form of news over the past week, you'll know that I dropped quite the bombshell at the end of it. According to Sebastian Hunter, AJ Silver did not die at Wildworld theme park in 1996 after all. AJ Silver is – potentially – still alive. We couldn't leave things like that so I've been hastily catching up with everyone involved to record this final bonus episode. Let's start with Sebastian and where that shocking news came from.

Sebastian: So, God, where to start? I've told you about the habit AJ and I got into, of having tea and biscuits and chatting about insignificant things. Once Lou arrived on the scene, he'd join us too. Apart from that time when Pea walked in, nobody knew about it, I don't think. Everyone else was so busy trying to keep things running smoothly, or as smoothly as possible, the whole time AJ was staying. And like I said, AJ liked that I had zero interest in his singing and his fame and all of that. It was like he got to have a break from being AJ Silver.

But then, after the first few times, he started opening up to me more and more. I wasn't used to that, and I found it quite uncomfortable, but I didn't know how to tell him that. Not because he was AJ Silver. Just because he was a person, I guess. I've never been great at interpersonal relationships. So he started telling me about how hard it was to spend all this time travelling but not being able to explore anywhere properly, that he felt like a caged animal. I remember saying that I imagined the money helped a bit, and he laughed. He said, 'I like you. You're not like the others.' Now, I'd been a bit of a loner, a bit of a weirdo, my whole life, and I was used to being bullied and teased. What I wasn't used to was people making it out to be a good thing. I got the biscuit tin out. Put the kettle on again.

I wouldn't have wanted to admit it at the time, or even really known how to express it, but there was something about him that I liked. He liked me because I wouldn't let him do or say whatever he wanted. I called him out on stuff, if he was out of line. And I liked him because he took an interest in me, at a time when no one else really did. He hated my dad, too, and although I didn't hate him, I couldn't see past my anger with him back then, so that was another thing that sort of held us together.

He talked a lot about how fame wasn't what he'd thought it would be, how he hadn't known what he was getting himself into. And how there was no way out. He talked about how pushy his mum was, that it was more her dream than his. He said that even if he stopped performing and recording, they'd still follow him around for the rest of his life. The paparazzi, he meant. I said he had a pretty high opinion of himself and that I thought they'd maybe get bored after a year or two, and he really laughed at that. I can picture him there, at the kitchen table, dunking a digestive biscuit and his face all twisted with laughter. He was just a kid, at the end of the day, wasn't he? He was out of his depth.

I don't remember when he first said he sometimes thought about ending things. That made me sit up and pay attention. Was he admitting to feeling suicidal? And if he was, what the hell was I going to do about it? I knew nothing about mental health. It wasn't a buzzword like it is now. I was out of my depth, too. But he must have seen my reaction because he clarified – he didn't want to take his life. But he wouldn't mind it if people thought he'd died. Because then he'd be free, and he could escape. I asked where he'd go, and he shrugged. Asked if I'd heard his song 'Island'. I hadn't. He said maybe he'd go to some of those places that he'd been to on tour but never seen. It's obvious now that he had the bones of the plan ready, even then. Him and Lou must have been working away at it, getting the money ready over months and months. He wasn't going to tell me where he was going, because he wasn't going to tell anyone that.

I don't remember quite how it went from this fantasy he talked about to an actual plan, but it happened pretty fast. He said he needed to 'go' in a dramatic, public way for people to believe it. It couldn't be something 'boring like an overdose'. Those were his words. He said he'd thought a lot about the logistics of it, that his private doctor would be on the scene and would insist on him being taken away in a private ambulance, that Lou would help him sort out the money for him to live on and pay off anyone who'd been involved, but he needed someone on the inside. And that was me. He started talking about the 360, about the accident that had happened before he came. I put my hands up. I said that if people believed someone had died on one of our rides, my parents could go to prison. And he nodded. He kept looking at me. It was eerie. He must have blinked but he didn't once look away. He said, 'Could you live with that, Sebastian? How about if you had a couple of million pounds to sweeten the deal?'

Dad and I were at loggerheads, had been for months, because he wanted me to work alongside him at the park, ready to take it over one day, and I didn't want to. I was young, and angry, and stupid. And I knew what that kind of money could do. So I said yes, I'd do it. I'd help him. And I told him about the engineer coming out after that accident, how I'd seen what had gone wrong with the wiring and could replicate it. From then on, those daily cups of tea were like military operations. Lou always there, looking on and interjecting occasionally. He was clearly AJ's right-hand man. Later still, the bodyguard started to join us. Lucian. He was in on it, too. We had our heads down, running through scenarios. I had to identify a day when I could cover the operation of the ride. Dr Haskins had to be nearby. We had to make sure he was the only one in the carriage that crashed. And we had to somehow find or make a dummy that could be mistaken for him. I didn't think it would work, if I'm honest. I said that to him more than once. And I'm pretty sure he was doubtful too. He said that if it all went wrong, he'd pretend it was just a prank. That's what I honestly thought would happen. But I got caught up in it. I remember asking about his family. Could he cope with his mum thinking he was dead? He said that he'd get in touch with them once the initial craziness had died down. He never did, though. And I've wrestled for years with whether or not I should come clean.

One night, I woke up in the early hours with a thought.

Dad had these life-size dummies that were used when a ride was new, to test it out before people went on it. He'd used them when we first got the 360, and then again after the accident. I knew where he kept them, too.

The night before AJ's Manchester show, we met after dark in front of the office – AJ, Lou, Lucian and me – and I let us in with the keys I'd taken from the hallway table. My hands were shaking. AJ had this little silver flask that he was swigging from, and he held it out to me once we were inside. I took it. Whisky. I've never liked the taste of it, but I had a slug of it to calm me. In the corner, behind the filing cabinets, there was a box. I pulled it out, ripped off the tape. And inside, there they were. Two dummies. AJ had brought this bag and he upended it on the desk. There were clothes inside. He took one of the dummies and dressed it as him. Oversized T-shirt, baggy jeans. He'd even got a wig from somewhere. I think that was the moment when I realised that he was serious about this. Part of me had thought it was just something he was toying with, but that night it felt like a line was crossed. It wasn't too late to back out, but I was definitely swept up in it. Curious about whether it could work. When he offered the flask again, I took it. I wanted to numb things, and I knew that's what alcohol could do. I wanted to pretend it was all a game. Because there was something in AJ's eyes that night. I'll never forget it. It was like desperation. And I knew he was going to do it, and I was going to be part of it, and our lives would never be the same again.

We both went into the park. I had a torch to light our way to the 360 and a screwdriver in my pocket. I went into the little booth. AJ followed me in, watched me as I unscrewed the over-ride button's casing and pulled off the plastic tubing the engineer had put in place to hold the wires together after the accident. I pulled them apart. Screwed the casing back on. Then I hid the dummy in the footwell of one of the empty carriages. On the walk back, I told him that no one else could go on the thing until he was ready to do it. I made him promise.

Danny: Can you tell us about the day itself?

Sebastian: Sure. Once I told AJ that I was going to be covering for Simon, he decided that was the day. He was going to suggest going on the 360 at some point in the afternoon, which wouldn't have been unusual, and then I told him about the challenge and said I'd bring it up. He said that his doctor, Haskins, would give him fast-acting laxatives to put in the others' food so it would end up just being him and Lucian for the 360 part of it. He was like a puppet master. All of them just did what he said. When they were ready to go on the ride, it was a bit chaotic, with Pea and Alex hanging around, and Dad too.

I wasn't counting on Dad appearing. For a horrible moment I thought he might insist on checking their seatbelts, but he let me do it. Dad started the ride up, and my heart was pounding. But then him and Pea and Alex left before I had to send the second carriage off. I had to time it just right, so that the collision happened in the undercover part. We didn't want anyone to properly see it.

And then Haskins was on the scene, and Lou, and they just took control of everything. It was pretty slick. I was half focused on the money that was going to land in my bank account once probate was sorted out, but I was thinking about where AJ would end up, too. How he'd live the rest of his life. I looked over at Dad, who was walking away from the ride, when the crash happened. I saw him turn back, saw his face. With that sickening sound, I think we both knew that our lives were going to change forever. But the difference was that I'd known it was going to happen. I'd let it happen. Helped make it happen.

Danny: This is some story, Sebastian. Since the last episode aired, the press has gone into overdrive about this. People have tried to track AJ down but with no success. I guess what I'm asking is, why should we believe you?

Sebastian: It doesn't really matter to me whether you do or not. I would never have said a word about it if it hadn't been for the fact that he screwed me over. He'd explicitly promised me two million pounds, but when the money came, via Lou, it was one point eight. Maybe that sounds petty, but we're talking about two hundred thousand pounds, and I'd put myself out for him in a significant way. Of course, I had no way of getting in touch with him, no way of fighting back, so I just accepted it. It was still more money than I'd ever seen or thought I'd have. I mean, he could have just not given me anything and I wouldn't have been able to do a thing about it. But then, when you appeared and started raking things up, I thought about it again. And I thought, no, fuck this, it's been nearly thirty years and I'm still a bit pissed off. Plus the fact that he went back on his word to tell his family he was still alive. That was pretty low.

Danny: How did they sort out a death certificate and coroner's report, once they'd declared him dead?

Sebastian: I don't know how Lou pulled some of that stuff off. I reckon Haskins would have signed a death certificate, and I read that the funeral was closed casket – that AJ had stated that in his will – so I guess they just paid the funeral directors off and cremated an empty coffin. I honestly don't know. But what I do know is that Lou must have had a lot of fingers in a lot of pies. Plus, these people had serious money, and with that sort of money, you can pull off pretty much anything.

Danny: What has your life been like, Sebastian? Do you regret your actions? How do you think your dad will react to this news?

Sebastian: Well, that's the question, isn't it. Was it worth it? The short answer is no.

Danny: What's the long answer?

Sebastian: I guess the long answer is that I sold out my family, and I can see now, with hindsight, that it was the wrong thing to do. I was so angry with Dad, but did I want to completely destroy his life? I think if you'd asked me back then, I would have said I did, but now? The man's a lonely alcoholic, and I wouldn't wish that on anyone. Mum's been okay, she's very resilient, but I'm not sure about Pea. She's in a good place now but for years she didn't settle down, didn't seem fully content. And I can't know, I suppose, whether she would have been in other circumstances, but it's something that plagues me when I can't sleep. Did I sell my sister's future happiness for one point eight million quid?

Danny: Has your dad been in touch since the last episode aired?

Sebastian: No, he hasn't. I listened to it when it aired, and then I waited. I thought he'd call immediately, actually. I thought he'd shout and scream at me. But I suppose that was the old dad, the one who was drinking and angry. And it hit me that maybe I don't really know this new dad as well as I thought, the one in recovery, who's presumably faced up to some of his issues. And perhaps I never will. If he's listening to this, I'd like to say I'm sorry.

Danny: One last question, Sebastian. What did you do with the money?

Sebastian: Well, you've heard that I gave some of it to Mum in the aftermath of it all, because she was struggling to make ends meet. It was a risk, because I knew she'd be curious about where it came from, but I couldn't see her stressed like that when I had all this money I didn't really need. I would have given it all to her if I could have done, but then her suspicions would have been too much. The rest of it is still sitting in my bank account. It became clear to me quite early on that what I'd done was wrong, and as soon as I acknowledged that, I couldn't really justify using it. Strangely enough, your podcast has made me realise what I should do with it.

Danny: And what's that?

Sebastian: I'm going to reopen Wildworld. Or, rather, I'm going to pay for Wildworld to reopen and ask Pea to run it. I mean, it's all still there, most of the rides, everything. Some of them were taken in the bankruptcy case but most weren't. I think it was just too much hassle to try to sell them on. It just needs a new lease of life. It feels like the right thing to do.

Danny: So there you have it. By the time I picked up again with Pea, Sebastian had put this to her. So to recap, the last bit of Pea's story we heard, it was 2009. She was running a dog rescue centre and she'd just seen Zak for the first time since 1996. Let's hear her reaction to Sebastian's suggestion that AJ Silver didn't die after all.

Pea: I mean, I don't know what to say. I believe him, Sebastian, because I don't see what possible reason he would have to lie about it. But it's just mindboggling to think that AJ might be out there somewhere. That Zak and his parents didn't have to do all that grieving, that we didn't have to lose Wildworld and break apart like that. If I think about it too much, I get angry with him for his part in it. Yes, he was young and he was pissed off with Dad and he wasn't the instigator, but still. He played his role.

Zak: Look, I know better than anyone what fame was doing to my brother. I knew how low he got sometimes, how trapped he felt. So if it's true, if Sebastian helped him to escape the circus that had built up around him, and AJ is out there on a beach or in a city just living an anonymous life, I'm okay with that. I wish we hadn't all had to go through what we did, thinking he'd gone so young and in such a horrific way. But if he's happy, I'm happy. And if he ever wants to get in touch, I would love to hear his voice, or see his handwriting, and find out what he's been doing these past twenty-nine years. He was so special, AJ. You don't get to that level of fame without having something incredibly special, and I'd love to know where he's put all that energy, all that talent.

I don't think Mom would see it that way, though. We all broke apart when AJ died – when we thought he'd died – but she suffered the most, I think. I'll never fully understand how it is sometimes between mothers and sons, at least not from the mother's perspective, but she hasn't got over it. I think this revelation will open it all up for her again, and she will spend the rest of her days looking for him, so I really hope Sebastian's telling the truth and not just fucking with us all. I don't see why he would, though. And that offer to reopen Wildworld for Pea, that's really something. He shouldn't have done what he did, and he shouldn't have profited financially from it, but it feels like he's trying to put that right. And after all, he's just the messenger, isn't he? AJ's the one we should be angry with about the whole thing, if anyone. Sebastian was just there and he had an axe to grind with his dad, and AJ took advantage of that.

Pea: I'm trying not to count my chickens, but yes, this would go a long way towards putting things right, for me. I've drifted a bit over the years, I can't lie. I grew up believing that I would be involved with Wildworld and when that rug was pulled out from under me with no notice, I flailed. It wasn't that I'd done badly at school, I just hadn't done the visualising that a lot of kids do about future careers. I thought that was all sorted, so I just didn't spend time thinking about it. So over the years I've been a waitress, a teaching assistant, a manager at a dog shelter. I trained as a hairdresser and did that for a while. It's fair to say I haven't found a career and settled into it. For the past few years, I've been trying to recapture the way I used to feel when I was at Wildworld. I've been operating rides at a theme park.

It's not easy work. There's a lot of standing around in the cold. It can be boring. People are dicks, sometimes. But of all those jobs I've had over the years, this one feels the most like me. So the chance to go back to Wildworld, to take it on the way I always thought I would? That's magical, to me.

After Zak visited, I started going back there sometimes. Parking in the empty car park and sneaking in through that side gate. It's eerie, when a place should be full of life and people and, in particular, children, and it's dead silent. But I still loved it. It still brought me comfort. I tried taking Dad there once. After he got sober, he was generally more even and content, but he would have these black periods. Depression, I guess. And during one of them, about five years ago now, I revealed that I'd been spending time at Wildworld and asked if he wanted to come along. He did, but it wasn't the right thing for him, looking back. For whatever reason, I could be there and think of all the happiness the place had brought me, but for him it was the opposite. He was tense the whole time we were on the site, and I saw him physically relax as we drove away afterwards. It just goes to show that people have their different ways of healing, of coping. And I know, deep down, that being back at Wildworld will be the best thing for me. Sebastian says he'll join me there as Assistant Manager, but that I'll be in charge. I like the idea of working with him, too. We've never been particularly close, but perhaps it's not too late. I feel lucky, hopeful.

Danny: So I know I'm not the only one who wants to know what happened to Pea and Zak after that last meeting?

Zak: After that visit, I knew for sure that I wanted to be with Pea. So I ended my relationship and started going back and forth as much as my income and annual leave allowed, which wasn't a great deal. For about three more visits, we kept up the pretence that we were just old friends going over our shared history. And then one day, she turned up at the airport to pick me up and she kissed me, right there in the arrivals hall. She kissed me like we'd never been apart. I liked that, that she didn't insist on having a big discussion about it. We just picked up where we left off, after a gap of more than thirteen years. But of course, we weren't the same people we'd been as teenagers. I was worried that it would fade out after the initial excitement of being back together, but it never did. Never has.

Pea: My relationship with Zak is the one good thing to come out of this whole mess. He lost a brother, and my family fell apart and lost its roots, its centre, and we can't change any of that. But if none of it had ever happened, we wouldn't be together. Wouldn't ever have met. And I don't know where I'd be. I mean, none of us do. But the thought of being without him again now makes me feel panicky, like I can't breathe.

We got married ten years ago, and last year, after we'd all but given up, we had our rainbow baby, Rose. Before Zak reappeared in my life, I'd decided I didn't think I would end up having children. The relationships I had after Zak – and before Zak, if you see what I mean – were fine but they all came up short. There was no one I could envisage starting a family with. I used to chastise myself for the fact that the only man I'd been able to imagine settling down and having children with was my first love, from when I was sixteen. I thought I was misremembering it all, giving it more weight than it deserved. I believed that I was just young and stupid. But that's not right. I know that now. It was just so good with Zak that I wasn't prepared to settle for something less. And thank God I didn't.

Zak: Becoming a father is really something. Rose just turned one and she's right on the edge of walking. She can do it if she's holding on to furniture, or if she's holding someone's hand or even just a finger, but she hasn't quite worked up the courage to let go and just go for it. I'm not worried or anything. I know this is how it works, and that she will do it in her own time. But just watching her, being there to catch her, feels a lot like a metaphor for the whole parenting experience. You do all you can but there's so much they have to do for themselves, and all you can do is be there to pick up the pieces if necessary.

The love is immeasurable. Here's this person who didn't exist a couple of years ago and I know, without question, that I would die for her. Pea and I send each other photos of her all day long. Early on, we used to send a message with the photo, but it always read something along the lines of 'Look at this incredible human being we made' so we stopped bothering after a while. Now we just send the photos, one after another.

I'm ready to have another one as soon as Pea is.

Pea: Of course Zak is ready for another one. If we're able to, we definitely will. I don't like to think about not having had Rose. Sometimes, I dwell a bit on the fact that if that story hadn't come out, if Nicole Waddington hadn't needed money and gone to the press with a bit of fabricated scandal, Zak wouldn't have come here, and we wouldn't have got back together, and we wouldn't have Rose. It makes me so scared I end up freezing and not being able to do anything for a minute or two. That's the power of thought. I try to remind myself how lucky I am, how lucky we are. And if Uncle AJ ever wants to pay a visit to his niece, the door is open.

Danny: I do love a happy ending. But let's not forget two of the other main players in this whole thing. How have Cathy and John reacted to Sebastian's bombshell?

John: If you'd come to me with this information from Sebastian at the outset, I wouldn't have agreed to do the podcast. But here we are, having trawled through the wreckage of my life, and I feel like things would be unfinished if I didn't respond. When I heard what Sebastian said at the end of the last episode, it sent me into a spin. AJ Silver – not dead? Did I lose everything over nothing? Was my demise just a cog in the wheel of his escape from the limelight – from the fame he'd courted? And did my only son really assist with that? I was listening in my flat, sitting at the table where I eat my meals, and I got up, went to the sink, and I was physically sick. So yeah, that was my initial reaction.

I've had time to think about it now, of course. It pains me that Sebastian hated me enough to do that to me. That our family business and our relationships meant so little to him. But one thing I've learned since getting sober is that when people do something malicious to you, there's usually a good reason. So I sat with it, and thought about what his reasons might have been. We'd clashed over his career plans, of course. He was becoming a man, learning all that that entails, and he'd obviously looked at the male role model in his life and found me wanting. And I was wanting, I was. I was an alcoholic.

Cathy: I don't know what to think. I called Sebastian the day after the last episode aired and just burst into tears. We talked for a long time about whether it was true and why he did it. For what it's worth, I believe him. And I forgive him, too. He was young, and he made a mistake. One thing he said that's been playing on repeat in my head for the past week is that he thinks he put the final nail in the coffin of my marriage to John. It was easy to reassure him on that point. Everything that happened culminated in me walking out with the kids, because I was worried for our safety, but that marriage had been dead for a long time. If there'd been no AJ Silver, or the visit from AJ Silver had gone well, or any other scenario you can think of, we'd still be divorced. He seemed relieved to hear that. I guess it's a worry he's been carrying around for a long time, and he was finally able to put it down.

I'm in a good place now. When I first left John, it felt like I was drowning, financially. But after Sebastian gave me that chunk of money to get us on our feet, I was able to start saving, and after the kids left home I was in a position to buy a flat for myself. It's just a small one, two bedrooms, but it suits me. I've made it home. I've got a cat. Dexter. I've been on a few dates, over the years, had a few short relationships, but nothing that's stuck. I don't know why that is. I used to worry about it, about the prospect of being alone forever, but I've got used to it now. There's something quite freeing about only pleasing yourself. I have an admin job at a nearby university. I like being around the students and the academics, like the buzz of it, the sense of possibility. I'm even taking a course there, which I can do for free as a perk of the job. It's an English Literature module, a Shakespeare one. When I was growing up, I didn't even consider going to university, but I think I would if I was young now. So why not? There's no pressure to do a whole degree, but I might. For now, I'm enjoying getting lost in worlds a long way from my own, reading beautiful words aloud when I'm alone in my flat, Dexter at my feet.

I think a lot about life, about what it's really for. What

matters. Maybe everything that happened was supposed to happen because it brought Pea and Zak together. It allowed for Rose to exist. And Rose is pure joy. I was as shocked as anyone when Pea told me he was back on the scene, but I can see now that they're perfect for each other. When she was a teenager, I was just trying to protect her, so I didn't stop to notice. I look after Rose when I can to give them a break. Sometimes I read my university texts aloud to her. She just gazes up at me, adoring, not caring what the words say. Just taking comfort from the sound of the voice of someone who loves her.

John: I haven't given up on Sebastian, no. You don't give up on your children. We'll talk, when we're both ready. I don't want our relationship to be defined by something he did when he was barely an adult. As for opening up Wildworld again, I don't know what to think about that. That place brought me so much joy, but it ruined me, too. If Pea thinks she can make a better go of it than I did, I wish her luck. I didn't fully realise, back then, how important the place was to her. But I think part of that is that it stood for something, for a united family. I hope it isn't painful for her to go back there and find that we're still splintered and broken. I'll be there on opening day, to show my support.

Danny: I'll leave the Hunters there. AJ's parents, Grace and Ken, declined to talk to us for this episode. BNT, AJ's record company, have told me they will be issuing a direct statement in due course. So for our last words, I'll turn to Maggie.

Maggie: Zak called me when he'd made the decision to move over there, to be with Pea. I told him I was happy for him. Sometimes, he sends me photos of Rose, and she's about the cutest baby I've ever seen. If they do get Wildworld back up and running, I'll definitely take a trip over there to support them. It's time to put the bad memories to rest, I think, and focus on the good ones, or even creating new ones. And as for AJ being alive? Well, if it's true, and if you're listening to this, AJ, well done. You got out. You were a pain in the ass to work with but anyone could see you were special. I hope you're being special somewhere beautiful.

Danny: I'm going to close with the lyrics to AJ Silver's 'Island'. Thanks for listening.

Island

There's an island out there in the ocean
And it's empty and waiting for me
Cos when I can't stand the crowd
And I'm screaming out loud
It's the only place I want to be

My paradise island

There's nobody there
No shopping malls, stadiums, studio
I can't wait to go
To my island

There's an island out past the horizon
And it's calm and deserted and free
So when it's more than enough
And I'm not feeling tough
It's the only place I want to be

My paradise island

There's nobody there
No shopping malls, stadiums, studio
I can't wait to go
To my island

I'll be all alone with no friends and no phone
And I might just remember who I am
I'll be by myself, I don't need no one else
And I might just discover who I could be

My paradise island
There's nobody there
No shopping malls, stadiums, studio
I can't wait to go
To my island

Sven_Kowalski
Anyone fancy a trip to Wildworld? #WhatHappened-
ThatSummer

Be_Linda
Wow. This podcast is going to leave a massive gap in my
life! Is a podcast hangover a thing? And any recommenda-
tions for getting over one? #WhatHappenedThatSummer

SueJohns43
I can't believe it's over. I'll miss these people! #WhatHap-
penedThatSummer

GowithGrace
I'm so happy that Pea and Zak ended up together. And a
baby. Love a happy ending. #WhatHappenedThatSummer

AlanaLlama
Anyone else planning to seek out AJ Silver? #WhatHappenedThatSummer

CarlySanders
AJ Silver, you are my Last Love! Always and forever.

A_J_5i1v3r
If Zak-man and Pea see this, I'm sorry. I promise I'll come and ride the 360 with you one day. I can't wait to meet Rose. #WhatHappenedThatSummer

Carly Sanders
AJ? Is that really you?

* * *

MORE FROM LAURA PEARSON

Another beautiful, heartfelt read from Laura Pearson is available to order here:

https://mybook.to/LauraPearsonNewBackAd

ACKNOWLEDGEMENTS

This novel has always felt like something of a gift, because the idea came to me out of nowhere while I was waiting for a Eurostar back from Paris with my family. I remember very clearly thinking 'What if an American pop superstar went to stay in a slightly shabby UK theme park while on tour, and died while he was there?' It was the most outlandish book idea I'd ever had, and I was – and remain – incredibly excited about it. I appreciate other people's enthusiasm about the project so much. Isobel Akenhead and Jo Williamson, my editor and agent, who are amazing when it comes to letting me run with my wild ideas, thank you so much.

Huge thanks to Caroline Hulse, who talked to me about this project on the phone when I was stuck with it, and helped me get unstuck. And as always, thanks to Zoe Lea, Nikki Smith and Lauren North who live through every day of every novel with me. Thanks for the early reads, the enthusiasm, and the pep talks. You're the best writing friends I could ever have hoped for. Thanks to Lydia Howland, Abi Rowson and Jodie Matthews for cheering me on from the sidelines and talking me through every day of my life. Thanks to Lisa Timoney for being a brilliant sounding board and friend.

Thanks to the readers and bloggers and reviewers. I wouldn't be able to do this job without you. I hope you'll get on board with this book, which is a bit of a departure from my previous ones.

Thanks to my family – my parents (this book was in the works before my mum died and I remember talking to her about how much a rollercoaster might possibly cost), my sister, my in-laws. I am so lucky to have the support I have.

Massive thanks to Paul, for being on my team every day. And to Joe and Elodie, for their love and their words of wisdom. Joe once told me that all I need to do is 'write more books, and make them better.' I'm doing my best to take that advice.

ABOUT THE AUTHOR

Laura Pearson is the author of the #1 bestseller *The Last List of Mabel Beaumont*. She founded The Bookload on Facebook and has had several pieces published in *The Guardian* and *The Telegraph*.

Download your exclusive bonus content from Laura Pearson here:

Visit Laura's website: www.laurapearsonauthor.com

Follow Laura on social media here:

facebook.com/laurapearson22

x.com/laurapauthor

instagram.com/laurapauthor

bookbub.com/authors/laura-pearson

ALSO BY LAURA PEARSON

BECOME A MEMBER OF

THE
SHELF
CARE
CLUB

The home of Boldwood's
book club reads.

Find uplifting reads,
sunny escapes, cosy romances,
family dramas and more!

Sign up to the newsletter
https://bit.ly/theshelfcareclub